WE ARE ALL MADE OF STARS

For my dear friend, Tamsyn,
one of the brightest stars in the sky

WE ARE ALL
MADE OF STARS

ROWAN COLEMAN

EBURY
PRESS

1 3 5 7 9 10 8 6 4 2

Ebury Press, an imprint of Ebury Publishing
20 Vauxhall Bridge Road,
London SW1V 2SA

Penguin
Random House
UK

Ebury Press is part of the Penguin Random House group of companies
whose addresses can be found at global.penguinrandomhouse.com

First published in the UK in 2015 by Ebury Press

www.eburypublishing.co.uk

A CIP catalogue record for this book is available from the British Library

Hardback ISBN 9780091951382
Trade paperback ISBN 9781785030727

Printed and bound in Great Britain by Clays Ltd, St Ives PLC

Penguin Random House is committed to a sustainable future
for our business, our readers and our planet. This book is made
from Forest Stewardship Council® certified paper.

Dear Len,

Well, if you are reading this, it's happened. And I suppose that I ought to be glad, and so should you. We've both spent such a long time waiting, and I could see how much it was wearing you down, as much as you tried to hide it.

Now, the life insurance policy is in the shoebox in the bedroom, on top of the wardrobe, under that hat I wore to our Dominic's wedding – remember? The one with the veil you said made me look like a femme fatale? You might not; you drank too much beer, and four of Dominic's friends had to carry you upstairs, you great oaf. It's not much of a payout, I don't think, but it will be enough for the funeral at least. I don't have any wishes concerning that matter. You know me better than anyone else will. I trust you to get it right.

The washing machine. It's easy, really: you turn the round knob clockwise to the temperature you want to wash at, but don't worry about that. Just wash everything at forty degrees. It mostly works out all right. And you put the liquid in the plastic thing in the drum, not in the drawer. I don't even really know why they have those drawers any more.

You need to eat – and not stuff you can microwave. You need to at least shake hands with a vegetable once a week, promise me. You always made the Sunday night tea – cheese on toast and baked beans on the side – so I'm sure you'll be able to keep body and soul together if you put some effort in. I expect at first lots of people will feed you, but you'll need to get a cookbook. I think there's a Delia under the bed. I got it for Christmas last year from Susan, and I thought, what a cheek!

Len, do you remember the night we met? Do you remember how you led me on to the dance floor? You didn't talk, didn't ask me or anything, you rogue. Just took my hand and led me out there. And how we twirled and laughed – the room became a blur. And when the song stopped, you kissed me. Still hadn't said a word to me, mind you, and you kissed me right off my feet. The first thing you said to me was, 'You'd better tell me your name, as you're the girl I'm going to marry.' Cheeky beggar, I thought, but you were right.

It's been a good life, Len, full of love and happiness. Just as much – more than – the sadness and the bad times, if you think about it, and I have had a lot of time to think about it, lately. A person can't really ask for more. Don't stop because I've stopped; keep going, Len. Keep dancing, dancing with our grandchildren, for me. Make them laugh, and spoil them rotten.

And when you think of me, don't think of me in these last few days: think of me twirling and laughing and dancing in your arms.

Remember me this way.

Your loving wife,

Dorothy

PROLOGUE

* *

STELLA

He was a runner. That was the first thing I knew about Vincent.

One hot July, four years ago, I saw him early each morning, running past me as I walked to work, for almost three weeks in a row.

That summer I'd decided to get up before seven, to enjoy the relative quiet of an early north London morning on my way to start a shift at the hospital. I was a trauma nurse back then, and there was something about the near stillness of the streets, the quiet of the roads, that gave me just a little space to exhale before a full eight hours of holding my breath. So I walked to work, sauntered more like, kicking empty coffee cups out of my way, flirting with street sweepers, dropping a strong cup of tea off to the homeless guy who was always crammed up against the railings by the park, working on his never-ending novel. It was my rest time, my respite.

At almost exactly the same time every morning, Vincent ran past me at full pelt, like he was racing some unseen opponent. I'd catch a glimpse of a water bottle, closely cropped dark hair, a tan, nice legs – long and muscular. Every day, at almost exactly the same time, for nearly three weeks. He'd whip by, and I'd think, there's the runner guy, another moment ticked off on my journey. I liked the predictability. The flirty street sweeper, the cup of tea drop, the runner. Sort of like having your favourite song stuck in your head.

Then one morning he slowed down, just a hair's breadth, and turned his head. For the briefest moment I looked into his eyes – such a bright blue, like mirrors reflecting the sky. And then he was gone again, but it was already too late: my routine was disturbed, along with my peace of mind. All day that day, in the middle of some life-and-death drama or in the quiet of the locker room, I found the image of those eyes returning to me again and again. And each time it gave me butterflies.

The next morning, I waited for him to run past me again, and for normality to be restored. Except he stopped, so abruptly, a few feet in front of me and then bent over for a moment, his hands on his knees, catching his breath. I hesitated, sidestepped and decided to keep walking.

'Wait … please.' He took a breath between words, holding up a hand that halted me. 'I thought I wasn't going to stop, and then I thought, sod it, so I did.'

'OK,' I said.

'I thought you might like to come for a coffee with me?' He smiled – it was full of charm; it was a smile that was used to winning.

'Did you?' I asked him. 'Why?'

'Well, hoped, more like,' he said, the smile faltering a little. 'My name is Vincent. Vincent Carey. I'm a squaddie, Coldstream Guards. I'm on leave, going back to the desert soon. And you never know, do you? So I thought … well, you've got lovely hair – all curls, all down your back. And eyes like amber.'

He had noticed my eyes – perhaps in that same second that I noticed his.

'I'm a very lazy person,' I told him. 'I never go anywhere fast.'

'Is that a weird way of saying no to coffee?' I liked his frown as much as his smile.

'It's a warning,' I said. 'A warning that I might not be your kind of person.'

'Sometimes,' he said, 'you just know when someone is your sort of person.'

'From their hair?' I laughed.

'From their eyes.'

I couldn't argue with that.

'Mind if I walk part of the way with you?' he'd asked.

'OK.' I smiled to myself as he fell in step next to me, and we walked in silence for a while.

'You weren't kidding about being slow,' he said, eventually.

The second thing I knew about Vincent was that one day I was going to marry him. But the first thing I knew was that he was a runner.

Which makes it so hard to look at him now: his damaged face turned to the wall as he sleeps, and the space where his leg used to be.

THE FIRST
NIGHT

CHAPTER ONE

* *

HOPE

I can't sleep. I can never sleep these days – not in here, anyway, where they don't let it be truly dark, not ever. But it's not only that; it's because I can't stop thinking about how I came to be here. I know, of course: I caught something – a bug, bacterial, which is dangerous news when you live with cystic fibrosis. I almost died, and now I'm here, in this place where they never really turn the lights out on the long and painful road to recuperation. I know that, but I what I don't know, what I want to know, is *how*. I want to know precisely the second that little cluster of bacteria drifted like falling blossom into my bloodstream. I can't know, of course, but that doesn't mean I don't want to or that I can stop thinking about it. The frustrating thing about my condition is that I have a lot of time on my hands to think, but not a lot of time on the clock to live. Time moves slowly and quickly at the very same time – racing and stretching, boring and terrifying. And you can live your whole life with the idea of mortality – that one day it will be the last day – and still never really know or care what that means. Not until the last day arrives, that is.

I was at a party, when Death came to find me.

I hate parties, but my best friend Ben made me go.

'You can't stay in all your life,' he said, dragging me out of my room and down the stairs. 'You are twenty-one years old, nearly twenty-two. You should be out every night, enjoying the prime of your life!'

'*You* are in your prime of your life; I'm most likely middle aged,' I told him, even though I knew he hated me referring to my short life expectancy this way. 'And anyway, I could. I could stay in all my life and listen to Joni Mitchell and read books, and design book covers, try and work out the solo of "Beat It" on my guitar, and I'd be perfectly fine.'

'Mrs K.?' Ben dragged me into the living room, where my parents were watching the same old same old on TV – some police detective, who drinks too much and lost his wife in a bitter divorce, chasing down some psycho-killer. 'Tell your daughter: she's a twenty-one-year-old woman. She needs to go out and have fun! Remind her that life is for living, and not for sitting alone in her room reading about how other people do it! Plus it's all the old crew from school, back from uni now. We haven't been together in ages, and they are all dying to see her.'

Mum turned in her chair, and I could see the worry in her eyes, despite her smile. But there was nothing new there: she'd been worried for every moment of my twenty-one years, constantly. Sometimes I wonder if she'd wished she could change my name, after I was diagnosed as a baby and the situation was officially hope-less, but it was too late by then; it was a name that already belonged to me – a cruel irony that we both have to live with now. My poor darling mum, she had enough on her plate. It wasn't fair to make her decide if I went out or not, because she'd spend the rest of the evening worrying either way, and later she would have torn herself to pieces with blame. So, making my own decision, that was one of the things I did right that night. It was just the choice that was wrong.

'Oh, fine, I'm coming out, I'll get changed.'

Ben grinned at me and sat down on the bottom stair, and I thought of him there, in his skinny jeans, an outsize jumper sloping off one shoulder, jet black hair and eyes lined with smudges of Kohl, as I rifled through my wardrobe, looking for something, anything, that might even nearly equal his effortless cool. It wasn't fair, really – that little odd duckling, the boy that the other kids left out or pushed around, had suddenly grown into a sexy, hip swan. We had used to be lame kids together. That was how we came to be best friends; it was part of the natural process of banding together, like circling our wagons – greater safety, even in our meagre number of two, than being alone. Him: the skinny, shy kid with the grey collars and worn-down shoes; and me: the sick girl.

I don't think it was then that Death entered, when Ben came into the house, though it could have been. He could have left a trace of a germ on the bannister or the damp

towel in the downstairs loo. It could have been then, but I
don't think it was, because near-death by hand towel isn't
even nearly fitting enough.

I dressed all in black, trying to hide my skinny frame with
a skater skirt and a long top, and wondered how many other
girls my age longed to put weight on. I rimmed my eyes with
dark eye shadow and hoped that would do the trick.

The moment we walked in through the door, and the
wave of heat and sweat and molecules of saliva, which I
know are in every breath I take, hit us, I wanted to go home.
I almost turned around right then, but Ben had his hand
on the small of my back. There was something protective
about it, something comforting. And these were my friends,
after all. The people I grew up with, who were always nice
to me and did fun runs in my name. Who I could sit and
have a coffee and a laugh with; who would always find
something for us to talk about, while carefully avoiding
those potentially awkward questions like, 'How's it going?
Still think you'll be dead soon?'

'Hopey!' Sally Morse, my sort-of best female friend
from school, ran the length of the hallway to engulf me
in a hug. 'Oh shit, it's so good to see you. You look great!
How's it going? What's new? You're like an entrepreneur or
something, aren't you?' She hooked her arm through mine,
briefly resting her head on my shoulder as she led me into
the kitchen, and I noticed the slight pinkness around her
nostrils: the remnants of a cold.

'I'm OK,' I told her, accepting a beer. 'I started designing book covers for people, and it's going quite well.'

'That's so cool,' she said happily. 'That's so totally cool because, you know, really university is a huge waste of time; there are no jobs out there, and you end up in loads of debt – it's a very expensive way to get laid and drunk. I emailed you loads, but you're shit at replying. Too busy, I suppose, being a businesswoman.'

She paused for a moment, scanning my face, and then dragged me into a hug, filling my face with a curious combination of lemon- and smoke-scented hair, and I hugged her back. I'd thought I didn't miss any of that: the people I once saw almost every day for most of life. I'd told myself that, anyway, but it turned out that I did. I was happy to see her in that moment, happy I had come. Perhaps it was then, perhaps in that little moment of optimism and nostalgia, in the midst of that hug, I'd inhaled my own assassin. I hope not. Although it would be just like the universe to try and undo you when you are happy, because in my experience the universe is an arse.

But the good thing about being amongst my old friends was that there was no need to explain – no need to have the eternal prologue of a conversation when I tell them about the CF, and they look sad and awkward in turn. It was a relief to be amongst the people who have been preparing for my exit, almost since the very first moment I made my entrance into their lives.

It wasn't long before Sally was tonsils-deep in some guy who I thought she'd most likely brought with her, because I didn't know him, so I made my way through the mass of people, looking for Ben.

'Hope!' Clara Clayton shrieked, planting a glossy kiss on my cheek. 'It's so good to see you! If you're here, that means Ben is here, and I want to see him. Bloody hell, he's grown up hot ... Hey, are you two ...?'

'Hello, Hope,' said Tom Green, the school heartthrob for so many years, and now no less sweet, blonde, or strappingly broad-chested. 'How are things? How are you doing?' He was still awkward, polite, kind, tall – all of the things about him that used to make me swoon when I was thirteen years old, though not anymore, I was interested to notice; now I thought he was lovely but sort of dull.

'I like your look,' he said, with some effort. 'Really... cool.'

As I made my way through the party, cigarettes being hastily put out as I approached, I relaxed. I felt at home here, amongst friends. I felt like a twenty-one-year-old woman at a party. I relaxed, and that was probably my mistake.

It could have been in any one of those miniature reunions that Death made its move, during that long hour of leaning in too close to people while they told me what degree they got, and what they were going to do next. It might have been then, or it could have been when the taxi driver coughed all over the change he gave me on the way over. But I don't think it was.

I think it happened when Ben kissed me.

Because, let's get this straight, I spend most of time in my bedroom in my parents' house pretending that designing a few book covers is a proper grown-up career, and reading books, lots of books. And a man kissing me would definitely be the cause of my demise in a Victorian novel.

I'm prone to dwelling. I'm a dweller.

✻

Ben was drunk, in the way that only he gets drunk, which is not at all, then all at once. And he'd gone from being uber-cool to dancing and laughing and spinning, and hugging, and playing air guitar, and chatting up girls, who lapped up his nonsense, while I stood in the corner of the room, watching him, smiling despite myself. He loves to think he's cool – the guy in the rock band, the 'I don't give a toss about you' rock star – but it doesn't take very much for him to be his great big dorky self: the boy I used to know. The one who'd fill his pockets with worms to save them from other boys stomping on them; the guy who might look like he could snack on bats' heads by night but who is an assistant manager in Carphone Warehouse by day.

Suddenly, he careered into me, grabbing hold of my shoulders, and we both fell back onto the sofa laughing – him a little too hard, and me a little too politely.

'You are such a dick,' I told him, reasonably fondly, though.

'Then why am I your best mate?' he asked me, winding his arm around my shoulder and pulling me even closer to him, fluttering his ridiculously long brown lashes.

'Oh, shut up,' I said, screwing my face up as he rubbed his cheek against mine, like an over-friendly dog. I made my move to protect him from himself, which was to make him think he was protecting me, which meant he'd stop drinking quite so much, so fast. 'You know what? This party, it's not really doing it for me. I think I'm going to go home. Will you take me home?'

'No, don't go!' Ben grabbed my face in his hands and made me look into his eyes, squeezing my mouth into a frankly ridiculous pout. 'You're always leaving places early. Stop leaving me, Hope. When are you going to get that I hate you leaving me behind? I want you around all the time.'

'Don't be a twat,' I'd said, although hesitantly, because the way he was looking at me just then was angry and hurt all at once. It was hard to read, and I am not a fan of ambiguity. Just for a moment, for the briefest of seconds, I glimpsed that perhaps something about the way he was acting tonight had to do with me.

'Just don't go,' he said.

'But Ben, I ...'

Which was when he kissed me.

I mean really kissed me. Ben, who I had known since I was five years old. Ben, who once waded into a patch of nettles to carry me out. Ben, who'd held my hair and made small talk while I hawked up globules of mucus, during my nightly coughing rituals. Ben kissed me, and it was a real kiss, urgent and hard, and with his tongue. It was physical, and awkward, and it took me by surprise, because I'd never been kissed like that before, with this kind of force or, well, *need*. As he pressed me back hard into the sofa, suddenly I felt like I couldn't breathe. I panicked and I pushed him away.

'Shit,' he said. 'I'm really drunk. Sorry. Sorry, shit.'

I got up and went to the bathroom. Flounced is probably a better word – I flounced off to cover my confusion, feigned fury and offence. I spent a long time looking at myself in the mirror, looking at my kiss-stained mouth. Somehow I knew that everything had changed, and that it wasn't going to be for the better.

When I came back, Ben had passed out on the sofa, his head lolling back in the cushions, his mouth wide open.

I got a taxi home alone and was in bed before midnight.

When I saw Ben the next day, he said he hardly remembered anything and told me to never let him drink again. He didn't mention the kiss, and I still have no idea if he has forgotten, or if he'd rather just not talk about it.

A week after that, I was admitted to hospital with a bacterial lung infection.

The pain, the pain, and the gasping for air, and the desperate need all the time for there to be more of it, took up most of my energy, but not all of it. There was a moment, just one, of perfect clarity, when I heard the doctor say to my mother, 'It's touch and go, I'm afraid.'

And I thought, I am not ready. I am not ready yet.

I made it, I'm still here, still alive, almost ready to go back to life. I won this round. But I can't sleep, you see, because even though I can't know, I want to know. I need to know the exact moment that I let Death in, and I can't sleep – because what if I'm not ready the next time it finds me?

Dear Maeve,

Kip and me, we always promised we'd write to the other's wife if it came to it. And well, Maeve, it came to it, didn't it? I am only sorry that it's taken me this long to write the letter I never wanted you to have to read. I wish, I wish I was good with words, that I knew how to say what I have to say. I wish I'd never made this promise to Kip, but I did. And he was the closest thing to a brother I ever had.

We did it all together. We were green new recruits together. Trained together. Kip was the worst recruit the sergeant had ever seen. But we all loved him. He knew how to make us laugh on days when everything could have been so dark. By the time we went on our first tour in Afghanistan, Kip was the best soldier.

He talked about you and little Casey all the time. You were the lights of his life. We used to hear what Casey had been up to, how she is more beautiful, funny, clever than any other kids, all day long. Kip was a soldier, but he was a family man first. I know he tried to be the best husband and dad he could be.

The day it happened started out like any other day. Routine patrol, defending the province against the Taliban. No intel or chatter to suggest we had anything more to worry about than normal. Not that normal wasn't enough to worry about. We all knew it wouldn't be long before we were allowed home on leave, but command told us: ears and eyes, stay alert, right up until the last second of our tour, and we knew that.

When the missile hit, it was ...

CHAPTER TWO

* *

STELLA

Whenever there is a moment of quiet, of stillness, I stop and I listen, and I wait for it to pass. It's hardly ever silent at Marie Francis Hospice and Rehabilitation Centre, even at night. Quiet chat, murmurs in the half-dark, laughter sometimes, sometimes singing. Sometimes a dream lived out loud. But it's hardly ever quiet. So I listen in those moments, and I wait for the noise again. And then I breathe out.

I feel a warm body wind itself around my legs and look down to see that Shadow, the very unofficial hospice cat, has emerged out of nowhere again. Pitch black with no markings and huge emerald-green eyes. No one knows where he comes from, or when he will come; he just appears when he pleases, knowing that when he does, he will be made a huge fuss of by everyone who meets him. He's large, clearly looked after by someone – someone who probably has no idea of the humanitarian mission he goes on through the day. He's young, I think, and kittenish still, despite his size. He sees a shadow from a flickering light and pounces on it, twisting and turning 180 degrees with every lunge in a bid to catch his prey. I reach out to him, and he bats at my hand playfully until I catch behind his ears with my nails and scratch. Suddenly mesmerised, and softly lambent, he lets me lift him onto my lap and hold him for a moment. I feel his small heart rapidly beating against my skin, and the rise and fall of his chest. This is the reason that the administration turns a blind eye to Shadow, and lets us keep a pack of Dreamies in the nurse's station drawer for him, because it's well known that contact with animals is therapeutic, soothing, comforting. And Shadow can do what most of our doctors, and us nurses and Albie, our chaplain's daft Labrador, can't, which is take himself from room to room, always seeming to know which patient needs his attention the most. Smiling, I smooth down his black silky fur in the long firm strokes that he likes, listening to the satisfying rattle of his purr. Lucky me, to have a few moments of his attention tonight.

'Tea, Stella?' Thea nods at my empty mug. 'You're due a break, surely – Shadow seems to think so. He was sitting with Issy till she dropped off.'

'No, I'm full to the brim,' I tell her. 'I've got my obs to do, and I've promised to sit with Maggie for a bit. She likes a chat and I said I'd write her a letter.'

'She could chat for England, that one,' Thea says, but without malice. There's a sort of inevitable closeness amongst the patients and their families here, a solidarity. It eases the journey, I think, for them just to know they aren't in this alone.

'How are you doing?' I ask her. Thea's answering smile is small and almost worn through, but steady. It's an expression I've become familiar with, a kind of all-defying hope in the face of certain disappointment. I've known Thea for eighteen months now. A single mother, she's been bringing her fourteen-year-old daughter Issy to the hospice since she was first diagnosed with a final stage case of a rare bone cancer, Ewing's sarcoma. At first it was for a brief burst of respite care, to allow Thea to have a little more time for her younger daughter, and for herself, but now after years of treatment, it's because it is almost time.

We aren't supposed to form bonds, or relationships, with the families that we care for, but sometimes it's impossible not to. Not when they are here every day, when they are living out the defining moments of their lives right in front of you, looking to you for reassurance and certainty where there is none. So she and I have become not friends exactly but companions in the midst of an endless succession of sleepless nights. And Thea keeps smiling, keeps hoping. If there's one thing I've learned while I've been working the night shift at Marie Francis it's that this is the one thing that sets us apart from other animals, the one thing that makes us human. Hope.

'I'm OK,' Thea says. 'Issy is smiling in her sleep. I like to try and guess what she's dreaming about. There was this holiday a couple of years back – we went to a water park with a huge great big slide. She shrieked like a banshee all the way down and then went back for more. Maybe she's dreaming about that.'

'I'll be in after I've seen Maggie,' I promise her.

On an average night here, there are maybe fourteen patients at any one time, plus two nurses, three health-care assistants and one doctor sleeping in the on-call room – all of us engaged in this kind of ballet, this dance that is something like a rain dance. Except, if we get it right, we're not calling down the rain but keeping pain at bay. This world, this night world, is the one we small crew inhabit alone, in between the busy, sunny days of outpatients, and counselling, therapy groups, music, dances and fundraisers. Family time, healing time, breathing time. Here during the night, no more than twenty of us are negotiating the path that at some point each of us will have to travel. But never alone if we can help it, that's the promise we make on the night watch. Although we can't come with you, you will never be alone when you take that final step.

And I always work the night shift. I asked if I could when I was offered the job. After some hesitation they let me, as long as I take enough days off in between, because no board ever wants their nurses only to work the difficult night-shift slots, even someone as experienced as me. No one ever asks me why I only do the night shift – because it's not like I have childcare to worry about. But, anyway, I only half understand the reason myself. I think it was a gradual thing. I think so, although it may have happened all at once. In the months since Vincent left the army, it's been hard to get a clear sense of anything very much, except that somehow the strands of our lives that were so closely woven together began unravelling into two separate threads – quickly enough for it to feel like I have no control over it. Perhaps taking the night shifts has been about holding up a white flag and declaring surrender, because if our house is the battlefield, then it's easier, less painful, less dangerous, if only one of us is in it at a time. It's my house during the day, and at night it belongs to Vincent.

Thea hesitates still, and I sense there is something she wants to ask me.

'How's Vincent doing?' she asks, and Shadow, suddenly tired of my affection, leaps onto the desk and nudges her hand up from where it is resting and onto his head. He has trained us all very well.

'Great.' I smile, nodding. 'He's doing really great. Never still since he got the new prosthetic fitted. State of the art it is, apparently. He got back from the sponsored bicycle ride last week, and he's already talking about training for the Marathon … He's doing great. He's barely ever still.'

'OK, good.' She stands there for a moment, and takes a breath. 'So you're writing a letter for Maggie?'

I nod.

I began it one night for a patient who could no longer hold a pen, and who wanted to make sure her husband would know how to work the washing machine after she'd gone. That's when the letter writing started, and it grew from there – each letter another story, another life, another legacy. Not every patient wants to put their final thoughts on paper, not every patient has to, but there is something comforting about leaving a physical relic of your mind in this world, something reassuring.

'Do they ask you, just before, you know … Is it like they know? They know it's time for a letter?'

And suddenly I know what it is that is terrifying her, what it is that she can't quite bring herself to articulate.

'Issy hasn't asked me to write a letter,' I say.

'Well.' She nods, dropping her gaze from mine as she holds up her empty mug. 'OK, I'd better get back to her.'

It seems like Shadow agrees: he drops down from the high desk with easy grace and trots off towards Issy's room, his tail high and purposeful.

'I'll be in soon,' I reassure Thea, with a smile. And I watch her go back to Issy's room, thoughts of a cup of tea forgotten as she quietly shuts the door behind her.

I take my pad of plain writing paper out of the desk drawer, and root around in my bag for my favourite pen: blue ink, ballpoint, smooth flow, looks like it could be a fountain pen, but doesn't smudge. I love the feel of it, gliding over the slight texture of the paper, filling it with swirls and loops that always, no matter what words they go towards forming, mean so much more than simply what they say.

Dear Franco,

I don't suppose you remember me. Why would you? It's sixty years since we met, and we didn't know each other for long. I have no idea if you still live in Monte Bernardi or if you are even still alive, though those spread adverts on the telly seem to say that Italians lives for ever, so I hope so.

It was 1954. I was twenty years old, and me and Margaret Harris from the bank where I worked had a day trip to Brighton. Down on the train, best dresses and hats. Mine was primrose yellow and had flowers embroidered on the pockets.

We were walking along the front when we saw you, although you didn't notice us. We thought you had to be a movie star or something: the way you stood there, with your sunglasses on – hair all slicked back, black T-shirt, white trousers. We went round the corner to peep at you, and then we put on some lipstick and walked past you again, swinging our skirts and giggling like we were ever so fascinating. You said hello in Italian. We ran away, screaming with laughter; what a pair we were.

I didn't see you for the rest of the day, not until the dance at the end of the pier. And there you were, in a pale blue suit. When you came over to talk to me I thought I might die, maybe from the excitement. Your English wasn't very good; my Italian was non-existent. But, oh, your accent.

We kissed all night, never stopped for a breather, or a drink. You whispered strange words in my ear, might have been a shopping list, for all I knew. I didn't care, because it sounded like music.

That's when I found out that Margaret had got the last train home without me – in a pique, I expect, because it was me you had eyes for. You walked me back to your bedsit and snuck me up the stairs without the landlady noticing. I'd never been with a boy before – I thought something dreadful would happen, that I'd get pregnant or catch some disease, but I was stupid and young and it didn't seem to matter more than that moment.

The next morning, you wrote your address in pencil in my address book and kissed me goodbye. I never heard from you again. I didn't catch anything or get pregnant. I wasn't brave enough to write. I married a good man a few years later, and I've been happy. It's been a good life. But every time I've changed address books, I've copied your address into the new one, once again. Monte Bernardi; a reminder of one night when I risked it all for a little excitement. So it would seem an awful shame not to use it just once.

Thank you for the dance,
Susan Wilks

CHAPTER THREE

* *

HOPE

'You still awake?' Stella checks her watch, as if I might not know that it is nearly 3 a.m. Why she's concerned, I don't know, as her sole purpose for being here is to wake me up.

'Looks like it,' I say.

'I just need to know ...'

'Yes, I know, I know the drill.' I tuck a knotted strand of hair behind my ear and let Stella take my temperature, my guitar cradled in my lap, as it often is. There's half a song in my head, and it won't go away, so I'm trying to write it – exorcise it, that would be a better term. It's a bloody stupid song, about as edgy as a kitten, about love and rainbows and all sorts of bollocks – not at all the kind of song I want to write, which is about ... Oh, I don't know, something profound. 'You need to know my temp, my oxygen saturation, my pulse rate, my blood pressure, blah, blah, blah. And then in another couple of hours you are going to watch as I take my hypertonic saline and then cough up the contents of my lungs in my ritual humiliation. You own me, basically. I'm your bitch.'

She raises an eyebrow and almost smiles.

'You might find it boring, but these are the ticks and measures that are going to get you out of here quicker,' she assures me, in this careful, quiet way that she has, gentle and soft, as if someone has found her volume control and turned it right down.

'I think I'm ready to get out now,' I say. 'I'm not dying any more, or at least, I'm not dying very quickly. It feels wrong to be here, taking up a room that someone else needs more than me, and I've got things to do.'

Before the weird kind of limbo that is Marie Francis, there were several weeks in hospital, and a lot of drugs and pain and fear. My fear, my parents' fear, my friends' fear, even Ben, who'd come to see me and tell me funny stories about the latest customers in his shop, but I could tell even he was afraid that this was it, because he wasn't nearly as annoying as he usually is.

Mum cried quite a lot and Dad brought me things: magazines that I would never read, junk food that I didn't want, soft toys holding stuffed love hearts proclaiming a series of increasingly inappropriate messages, not to mention the fact that they were soft toys and I am a grown woman, even if I am one who can sometimes wear a bunny-rabbit onesie all day. The last one said 'You Are My Sweet Heart' – an on-sale remnant of Valentine's Day, I presume. I appreciated the sentiment, but still, I tucked the bear right at the back of my growing pile of plush bodies, underneath the blue rabbit that assured me: 'It's a boy!'

Finally I was transferred to the Marie Francis Hospice and Rehabilitation Centre for the final part of my recuperation before they will let me go home. I should have been in the specialist CF unit, but my local hospital had seen a ream of cutbacks that meant cutting two beds, and the other four were full. So, not well enough to go home, and the next CF specialist bed half a country away, they found me a bed here, close to my parents, for my final phase of close-care recuperation. I've ended up here, but at least I am not *ending* up here. The drugs worked, my body fought back. I am on the mend, or as mended as I will ever be, considering that I was born faulty.

I mean, every breath hurts. It's still a gargantuan effort to suck air and push it out again – a sort of crazy catch-22 where breathing exhausts me so much that I only breathe harder, desperate for more air. But I'm past the worst: the part where my lungs each had less capacity than a can of coke. And, although acid still swirls up my throat and into my mouth from my inefficient gut, and it's hard to pretend it's not me giving off noxious gasses when there is no one else around to blame it on, I feel better, a lot better.

I said no thank you, Death, I'm not ready and I am still alive. And bored out of my mind.

Stella glances at the notebooks open on my bed, and I hope she can't read my sappy lyrics upside down; if she can, she'd probably change her stance on euthanasia.

'You should try to get some sleep. It's late,' she says.

It's like her mantra – she says it almost every time she sees me, even though she looks like she never sleeps: she is pale and wraith-like, like what she needs most in the world is a good sunbed.

'Is it?' I glance out of the window, but only the reflection of my room bounces back at me out of the dark. 'It's hard to tell in here. It's like time stands still, or the seconds move very, very … slow-ly.' Stella watches as I stretch the last word out for a long, long time, benignly tolerant of my show of immaturity – because I am, after all, only twenty-one.

'If you need stuff to do, you could join in with any of the activities in the daytime.' Stella completes her notes carefully. 'Or take a look in the library. We may rely on donated books, but we get lots and we always seem to have the latest bestsellers … There's some good stuff in there, I've heard.'

'Yes, I had a look,' I say, thinking it would be churlish to mention that I'd already read anything worth reading, and everything else was twaddle, because that would make me seem like a snob. Stella probably wouldn't guess the large percentage of the limited hours of my life that I have devoted so far to reading; she couldn't know that while other girls my age are partying all night in Ibiza, engaging in wild no-strings sex with virtual strangers, training to be track stars or packing for Bali for some kind of sponsored adventure, I am sitting at home, living in another world that exists only between the pages of a book and on the internet – the only place where I am really allowed to talk to other CF people, as we can't meet in person. You put two CF people together and there's a chance that one of the bugs they carry around all day might just kill you off, and vice versa, so we stay apart from each other.

There are chat rooms and blogs, and support groups, but I've started to stay away from them, ever since this girl whose blog I loved to read started to blog about planning her marriage at an insanely young age, to a man she barely knew. Although no one mentioned that, of course, because, you know, she probably wouldn't have time to find out they were deeply incompatible. I'd check for a new post every night; I loved it. I loved her endless bubbles of enthusiasm, and how getting married made her just so happy. I loved how she'd made a little bridesmaid dress for her wheely oxygen tank, and how she talked about wanting to honeymoon in Australia and see Ayers Rock, like William and Kate.

I loved her endless debates on nail varnish and tiaras, and how long she could wear high heels for without needing a sit down. She talked about how her health was declining, how she'd been moved to the top of the transplant list, but that somehow even that just filled her full of hope. Because a transplant meant so many more years to be with her husband, and if they had to the put the honeymoon off for a year, it didn't matter. She posted about how the wedding wasn't going to be in a church after all, or in the summer, but in a hospital chapel, in the next month, and how she was so certain that when a person was as loved as she was, and who loved life as much as she did, that fate would bring her the life-saving operation that she needed. And then, about a week before her wedding was due to take place, she stopped posting. And she never started again. And I don't need to google her name to find out what happened, or even read the hundreds of comments under her last blog post. So anyway, since then, I've started to stay away a little. One sad ending is about all I can take.

'Anyway, I'm sure they'll check you out soon enough. We just need to be sure that you're stable and OK to go home. We don't want the infection taking hold again, and the doctors will want to see that your lung capacity has come back up to safe levels.' She pauses. 'You were very ill, you know. Your body has been seriously weakened. We don't want all our good work to go to waste because you can't sit still long enough.'

'I do know that,' I tell her. 'I'm not a child, plus all this pain I'm in is a pretty good reminder.'

Stella tips her head to one side and looks at me.

'You're very grumpy – are you always like this? Like a teenager who's been grounded?'

I want to be offended, and for a split second I am, but I find myself blurting out a guffaw instead.

'Yes,' I say. 'Yes, I am. Look, I'm sorry. I have a way of dealing with it all, and it's mainly this. I'm not a chirpy sort of a person. Sorry.'

This time she laughs.

'Ha, well, then, we have that in common. But I do always try to be polite. As my mum says: good manners cost nothing.'

'I am sorry,' and for a moment I do feel as awkward as a teen. 'It's the word "hospice",' I say, picking up my guitar. 'People die in hospices.'

'People die everywhere, and not especially here. You aren't our only recuperation patient, you know. Or even our youngest. And "hospice" is really just another word for hospital. It is about offering hospitality to the needy – just in these modern times we think it has to be about death, but it doesn't, it isn't. It's about life.'

'You've read the fundraising material, then,' I say, and she smiles a little, perching on the edge of the armchair my room comes equipped with. It's blue, with a white cushion covered in tiny little blue flowers – homely, see? Comforting. Not at all like somewhere you are most likely about to pop your clogs.

'You're very … cynical, aren't you?' she says, examining me with these crazy, huge, bush-baby eyes that look like they could see in the dark without any trouble at all. 'Most people that pass through here, they are so …'

'Much less annoying?' I make a joke of it, but I know it's true. Sometimes, trying very hard to appear that you don't care, exhausting as it is, can make you rather tiresome for all the people whose lives revolve around caring for you.

'Happy to still be breathing,' she says.

'I am happy,' I say. 'I just hide it really, really well under this veneer of endless misery.'

'That song you were playing when I came in was chirpy,' Stella observes, and she's right, damn her.

'Yeah, I don't know how that happened,' I say with a small smile.

'Maybe the hospice is inspiring you,' she says. 'Our chaplain would love that; he's in a band, you know. Prog rock. He played at our last Christmas party. I mean, you'd think that it would be impossible to bring down a Christmas party. But you'd be wrong.'

'If I was ever going to be religious, I'd want my chaplain to be in a terrible prog rock band,' I say, crossing the room and resting my forehead against the window to see past my own reflection and out into the dense night.

The hospice is in a couple of acres of garden, which slope gently down to the canal – the railway pulsating away regularly on the other side of it. An old Georgian building skirted in a modern purpose-built extension, Marie Francis is a strange little oasis of walled-in greenery in the midst of the neon and vulgarity of the place I grew up in. Outside, it feels as if the trees throw up an invisible wall between us and the rest of this dirty old Camden town.

Now, in the depths of the night, it's easy to believe that you could be in the middle of nowhere – cut loose in the dark, floating through space where the sun never rises; cut loose amongst the constellations. I wonder if Stella has to remind herself that the number 253 bus trundles down Camden Road, while behind the brick-built wall is the sanctuary of Marie Francis. Behind that green-painted wooden door set into the brick wall – the door that staff and patients' families soon learn is a better way in than the brightly lit, all-glass foyer, which closes at 5 p.m.

And then unexpectedly I feel the weight of the night, pressing down on my vertebrae, and I'm suddenly exhausted.

'Actually, I do really want to sleep now,' I tell her. 'I'll do my physio and then try and get some rest. You don't have to watch me, I've done it a million times before.'

She hesitates for a moment, a frown slotted between her eyebrows, assessing what would most likely happen if she forces this issue and demands to stay.

'OK,' she says eventually. 'I'll leave you to it. See you at five for your next lot of meds.'

There is no reasonable, rational reason why I climb into bed and lean back, sitting up against my many pillows especially brought in from home. There is no sane explanation why I know that I won't take my aspirator tonight, or beat my own rib cages until I cough up fat slimey balls of mucus. There isn't a sensible argument for why I will sit here, taking every increasing shallow breath as I fall asleep until an explosion of coughing wakes me up, as it inevitably will – tearing at my body, like a hurricane that's keen to be released from inside my chest. There is no reason, explanation or argument for why I don't do my physio, except that sometimes I just like to pretend I'm normal. I like to pretend I'm not sick.

And, yes, I know how ridiculous that makes me.

But that's the thing about living with your own mortality for as long as you can remember. It makes you a little bit crazy.

Dear son,

I worked hard for a lot of your life. It's what you did in my day. Men went out to work and came home when the kids were in bed. Your mother took control of the home; I took control of the money. We had our ups and downs, like every couple, but it seemed to work, or I thought it did. I've watched you grow up and do things I could have never dreamed of. Going off to university, starting companies from scratch. Not that I really get what it is that you do still, which I know annoys you, because you think that means I don't care or that I'm not proud of you. But that isn't true. I do care, and I am proud. I'm just from another age, and I couldn't understand even when I tried to.

You don't go to work in an office, on a cooked breakfast. You work from home, you go and pick Gracie and Stevie up from school. You cook for them, and nurse them when they are sick. And when they were babies, you changed their nappies and stayed up all night feeding them. I'll admit, it baffled me a bit.

But I've had time to think, and I was thinking about our last big family lunch – the last one before the tumour changed all the time we had together. I was thinking about the way your children looked at you, the way they love you, the way they laughed, the closeness between you. You are more than their father; you are their parent. And I wished things had been different back when you were a boy. I wish I'd been home sometimes before you were asleep; I wish I'd been the sort of father that you are now. I wish I'd been a better dad for you, son. I wish I'd told you how very much I love you, and that every single time I've seen your face, it's filled me with pride and joy – more joy than I have known in my life. And the greatest pride I take is in the kind of man you are: kind, thoughtful, not afraid to be loving or loved.

You've given me more than I deserved; I only wish I'd done the same for you.

Dad

CHAPTER FOUR

* *

STELLA

A little after four, I am sitting with Thea for a while in the patients' lounge, just sitting in silence. I watch her watching the moon out of the window. Shadow is curled up on her lap, curled into a tight, black, featureless ball, as she rests her palm lightly on his back, her eyes slowly closing. It's something all the families need: that moment, that rest from the vice-like grip of waiting. As we sit there I watch her visibly relax, just a little. Her shoulders drop, the creases in her face become less deeply etched. And then it is over and she remembers, and her body clenches again, steeling herself for whatever is next.

The odd thing is that by being here I feel relaxed and at peace, useful and wanted. It's when I tie the laces of my running shoes and get ready to go home that my body clenches in self-defence.

We start as an unexpected flurry bursts into the corridor outside, voices and noise; they communicate an urgency. Shadow shoots off of Thea's lap and out through an open window. I get up, and Laurie, the other night nurse on shift tonight, stops just outside the room, looking at what I can see.

'New admission?' I ask.

She looks at me and shrugs. We are not an emergency unit; people don't just turn up here, they are always referred and expected. Glancing at Thea, I follow Laurie into my serene kingdom of quiet corridors, which are now are filled with paramedics, a patient on a gurney and, at the heart of the activity, a face I recognise, although I've seen her only once at my interview: my boss, Keris Hunter.

'It's Grace Somner,' she tells me through the crowd of people as they wheel her into our only vacant room. I know the name, although not the woman. Grace has been a stalwart of the Marie Francis fundraising team as a kind of uber-volunteer. There's a photo of her in reception: a woman in her late fifties, with an abundance of blonde hair piled atop a face that's seen harder times. She also runs the teen resource centre, not only for teenagers suffering from terminal illness, but also for those who have lost someone. She gives them a place to go and shout and swear, or play videos games endlessly, or talk or paint. 'She doesn't have any family so it was me she asked the hospital to call when she collapsed. End-stage stomach cancer. I don't know why she's hidden it from us for so long, or even how. I brought her here. What else could I do? Otherwise she'd die in hospital without anyone she knows, or who knows her.'

'It's fine,' I say. 'No need to explain. Go and have a cup of tea. Laurie and I will settle her in; we'll take care of her.'

Our on-call doctor arrives, a little flustered as the

paramedics officially hand over care, and Laurie and I follow his instructions for Grace's medication: set up the drip, deftly, painlessly insert the cannula in the back of her hand, smoothing down the cool sheets, adjusting the pillows to support her neck. But through it all she remains in a deep, quiet sleep, probably because of the level of pain medication they gave her at the hospital. Soon enough, the new levels will kick in and she will likely wake up and wonder where she is. After a word with Laurie, after the room is cleared, I sit down next to the bed and wait for Grace's eyes to open. I don't want her to be alone when she wakes up and remembers.

Remembering is the worst part.

Shortly the day shift will come on, and I will change into my running shoes and make my way home to the house, where my husband will have been up and awake for hours, crying until his eyes are red raw – unless he has drunk himself to sleep. And it is always now, at this point of the night, when dawn seems like a possibility, that I remember.

I remember that my husband can't stand to look at me any more.

*

It's just before six when I turn the key in the lock and open the front door very slowly so that it does not creak. I hold my breath. The house is quiet. I can hear the needle on the vinyl that Vincent has always preferred over CDs or downloads click, clicking away. I breathe out as I see he is sleeping on the sofa, still wearing his gym uniform, his

Beats headphones, which he bought to stop the neighbours reporting us for the loudness of his music all night long, still covering his ears. He must have taken his prosthetic off at some time last night; it is propped up against the coffee table, where several cans of pre-mixed Jack Daniel's and diet cola lay discarded and crumpled.

Reassured that he is sleeping deeply, I tiptoe into the room and look at him, my heart in my mouth and full of longing and love. Oh God, how I miss being able to just look at him, never mind touch him, or feel his touch. His head is tipped backwards at an awkward angle that will surely cost him a stiff neck when he wakes up, and I see the long tanned stretch of throat, laced with scarring on the right side which extends up the side of his face and into his hairline, where the hair grows unevenly now. Edging closer, I sit in the armchair opposite, taking in the sweep of his thick, dark lashes, his wonderful, slightly crooked nose, his arms – muscular and toned, crossed over his chest, tightly hugging one of our sofa cushions.

The yearning to feel the warmth of his skin is almost unbearable. I wonder what would happen if I let myself carefully unclasp his arms, took away his protective cushion and slid my hand ever so gently under his T-shirt, feeling the firm abs that he works so hard to maintain, rising over the ridge of his pectoral muscles, tracing my fingers over the web of silver scars that track down his back and side. For a moment, unbidden and of its own volition, my hand floats upwards and out, stretching towards him. But I stop. I can't risk it. I can't risk him turning away from me again. Somehow I need to find out what happened the day he was injured that changed everything between us, because when I know what it was, then I will know why he can't stand to be near me, why he can't sleep unless there is rock music drowning out his thoughts, and if … I almost can't bear to think it, but I must … if we have a chance to stay together.

So I don't touch him. I sit back in the armchair and watch him for a few moments more, until just minutes before I know the alarm on his phone will go off to get him up for work. Then I leave him and trudge silently upstairs to our bedroom, hoping to dream of him instead.

Dear Keith,

No, wait, darling Keith.

Darling Keith, you are the one I have always loved; I hope you know that. I think you do, but I should have told you, shouldn't I? What a fool I am for not telling you more, louder, longer, ever. But I always thought you knew.

There'd be a look between us, a touch, a moment when the air just hummed with it, with our love for each other. We never needed to shout about it, did we, Keith? Shouting was never for us. Well, except at the footy, every Saturday afternoon – just our poor misfortune that we have to support the worst team to never grace the Premier League.

Every Saturday afternoon, we laughed, didn't we? Laughed and sang and had a drink on the way home. When all the others had peeled off, and we were the last two with the furthest to walk, our fingers would find each other's, and we'd hold hands for those last few yards.

Well, Keith, I have always loved you. I've never shouted about it, but now the words are here, on the paper. Put them in frame if you like, copy them a thousand times, and stick them to trees. Take out an ad at the ground; tell the world that I love you, Keith, and that the greatest joy of my life has always been knowing that you love me back.

I'll be yours always,
Michael

THE SECOND
NIGHT

CHAPTER FIVE

* *

HUGH

'Hello?' I let myself in and listen. And to my relief I discover there is no one else here, except for the cat – the only gift I have ever been given that I cannot return. The girl that stayed the night, a nice-enough girl called Joy, has let herself out and gone. I'd been worrying all day that she might have decided to stay and cook me something in a wok, because a lot of single women seem to like to cook things in woks, but she's gone.

The cat sits on the bottom step and regards me with a take-it-or-leave-it indifference. So deeply black that he almost has no edges, no features apart from his luminous green eyes, he regards me with what seems to be a habitually deep dissatisfaction.

'Jake.' I nod at him politely as I go into the kitchen. It was never me that wanted a cat, it was Melanie, an ex-girlfriend who assured her permanent place in my life by leaving me this pet behind when she left. She bought Jake for me for Christmas as a surprise, a tiny black mass of fluff in a cardboard box. She cried when I said that I really didn't want a cat, and that actually I was a bit allergic. She cried and wept – big snotty, raspy sobs – so I gave in, thinking that after a couple of weeks I could take him to a shelter and pretend he'd been run over. But, as it turned out, Jake lasted longer than Melanie. I was just getting used to him when one night she said she couldn't bear my cold-hearted indifference for a moment longer, and stormed off to find the happiness she claimed to deserve. And I thought, am I really that much of a git? Because I don't feel that way inside; I feel like I have a regular warm-blooded beating heart. Although I wasn't that sorry to see her go; in actual fact, I was kind of relieved. But anyway, I thought I'd keep the cat, just to show the world that I do have a heart, should they care to look.

Jake follows me into the kitchen at a slight delay and looks pointedly at his food bowl, prepared for disappointment. Melanie, during her short tenure, bought him all sorts of food, different-coloured gourmet tins, special treats. We had an entire kitchen cupboard devoted to his dietary requirements, which were complex and many. He ate better than I did – mostly because Melanie was one of those very women that love to stir-fry vegetables. I grew up on oven chips. Now, though, since she's no longer cluttering up the fridge, I feed him the tuna every day that I bulk-buy at the supermarket. Take it or leave it. He takes it, and supplements his diet with small birds or mice, which he finds during the night and often brings home to murder in the kitchen. Carole, one of the other curators at work, told me that this means he loves me. I just assume that every mangled animal I sweep into the bin is some kind of death threat. It's safer that way.

I put a frozen pizza in the oven and crack open a beer, take my research notes from work and put them on the kitchen table. I switch on the radio to LBC and turn it down low, because I just like the sound of the voices in the background – not what the people say, because most of what the people say makes me want to dig a bunker in the middle of a remote forest, hoard tinned food and wait for the apocalypse.

Tonight I am researching the Victorian spiritualist movement, and the wave of table tipping and séances that swept across the nation, the Empire and the world, for a special exhibition at work entitled 'Afterlife: How science tried to solve the mysteries of death'. It's a working title; something more catchy will come – that's what I keep promising my bosses. It's all got to be immediately catchy, these days; it's got to be a *Daily Mail* headline, even history. Which is fine, because that's what I'm good at: making the subject I am passionate about seem interesting to people who normally are mostly passionate about TV talent shows. It also comes in handy when meeting girls.

When I was a kid, and I mainly pretended to be Spider-Man or Eighties Flash Gordon, I never would have foreseen anything as prosaic as a career as a historian, specialising in nineteenth-century social culture, in my future. It was one of those things that I felt like I alone had discovered. A subject that I caught the corner of, and kept pulling at, peeling back layer upon layer until it transformed from an interest into a specialism and finally, I, in my little two-bedroom London terraced house, was listed almost everywhere as a world expert.

The Victorians loved to congregate around tables and talk to ghosts.

It's not lost on me, as I sit at the table that's been in this kitchen since I was a baby – this very table where my mum used to feed me mashed-up carrot and my dad would sit after work, and roll his shoulders, and wince if he got up too quickly – that I am surrounded by ghosts, if only metaphorical ones. This is the table where Mum would let me draw on the tablecloth, where Dad would explain to me the finer points of making a fly, for the purposes of fishing. This was the table where I first asked out a girl, and was spectacularly turned down. And it was here where Mum left her wedding rings.

This is a table surrounded by ghosts, covered in the fingerprints of the two people I have loved most. The people that exited, stage left and stage right, before their time, before my time, all gone now, leaving me here alone with a table full of long-dead people's exploited hopes. And a slightly resentful cat.

'Knock once for yes, twice for no,' I say out loud to Jake, who has climbed onto the table to sit on my papers. It's a peculiar habit he has developed of liking to sit on whatever I am trying to read. As far as I can tell, it's designed purely to be annoying. There is nothing – no reply but the soft chatter on the radio, and the distant sound of trains somewhere. No secret smoke or mirrors. No other realm, full to the brim of the dead who have something very pressing to say to a Celia, Cecil or possibly Cedric.

'Is there anybody out there?' I say to Jake, who blinks in slow motion, and then, hopping down off the table, taking a ream of my research with him, disappears through the cat flap, as if he's going to check.

It's not until I go into the living room a couple of hours later, my head full of stories of long-ago mediums that once held court every night at every fashionable address in London, that I see there is a message blinking on the answerphone, and the sight stops me in my tracks.

The device is a relic, seriously outmoded technology, at least fifteen years old, perhaps even older. So old it has one tiny analogue tape that has been rewound and recorded over a thousand times – but not recently: no one calls my landline any more. I keep it really because it was Dad's. It even still has his greeting message recorded on it. Not that I've played it for a very long time. I just like to know it's there, that I can still hear the sound of his voice whenever I want. Fishing my mobile phone out of my pocket, I look at it. Nothing. No missed calls or texts. The landline wasn't a last resort, a final attempt to try and reach me. Perhaps it was a random cold caller.

I don't know why I feel so nervous as I press it, and wait for it to go through its various machinations, whirring and clicking. Finally the long beep that precedes the recorded message sounds, and I wait, but it's just – silence. No, not silence. I rewind it and play it again, kneeling on the carpet so that my ear is level with the speaker. This time I hear crackling, a distant sound of cars, perhaps the sound of an intake of breath. Someone is – was – there on the other end of the line. But there are no words.

I am gripped by a need to know who it was who called. Yes, probably some scam selling me something, I tell myself as I dial 1471. A cold call from New Delhi, or something about a car crash that I may be eligible for compensation for, but I have to know. The phone rings and rings on the other end of the line, and I let it, unable to break this tenuous link between me and someone who wanted to talk to me. It seems like a lifetime until it is picked up.

'Er, yeah?' A male voice, young and unmistakably London, on the other end.

'Oh, yeah, I had a call, from this number?' I say, trying to sound nonchalant, concealing the strange, sickening irrational urgency that seems to have gripped hold of my gut. 'I had a missed call from this number, today?'

'It's a phone box, mate,' the voice says. He sounds young.

'Would you mind telling me where it is?' I ask him. 'If you wouldn't mind?'

'End of Shapland Road, opposite the burger place,' he says and hangs up. I listen to the dial tone for a few moments more and put the phone down. I turn around and start to find that Jake has returned and is watching me, curiously, from the banister on which he is somehow poised, apparently able to defy the pull of gravity.

'Who would call me from the phone box at the end of this street?' I ask him.

He hasn't got a clue, either.

CHAPTER SIX

* *

HOPE

'I'm going in,' Ben says, rubbing his hands together like a Bond villain.

'You bloody are not.' I drag him back, but he shakes me off and heads out into the hallway, clutching my guitar by the neck, knowing that eventually, like a Shaggy to his Scooby, I will inevitably follow. Today is the day when a selection of volunteers come to serenade the inmates, I mean patients. Last week we had this guy who played acoustic guitar and wore very tight jeans, which meant that when he was sitting on the stool he'd borrowed from the coffee bar, you could see exactly the outline of his penis. No such luck this week, though. This week we have the man with the accordion, who is singing 'Here Comes the Sun'. Singing might not be exactly the term – it's like Terry Wogan has been resurrected from the grave and he's gone a bit folksy. Oh, wait, I don't think Terry Wogan is dead. Well, you get what I mean. I thought about hiding in my room, waiting for the utter horror of having to watch someone else be dreadful to blow over.

But of course Ben is going in; he never can resist the urge to grab the limelight. He sucks up adoration like a bone-dry sponge, so it's lucky that almost everyone who meets him likes him at once. Sometimes I wonder if it's a talent he developed while trying and failing for his entire childhood to get his mother to notice him.

Ben strides into the patients' lounge, and I loiter in the doorway, waiting to see what he does before I actually commit to entering, not just because of the awful mind-bending embarrassment of witnessing his utter lack of embarrassment in action, but also because I need that moment to wait for my heart rate to slow, as the short walk seems to have made my body think it's running a marathon. The pain that holds me at all times intensifies for a while, and I concentrate on breathing, waiting until it becomes its usual background grind again, one that with enough concentration I can fade almost out of existence.

The room is full of families and children, sitting on sofas, curled up on beanbags, toys spread across the floor, flooded with a kind of warmth that doesn't come from the underfloor heating. My own small family of Mum and Dad aren't here tonight. They left as Ben arrived, handing over the baton of keeping an eye on me in one seamless, almost invisible, move – Mum turning pink as Ben shamelessly flirted with her. Suddenly, I miss them, with a pang that isn't like me at all. I look at the families brought together this evening, courtesy of Death and the accordion, and you feel it: all the hours of care and teetering anxiety, but mostly a sort of optimism. That life can't be too bad, if it can be exactly like this, even just for a few rare perfect moments at a time.

Ben isn't exactly the world's best singer, but what he lacks in tuning he makes up for in charm. Accordion Man looks more than a little put out as Ben joins in with his performance, but seeing the welcoming smiles of the faces of his captive audience, he grins and nods, and bobs up and down on his knees. I stand in the doorway and watch a little girl climb off her mother's lap and dance in circles at Ben's feet. And I see how it makes her mother, who's wrapped in a bright purple dressing gown, smile, which in turn makes the girl's father smile, and his expression of intense worry lifts a little for a while. That might be Ben's greatest gift: the knack he has for making almost every person he encounters stop thinking about themselves and start thinking about him instead. He really should be doing something else apart from persuading unsuspecting people to upgrade to phone contracts they don't need. He should be shining somewhere; he should always be the star. I think – I don't really like to admit it, because it's pretty shitty – but I think there's a little part of me that wants him to stay small and disappointed, because if he suddenly knew, if he suddenly saw what a talent he has for living, then of course he'd leave me far behind in my tiny four-walled world.

Silently I sing along with Ben, and Accordion Man. I feel each note vibrating internally, knocking against my bruised and battered insides like a pinball in a machine of flesh and blood, and I know that even as weakened as I am, I could still sing better than both of them. But I don't. I just watch and smile as Ben, one of the ballsiest buskers ever to be unleashed on unsuspecting Saturday-morning shoppers, flirts with the women, winks at the men and plays the fool with the kids, making the room come alive with smiles.

'How about this one? Know this one?' he says as the song ends, to laughter and clapping. He starts to play 'One Love' by U2, and, out of his depth, Accordion Man shrugs and takes a seat. But even he's not that offended by Ben, because that's his gift – the whole world loves him in an instant, and he loves them right back. There's never a moment with Ben, not even a second, when he isn't certain that everything is good.

'Why don't you go and sit down; join in?' Stella comes in and stands behind me. 'Your friend is joining in. He's … very flamboyant.'

I turn to look at her. Her dark eyes in a slim narrow face give her a particularly intense edge – like she feels everything a little more keenly than other people, even than me. I wonder what secrets there are that keep showing shadows in the hollows of her cheeks and eye sockets.

'Ben doesn't join in,' I tell her. 'The world joins in with Ben.'

'Well, don't be the only one left out, then,' she says, watching Ben throw back his head and holler. 'It's really sweet that he comes every night to see you.'

'He's weirdly chivalrous about that sort of thing; he promised, you see,' I explain. 'He never breaks a promise. I told him he didn't have to, that I am perfectly happy reading and watching movies, but he thinks I can't go twenty-four hours without seeing him.'

Stella smiles, tentatively. 'When I first started seeing my husband, I remember he couldn't stop showing off to impress me. He'd do anything to make me laugh, or scream or hit him. He loved it, loved the attention; and I've got to say, your Ben reminds me a little bit of that time, right now. Look at him! He so alive, isn't he?'

We both look at him, head thrown back as he sings, throat exposed, eyes closed, feeding off the energy in the room.

'He's not *my* Ben,' I say uncomfortably. 'And, anyway, Ben just likes to be in the spotlight. He's just your average attention-grabbing monkey.'

'Or maybe he likes to be in your spotlight, have you ever thought about that?' Stella asks me, with a mischievous edge I haven't seen before.

I snort. 'Ben and I are not in any way romantically involved. He fairly often witnesses me cough up mucus, and I've wiped vomit off his chin after a big night out.'

Those dark eyes regard me for a moment longer, keeping secrets, holding back thoughts.

'See Issy over there in the corner?' she says, nodding at a girl huddled in an armchair that somehow swamps her. 'She's fourteen years old. You are the nearest thing to someone her own age in here. She's got the room opposite you, and she is obsessed with you. Every time I go in there, she tries to find out more about you. She thinks you look so pretty and interesting. Would you go and say hello? You'd make her day.'

I hesitate and look over at the girl, slight and slim, clearly mortified by the handsome young man cavorting in front of her. It seems awfully unfair to me that even when a person is so gravely ill, they are still at the mercy of adolescence. I feel her pain.

'Or we could talk some more about Ben and his true intentions towards …' Stella teases.

'I thought you were sensitive,' I tell her. 'I thought you were like Anna Karenina in scrubs.'

'No idea – is that a film?' Stella asks me. 'What film character would you be? Maybe you and Ben would be like Baby and Patrick Swayze …'

And suddenly it seems like the best idea to go and sit next to Issy and ask her what bands she is into, and try not to draw attention to her grave health, which at least is something I am adept at.

'So on a scale of one to ten, how awful is this?' I ask, nodding at Ben wailing away.

'I like it, actually,' Issy says. 'I like noise, almost any noise, but not Accordion Man – he's just wrong.'

'Ha! I call him Accordion Man too.' We grin at each other. 'What music do you like?' I ask.

'Oh, I don't know, whatever is on Mum's iPod. I prefer to read, really.'

'Me too,' I exclaim, and this time she beams. 'You have great taste.'

'I don't really have any taste at all,' she confesses. 'Just a lot of time on my hands – and not enough, all at the same time … I'll read anything and mostly I like it, but I do like some authors better than others. Books are a bit like time travel, aren't they? They can pick you up out of your life and put you in someone else's. It's just a shame that at some point you always have to come back. So what's wrong with you? You look OK, to be honest.'

The question takes me by surprise.

'Me? Cystic fibrosis. It's like having a really shitty lung infection and constipation for your entire life, which is usually quite short. But, you know. It's not …' I gesture vaguely, realising that I've taken us down a path that only a minute ago I had been reminding myself not to engage with. Do not mention mortality to the dying kid.

'Cancer,' she says. 'Which is fucking shit.' She widens her eyes a little after swearing, looking as if she might get into trouble. I glance at her mum, who is sitting next to her with what I assume is Issy's little sister in her lap, and I lean in a little closer.

'Yeah, what a cunt,' I say, and she laughs, clasping her hands over her mouth.

'You can't say that!'

'I think you'll find I just did.' I lower my voice a further notch. 'But don't tell your mum.'

Ben has the room in the palm of his hand; there's a little boy, someone's grandson, I think, dancing around his legs, and he's got Edward and Saul, two of the older patients, clapping along – even if they are each keeping their own particular time. Without warning, I feel this unexpectedly intense rush of affection towards him for rescuing this evening from a well-meaning but undertalented volunteer and filling this room with laughter, instead of the usual polite enduring applause. Sometimes I forget how wonderful he can be.

Sensing Issy watching me watching him, I drop my gaze.

'He's good looking.' She nods at Ben, who is still caterwauling at the top of his voice. 'Is he a good kisser?'

'He's not my boyfriend!' I say, sounding about fourteen myself. 'Plus, boys are overrated. Books are so much better than boys, trust me.'

'Have you had a lot of boyfriends, then?' she asks me curiously.

'At least eighty-seven,' I tell her. 'Well, OK, two, and both of them were …' I glance at her mother, who is pretending not to be listening to every word, as her younger daughter gets up and joins the little boy in frantic dancing. 'Cunts.'

Issy laughs again, this time loud enough to make Ben raise an eyebrow at us, which makes her laugh even more and blush, the splash of colour bringing her pretty features into full focus, allowing me a glimpse of the girl she should have been. When she laughs, her eyes sparkle and she has two little dimples that form in her cheeks. Neither of us acknowledge the medication that flows steadily into her slight frame from the IV by her side; we both just want to pretend it's not there.

'This is a great experience,' she tells me. 'This is a good moment.'

'Yeah, it's a laugh,' I acknowledge, smiling at Ben as he twists and grooves with the two little kids.

'No, it's more than that,' Issy says. 'It's a happy thing. See?' She nods at her mother, who is laughing at her little sister. 'I haven't seen Mum like this in such a really long time. I'm so glad I'm seeing it now.'

Finally Ben's impromptu set list runs out, and he takes a bow, and then another, and one more just for luck, coming over and flopping down on the floor next to us, blowing his fringe out of his eyes, and grinning.

'Did you like that?' he asks Issy, who is at once a melting mess of mortification, unable to look up from her lap.

'I've got a book I think you might like,' I tell Issy, desperate to rescue her from the excruciating awkwardness of being around an attractive male. 'I'll be back in a second. Ben, come with me.'

Oblivious, he gets up and follows me, waving to his fans one last time, even though they are now more interested in the night's main attraction: Albie, the therapeutic Labrador.

'That was a massive laugh,' Ben says, dropping his arm around me as we go into my room and dragging me into a hug, so that my nose is smooshed against his chest. I let myself rest for a beat, let myself take strength from him as I feel the weakness and background pain intrude into my thoughts again, and then doggedly fight my way out of his embrace, because it is far too tempting to stay there, which would be a little bit awkward after the actual kiss-of-death (alleged) incident.

'I was awesome,' he goes on. 'They were a great crowd. Hey, maybe we should do a full-blown gig? I could get the band in? We could put a show on right here!'

'You are nuts,' I say fondly, knowing that he would do exactly that. 'But also fairly cool. Thank you for saving us inmates from Accordion Man.'

'The pleasure was all mine.' He takes a step back and appraises me. 'You look better, you know. Yes, there's some colour in those chubby little cheeks.'

'Oh shut up, I've been on the verge-of-death diet,' I protest, finding the book for Issy. 'My gut can barely absorb nutrients! I'm not chubby, I am just very short. It's different.'

'You aren't chubby, anyway. You are as slender as a willow wand,' Ben says. There is a beat filled with awkward silence.

'Weird,' I say.

'Let's go out for a pint.' He dips his chin and looks up through his lashes. It's his killer move – I've seen it stop a girl dead in her tracks a thousand times over. 'Let's go and sample the night air.'

'Don't be stupid,' I say. 'Didn't you hear all the verge-of-death stuff? I can barely walk to the end of the corridor without feeling like the inside of my chest is on fire.'

'I know, but the aim is for you to get out of here, right?' He grins. 'There's a pub literally across the road, and it's a nice one. And it's pretty mild out, and dry for once, and a bit of fresh air and a walk would do you good, build you up a bit. And I checked with the intense-looking nurse and she said OK, as long as you are back by ten. So, a quick one? Doctor's actual orders? Or nurse's, anyway.'

'I've got pyjamas on,' I say.

'So change!'

'And I've got to drop this book off to Issy.' I grab the book I was thinking of from my bedside and hold it up, like a shield. 'We were going to talk about it.'

'Is Issy the young girl you were talking to?' I nod. 'Give her the book on the way,' he tells me. 'Catch up with her tomorrow.'

'She might not be here tomorrow,' I say, and his expression softens.

'She will be. I saw how you made her laugh,' he said. 'Her eyes sparkled; she'll be here tomorrow. And, by the way, I think you are extremely cool for talking to her, and letting her have a laugh.'

'And I hate it when you do this,' I say.

'Do what?' He is going through all the clothes that I left on the back of a chair, and throws a pair of jeans at me.

'Trying to bring me out of myself,' I say. 'I don't want to come out of myself. I like it in here.'

'Yes,' he says, accosting me to drag a sweatshirt on over my vest, dressing me like I am an awkward child. 'But you are completely failing to notice the obvious.'

'Which is?' I ask him.

'When you are stuck inside your own head, I miss you.'

And just like that, he's won.

CHAPTER SEVEN

STELLA

It's 6 a.m. and still dark outside – too late in the year for there to be even a hint of dawn before I make it home. The night sky is still dense above the hum of the street lights, except for glimpses here and there of the fattening moon behind the cloud. I tie my shoes with precise care; the last thing I want is the knots coming undone as I run, because once I've started, I don't want to stop. The beat of my feet on the pavement, vibrating through my soles into my thighs, becomes my heartbeat. If I stop, I falter, and I find it hard to start again.

I never used to run anywhere. I never used to walk anywhere, either, except for that summer I first met Vincent. I liked my car. I liked the power and the freedom it gave me – the idea that whatever else was going on, if I wanted to, I could pick up my keys and be miles away by nightfall. I could start over, start a new life again, where nobody knows me. Back in the day, back before I had someone else to care about, and starting again stopped being an option.

My mum and dad, well, they have always been so in love with each other that it sort of felt more like they were fond and benevolent guardians to my brother and me than parents. When my brother fell in love just as hard, and went down to Devon with his new wife, and my parents retired to a cottage where at last they could simply enjoy each other's company uninterrupted, I was quite content to be alone. Because I was full of expectation that one day that sort of happiness would be mine.

And I was right. I met Vincent, big, strong, wonderful Vincent, with his long powerful thighs and a backside that was so firm you could bounce a penny off it. I know because I tried once. Back then, we were nearly always naked, always engaged in some activity that would keep us physically close. His fingers always laced in mine, my arms always around his waist, the length of our thighs always touching, our bare skin gliding over one another in a delicious silken warmth. We gravitated towards each other all the time. I was the moon to his earth, or perhaps the earth to his sun, because back then Vincent radiated heat – he shone with life force. He still does, I suppose, but it's a different kind of force: an all-encompassing hurricane of fury.

Being at the peak of fitness mattered to him; he loved being strong and efficient. In that first summer, that golden time when we first met while he was home on leave, he'd use any excuse to strip off and stride around, skin glowing. Lots of his mates had tattoos, but not Vincent. His skin was clean and as fresh as the day he was born. Outsiders might have thought he was vain, because they didn't know him. If I were another girl, sitting in the park, watching him strut past, cock of the walk, I'd have thought: he loves himself, that one. I'd have looked at me: short, dark, nothing special, and thought it must be a nightmare being her and being with him. But I never felt that way about Vincent, because I knew him. He wasn't vain. He didn't care what he looked like, or what other people thought of him. Plenty of girls would give him the eye when we were out; he never noticed. It wasn't about showing off for him; it was just that he so loved to be as alive as he possibly could. He loved feeling his muscles ache and his heart beating, and the sun on his back or the rain in his hair. He loved every moment of it. I've never met a man that inhabited his body as well as Vincent, at ease right down to the tips of his fingers.

He'd laugh at me, sitting naked in bed eating crisps while I watched him do press-ups, and I'd laugh at him.

'You should come running with me,' he'd say, early on in our courtship, and I'd shake my head.

'You should love me the way I am,' I'd tell him. 'With wobbly bits! I told you on the day we met that I'm lazy. I don't sit down at all at the hospital, so when I'm not working I like to lie down. And eat.'

'I know, and I do love you the way you are.' He'd grab me around the waist and lift me up, clean off the floor, like I didn't weigh quite a lot more than twelve stone – even potentially thirteen if I ever got anywhere near a set of scales, which I didn't. 'Especially your wobbly bits, actually, but it's not about that. It's about the feeling you get: the road beneath the soles of your feet, the smell in the air. It makes you feel strong, somehow, invincible. Exercise is better than any drug. I want you to feel that too.'

'And how would you know what's better than a drug?' I'd tease him. 'Your body is a temple. You don't even take caffeine.'

Sometimes, on days like that, he'd drop me on the bed, sometimes on the rug, and kiss me all over until I pleaded for him to stop. We laughed and laughed and laughed in those early days. Every day we were together was like the first day. Perhaps it was because he was away so much, because we spent so much time apart, that when we were together we were starving for each other – desperate and hungry for every second that we were connected.

The day he bought me these running shoes was a fiercely bright one, full of sunshine and arching faultless sky. He'd presented them to me on one knee, offering the shoebox like a ring on a velvet pillow.

'Top of the range,' he told me, proudly.

'And pink!' I cried out, looking at the neon articles. 'You bought me pink running shoes because I'm a girl – sexist!'

'You like pink,' he said, still on one knee. 'Your curtains are pink, your duvet is pink, you have a pink toothbrush and loads of pink underwear. I got you pink because you like it, babe.'

'Yeah, when I choose pink it's a choice. When you choose pink it's a patriarchal statement of expecting me to conform to your masculine ideals,' I teased.

'Fuck off,' he said, laughing. 'Your fucking car is even almost pink – well, purple! Anyway, whatever colour they are, they are exactly the right size for running: your shoe size plus half a size so your toes don't get rubbed.'

And that made me love him just a little bit more, so I accepted the shoes.

On the first day we went out running together, I dragged my feet and complained. I whined like a toddler, and he promised me an ice cream as he ran circles around me. He finally left me waiting for him on a park bench in the sunshine, with my rapidly melting prize, as he disappeared over the brow of the hill. I was still there, dozing, listening to the sound of children complaining and dogs barking, when he came back, shining with sweat, grinning from ear to ear as he collapsed on the bench next to me.

'How was that?' I asked him, letting him take my ice cream and finish it.

'Like flying,' he told me. 'Like launching off a cliff and taking to the air! It's better than ice cream, it's better than sex ...'

I saw the teasing glint in his eye as I launched at him, and some of the ice cream was smeared between us, sticky and cold. He caught me and held me and we laughed so hard I had tears running down my face. An old woman walking by took one look at us, tutted and shook her head. You could almost hear her saying, 'They'll learn.'

But I decided then and there that I never would learn. I *could* never learn not to love this man. There would never be anything that would come between us.

'You look beautiful,' Vincent had told me, suddenly quiet and still, looking hard into my eyes, that way he often did, when suddenly everything was so intense and so important, especially to me. 'You are everything that matters, you know. I never knew, I never knew what it was like to be afraid of dying, until I met you.'

'Poetic for a squaddie, aren't you?' I'd said, looking away because for a moment being loved so much felt a little dangerous, as if we were inviting fate to come and punish our joy. Vincent had kissed me hard, leaving his sweat all over me. We were so connected, it felt like every molecule that made us up vibrated in unison.

Which is maybe why I tried harder, the next time he took me running. It still felt like having my lungs clasped in some great iron clamp, and I told him I thought I might be having a heart attack. He told me I would do, too soon, if I spent my life sitting on my arse. He said he needed me to be alive longer than he was because he wouldn't be able to live without me, so I kept going – he romanced me into trying. I followed him doggedly, praying for the moment to come when he would let me stop.

One time after that it rained and I got soaked through to the skin, mud all over me, turning my girly trainers black. When we got home, he peeled my wet clothes off me, pulling me into the shower with him. I'd stood there, too exhausted to feel sexy, while he washed me down, kneeling in front of me, the water cascading over his shoulders, massaging my aching thighs, kissing the places in between. I decided then, I didn't care how far I ran or how much it hurt. It was worth it because I knew then I'd follow him everywhere; I'd never leave him.

Then one day, just a few days before he was due to go back overseas, I was following him along the canal towpath, with the spring blossom pouring down from the trees, the sun warm on my back, and I felt *joyful*. It stopped being his thing and my torture, and started being *our* thing. The thing we did together. Oh, what a smug couple we were, out running together every morning he was home on leave. If I even mentioned it to our friends, they'd stuff their fingers down their throats and pretend to vomit. Our friends: we had a lot of friends then; people circled around us. We don't have the same friends now; we moved when he came out of the army, and he never wanted to keep in touch with any of the old crew, not my friends, anyway. His relationship with his unit is different – they are the family that he never really had.

Now, Vincent has a lot of wonderful people who are around him all the time, pulling him forward, giving him the purpose, focus and dedication that he displays every day to the world outside our front door. But somehow I don't have him any more, and he doesn't seem to want me. And I am not really sure how that happened, except that after the injury everything changed, including him and me. I changed because he did, because when he didn't want me any more, I discovered I didn't want to be me.

And from the outside, everything looks if not good then OK. It's eighteen months since a rocket launch attack killed one and injured three in his unit. Eighteen months since Vincent escaped death, and now he is fully rehabilitated, at least physically.

I remember when the news came.

I was working, part of a team in A&E, trying to save the life of a little girl who'd walked out in front of a car, while her mother had stood by screaming as her daughter had been flung into the air. She had head injuries, massive internal injuries – the broken bones were almost incidental – and we were working, just like we always did, to reverse death, to defeat it and send it away again. We knew what we were doing, the trauma team. We were gladiators, experts: fearless, brave, perhaps a little bit cocky; each of us was certain that if we played our part, followed the rules, we had a very good chance of sending Death away empty-handed. And that day, the day that I heard the news about the love of my life, we knew we were on the road to saving that little girl. It would be hard, but we could do it.

And then I was called away, and they told me Vincent had been badly injured, that he was being airlifted first to Camp Bastion to be stabilised, and then to Birmingham. And the first thing I thought was that I couldn't go back to working on the little girl. I couldn't because, if there was only one life that was allowed to be retrieved that day, I didn't want it to be hers.

It was a dark thought, a terrible, irrational, selfish thought, but I had it. And sometimes now I have to think about it; I make myself think about it – about the strange cosmic choices that we think we have, the vows we will make, the prayers we will send out to a god in which we don't even believe. Take her, not him. Please, God, don't take him.

They sent me home, of course. Another nurse stepped in and took over my role, and the little girl was saved. I remember it seemed like years for the call to come through that Vincent was stable enough to be brought back to the UK, that the doctors felt that he was going to make it. I got in my purple car and drove up to Birmingham right away. I wanted to be at his side the moment he arrived.

Things were touch and go for a while, but at the hospital everything was taken care of with military precision, even though it wasn't a military hospital. The nurses took me under their wing, looking after me especially well as I was one of their own. They told me they ran the wards with the servicemen on as if they were in the army. Having people in uniform, having a routine, comrades in arms, it all helped the men and women they treated get better. When Vincent had healed enough, he was transferred to Headley Court to be fitted with a prosthetic leg and to learn how to walk again. I didn't see him so much then, in those four months; he didn't want me to come. He said he didn't want to see me again until he could be standing on his own two feet.

I fought him on that, of course. Even if he didn't want to see me, I wanted to see him. To know what he was going through, to know that I could be near him, to see him, touch him, while he went through what was almost unbearable. But he was insistent, cool to my pleadings. I thought it was his way of coping, of maintaining dignity. I thought, what's a few months out of a lifetime if it makes him feel better? We talked every day. We emailed, we skyped, and it was like we let ourselves believe that nothing had changed, that everything was the same, because, after all, ours was a romance that had always been lived down the wire.

And then on the day I went to pick him up, he greeted me at the top of the steps, standing tall, and I ran into his arms. And as I ran I thought, this is it, the proper beginning of our real life together as man and wife. We've been granted a miracle: he lived when others died. He'd survived and healed, and he could go on to do anything he wanted. The few months of pain, and worry, and uncertainty, were over; this was the minute that everything was back to how it should be.

It was in the car on the way home that he told me he was leaving the army.

'But you don't have to?' I'd been shocked. 'They haven't … I mean, have they said you have to?'

'No,' he said. 'I could stay on. They've plenty of roles I could take. They don't even rule out you going back to active service, these days.'

'Yes, when I was in Birmingham with you, during those first bad weeks, I found out about what could be next for you. Liaison officer is one thing. Working with other veterans, support roles – you can even go back to your unit, with the right support …'

'I know.' His tone was terse. 'I thought you'd be pleased. To have me home, out of harm's way. I … I don't want to go back. I'm not …' He paused and I thought he was going to say something more, to tell me what it was that had changed in him, but he finished the sentence making it clear the decision was already made. 'I'm not going back.'

'Of course I'm pleased.' I reached over to touch his knee, remembering just a little too late that one of them wasn't there any more, and stupidly withdrew my hand. 'Of course I am, it's just … what will you do?'

'Well, I can do anything I want to,' Vincent said, turning his gaze out of the window. 'Everybody says so.'

'So what do you want to do?' I asked him.

'The first thing I want to do is have a beer,' he'd said. 'And then after that, have another one.'

THE THIRD
NIGHT

CHAPTER EIGHT

* *

HUGH

I'm not big into winter: I don't like the dark afternoons or the cold walks home from work. I like a proper hot summer: shades on, girls in summer dresses, glimpses of brown skin and cleavage. But not my mum. Winter was the season she always loved best when I was a kid. She used to say she loved drawing the curtains and turning on the lights. She'd put the gas fire on and lay out a blanket, and we'd have tea together before Dad got in from work – crumpets or toast in front of the fire, its plastic coals glowing orange and red. Sitting cross-legged, her long blonde hair still tangled from an afternoon that she had slept away, Mum would tell me stories while I watched kids' TV.

Her stories came straight out of her head, and were probably far more scary and bloody than a boy of my age should have been listening to, but also they were magical, fantastical, epic and far-ranging and full of wonder. My dad was the finest man that I know – the best person – but I think that my curious mind, and what academic brains I have, came from Mum. It was just that she never had the kind of life where she could explore her potential. And anyway it didn't matter if she was telling me stories of knights lopping off heads, or witches chewing on the bones of children, somehow it didn't matter, because my mum had this way, this warmth, this enthusiasm, that made everything seem OK.

I was never afraid of monsters under my bed, or demons lurking in the wardrobe, because I assumed that nothing scary would ever be so stupid as to try and come face to face with my mum and her stubborn determination to laugh in the face of any kind of danger. Her fierce brightness would obliterate any shadow – that was how I thought of her: she was like a night light personified.

After crumpets and stories, she might fall asleep on the sofa, and I'd play, happy to be solitary, until Dad got in from work and made proper dinner. I remember it would take him some effort to wake her up for supper; he had to shake her and call her name, a little louder each of the many times. But eventually Mum would wake up, her pretty hair messed up and her eyes sleepy, and she would come to the table – the same table I still sit at. She would smile at me all through dinner, barely eating a bite before going to bed, while Dad talked at length about his day and would ask me about mine. I don't think I realised that he rarely spoke to Mum directly during those times. I don't think I realised it until quite recently.

Dad would tuck me in, and read me a story, and brush the hair off my forehead before planting a kiss on my cheek. And sometimes I asked him why Mummy never put me to bed, and he said, 'Mummy is just very tired, son. She needs her sleep.'

I suppose that's why during the summer I always think of Dad. Of long, hot afternoons on the canal bank, the sunlight dappling the water, midges flitting over its still surface. Waiting in quiet content companionship for that thrill of movement in the water: a sharp tug on the line, knowing that one of you had caught a fish. But in the winter, at times like this, it's her I think of – the way that she could reel you into her world and make you feel so special and wonderful and wanted. How sometimes she'd wake me up and take me out into the garden, gone midnight on a crisp, frosty night, and lay me down on the brittle grass, and we'd paint pictures in the constellations in the sky. And then, after she went, it's always felt like that part of my childhood was never real – that it was just one of the fairy stories she made up. And then I have to remind myself that I am a grown-up now, that I have a great job and a nice house, and only really pathetic men dwell on the holes that their mother left in their life twenty-five years ago.

Maybe I should have gone for a drink with that girl from the British Museum tonight after all. She has an ability to talk non-stop without breathing. It's not exactly beguiling, but it works very effectively as an anaesthetic of the mind; plus she is extremely pretty. Still, I'm nearly home now, so a quick spag bol with Jake – if he's got room in his diary between his daytime roaming and night-time adventures – and then maybe a pint in the pub down the road before bed.

I always forget to leave the lights on when I leave for work, so the house is dark when I get home, with the lights in other neighbouring houses burning so brightly either side of it, lit up with a welcome.

As I approach home, I stop at the gate, noticing that tonight next door's house is in darkness too. And there's something else. A boy, next door's boy, is sitting on the doorstep, huddled up in what looks like a tracksuit top. Whatever it is, it's not enough of a defence against the chill in the air. More of a hoody, if anything. I think about pretending I don't see him, but oddly he reminds me a bit of Jake when he comes in from the rain: half his normal size and shivering; it's the one time he'll let me make a fuss of him, wrap him in a towel and rub him down, huddling close to me for warmth.

They haven't been in there long, the new neighbours. The house was bought by a housing association a couple of years back and seems to be fitted with revolving doors: there's a new face every few months, and this kid is another one of them.

'Er, hello?' I say. 'You all right?'

He does not look up from his phone, which floods his face with artificial light, throwing the shadows of his eyelashes in upward spikes.

'OK?' I ask again, not because I really want to know, except that he looks vulnerable sitting there – about ten or eleven years old, I'd say.

'Why do you want to know?' he asks me. His voice is sharp, managing to sound nervous and angry at the same time. He is suspicious, and I don't blame him.

'Well, it's dark and cold, and you're sitting on your doorstep on your own. Isn't your mum in?'

'If she was, I wouldn't be out here, would I?'

'I suppose not. Will she be back soon?' While he doesn't appear to be in any imminent danger, and I'm starving for microwaved pasta and a beer, I don't feel like I can just ignore him; my dad would never have ignored him, and he is the benchmark I strive for.

'I forgot my keys, didn't I?' he says, unconcerned, but he shudders despite himself.

'How long have you been there?' It's gone seven. School will have finished hours ago.

'I dunno, couple of hours,' he says. 'I'm flipping freez-ing.' Somehow the phrase sounds comical in his high childish voice.

'Did you call your mum?' I ask him.

'Yeah, but she works shifts, and if she comes home she doesn't get paid, and it's like, oh I dunno, you have to go every day to keep your job, or something, or they give it to the next person. So I said I'd be fine. I told her I'd go round a mate's house, but there wasn't anyone about. When she gets in, I'll just say I was here for a minute or two.'

'So that she doesn't worry?' I ask him, touched by his concern for his mum.

'Are you a pervert?' He looks me suddenly, sharply, as if he's just remembered he isn't supposed to talk to strangers.

'No … I'm your neighbour. I live here – next door.' I jangle my door keys.

'That doesn't mean you're not a perv,' he says, standing up, defensive now. 'Pervs are everywhere. They even look normal. You're wearing a bow tie; perverts wear bow ties.'

'I …' My hand travels involuntarily to my neck, protectively covering the offending article. 'I am a professor of history,' I tell him. 'My bow tie is ironic.'

'Er, no it isn't,' he says scathingly. 'If you weren't a professor, then it would be ironic, which doesn't make it un-pervy.'

'Well, I'm not a perv,' I say, feeling frankly ridiculous. 'I'm not. I'm Hugh.' I offer him a hand to shake, and then realise how ridiculous that is, inviting him to come all the way down the path to shake my hand, out of the shelter of his doorstep, so I tuck my hand back in my pocket. 'I was just worried about you sitting there, freezing. I could make you a cup of coffee if you like, bring it out?'

'Coffee? I'm only ten!' he says, affronted by the suggestion, and I can't help but grin.

'Er, hot chocolate? I think I might have some left over from this girl … this woman, adult woman, I used to date.' He looks like he is considering the offer, when we are interrupted.

'Can I help you?' I turn and find his mother, home at last. Small, short and petite are words that might describe her; she's barely five foot, with a tiny build, huge dark eyes and long, straight black hair. Her heart-shaped face is almost dwarfed by a thick woolly hat pulled down to her eyebrows, which are drawn together fiercely. I sense she's used to defending her small family with quite some vehemence.

'No, I was trying to help your son. I'm Hugh. I live next door? I came home from work and found him sitting on the doorstep. He looked freezing.'

'I've been here for two minutes,' the boy says, staring hard at me. 'He wanted to make me a cup of coffee!'

He makes it sound as if I tried to entice him inside my lair with a packet of sweets, and suddenly I wish more than ever that I were in my dark empty house enjoying the prospect of an evening with my beer and my microwave.

'He's fine. He lost his key, he's been round a mate's,' she says, defensively, bustling past me on her side of the fence, fumbling for her keys. 'You don't need to worry about us. We're fine. We do really well, actually.'

'I wasn't questioning whether or not you are a good mother …' As soon as I say the words out loud, I can see I've touched a nerve, frightened her somehow, and I don't blame her. What a stupid thing to say. Why didn't I just take him at his word and go inside ten minutes ago? This is what happens when you engage with the world at random – it starts engaging back.

'He's fine, we're fine. Mind your own.' She fumbles with the keys and drops them. I am making her nervous, and I feel sorry. The best thing I can do is simply get indoors and we can all pretend we never had this conversation.

'Well, you're home now,' I say. 'I'll let you go. Goodnight.'

'Is he a pervert?' I hear the boy asking just before she slams her front door shut.

Jake is there sitting on the bottom stair, mercifully speechless.

'How was your day?' I ask him. 'Sex, drugs, sleeping on the radiator?'

He looks like all three were entirely possible and follows me begrudgingly into the kitchen. I stop without thinking and check the answerphone, but there is no light blinking – just a dusty, empty faux-wooden box, not the portal to mysteries that I don't understand at all. I don't know what I was expecting, or hoping for, from that missed message last night. Or who I thought might have stood in a public call box trying to reach me. But it had given me something I didn't expect: a sense of hope, of something different. Although what I think I might be missing escapes me. I have everything I want. A great job, my freedom, no financial or emotional tangles – everything is exactly how I like it. And that stupid silent-but-not-quite phone message makes me feel like I do when I've left the house and I can't remember if I left the shower running. Some important piece of missing information that is just out of my reach. But it's ridiculous. I'm being ridiculous. I'm thinking like a girl.

Probably all this research into séances and spiritualism isn't helping. Perhaps after spending so many days dissecting messages from 'the other side', I'd half hoped it was Dad, checking in to see how I was doing, if I had become a better fisherman overnight, or built that new rod stand we'd planned together. But it was probably just a wrong number, which led to a blinking light in an empty house. Which might be a metaphor for my life: the man at the end of the line that only a stranger might call by mistake. A man who is perfectly content, I remind myself, sharply.

A knock at the door makes me jump, and Jake speeds out of the cat flap before I've even opened him a tin of tuna. I sigh. The last time I opened the door to strangers, it was to Christians who did not know the Bible as well as I do, and who certainly weren't expecting to have every quote they gave me returned with one from *The Origin of Species*.

'If you're a politician …' I grumble as I walk down the hall, but I know the answer to that as soon as I see the distinctive outline on the other side of my bubbled glass. It's my very short neighbour, in her large woolly hat.

Oh, Christ, I hope she hasn't come round to be confrontational. I hate confrontation. I am a person who is really happy to be dumped by text, or to be given negative feedback in an email. I don't care for face-to-face angst at all, but it's too late to pretend that I am not here: if I can see her, that means she can see me. Perhaps if I apologise as soon as I open the door, she will go away quickly.

'Hello, I'm sorry about before,' I say hastily. 'I realise that adults aren't supposed to talk to kids any more. I didn't mean to make either of you uncomfortable.'

'No, I'm sorry,' she says, and I am taken by surprise.

'Oh.' I don't really know where the conversation can go from here, so I simply wait, holding on to the door.

'About before …' She gestures at her doorstep. 'I'm sorry about that. I didn't meant to be rude and that, it's just, you know, where I lived before, people always had an opinion, and thought if you are on your own with a kid, living in a housing association place, you have to be either sponging off benefits or neglecting the kid. I work. I pay rent. I love my son. I guess I'm touchy about it, but I know you were trying to be nice and that.'

'Well,' I say inadequately. 'Not to worry … Cheerio, then!' Cheerio?

'I do take good care of him, though,' she says before I can close the door. 'Just so you know. I do, and he should have told me he didn't have a friend's house to go round, but he tries to take care of me too, and he didn't want me to have to leave work early, because he knows that I struggle to pay the bills. Normally, I'm home an hour after school finishes. But today there was some overtime, cleaning at this hospice up the road, and I heard they might be looking for permanent staff ... and if you say no, you don't get offered it again ...'

'You don't have to explain it to me,' I say, finding my voice at last, and frankly feeling like the world's biggest shit for making this young woman feel that way, even if it was by accident. 'I'm glad he's OK. I'm glad you're OK. I don't have an opinion about your skills as a mother, except that I am sure they are very good – I mean, to come round here ... I wouldn't have done it.'

'Really?' She looks relieved. 'So we're OK, then?'

'Sure,' I say, sort of touched that she should care what I think about her or her kid. There's something heartening about it.

'Great.' She gives me two thumbs up, which hover there in tableau for a few awkward seconds, neither of us sure of what comes next. 'I'll be getting back, then.'

'Me too, I've got stuff,' I say, as if spag bol and beer counts as stuff.

As I close the door I see that Jake has slinked in from the garden again.

'You're all meow and no claws,' I tell him. 'She seemed all right, to me.'

But, as I pierce the cover of my ready meal and whack it in the microwave, I wonder if the blinking of the phone message and the knock on the door tonight are ways the universe is reminding me that this perfect, carefree, no-strings life I've made for myself can be kind of disappointing sometimes.

Dearest Lizzie,

This is a to-do, isn't it? Here I am about to be carried off into the wide blue yonder and, well, to say the way that fate is taking me is a bit of a joke is to say the least!

You have been a remarkable daughter, a remarkable person, actually, and I know you don't get your patience or tolerance from me. I was never so selfless, kind or forgiving as you.

You were fifteen on the day I said I was leaving home to become a singer on a cruise ship. I suppose that had something to do with my age – approaching forty and still I felt like a stranger in my own skin. You do see that, don't you, darling? You see that it was never you I was running away from? It was me I was running to. Oh dear, and now I sound like that awful song about having never been to me. God save us from hippies.

You could have hated me then; you had every right to, but I told you what was happening and why, and you listened and you – well, you've always been wise beyond your years – you decided to understand. I don't know if you really understood then, or if it was years later, but it hardly matters, because you were there, on my opening night, when I came back to shore, in that smoky godawful dive. You'd even brought your pals.

Knowing you were there made me feel like a million dollars. I wore my sequins and false lashes with pride. It was the first step on a long journey, and you helped me take it – your love for me never wavered.

You never shied away from telling your friends that you had two mothers now, that one of them used to be your dad. You lifted your chin up high and held my hand, and helped me through. I am so lucky, so, so lucky, that I had you in my life. I don't think I would have lived this long if you hadn't shown me that it was OK to be me.

Prostate cancer – well, it's a laugh, isn't it? The woman with the finest manicure in town is getting taken down by the biology that she never wanted. Bury me in a silver coffin, darling, cover me in glitter from head to foot, play Dean Martin and dance. Make sure you and my grandchildren dance for all you are worth.

And, as for me, don't you feel sad. There cannot be a happier person than me, knowing, as I do, that the same biology that's finished me off is what gave me the chance to create you – the most wonderful woman I know, apart from your darling mother.

Dance, just dance every day. Dance on my grave – I shan't mind a bit.

With love,
Mum

CHAPTER NINE

* *

HOPE

I'm not entirely sure what I've agreed to, but somehow it's happened, and all in that one hour in the pub. Ben left me at my room door last night, and I haven't been able to stop thinking ever since. Not just normal 'Oh God, I feel like hell, and I wonder what they are giving us for dinner' thinking, but stupid, crazy, fast-thoughts-type thinking, where you keep on wondering: did that really happen? And, if it did, what was it exactly that drove me to the point of temporary insanity?

'What about Glastonbury? We should do that. I'll get tickets now – something for you look forward to, when you get out of here,' Ben had said about halfway through our pint – or should I say his pint and my J2O. Beside his drink there was also a vodka chaser. (I don't know why for just a quick drink he felt like he needed an extra shot of spirits. I think it's almost like a badge of honour with him – look at me, with my chaser; I'll be playing the O2 next year, wait and see – me with my edgy lifestyle and my vodka shot.)

'All the tickets will be sold now,' I'd told him. 'They'll have been sold out months ago. Besides, I'm not exactly keen on the whole toilet situation, or the mud, or the rain, or the camping.'

'Don't be stupid, that's what festivals are all about. OK, so if this year is too late, what about next year, then?' he'd said, and I'd looked sceptical. 'Also, you know, with you on board we might get disabled access.'

I'd given my best withering stare, and he'd shrugged.

'Seems a bit optimistic to plan that far ahead,' I'd said. 'Be a shame to spend all the money on something and then I die before I get to go. And I really do hate the rain and the toilets and the camping. We could watch it on telly again.'

'You're too young to always be the voice of doom, you know,' he'd said. 'I've become an expert on CF, and when you are well and it's under control, you can do anything, including rock festivals. And it's not a death sentence any more. When you were born, everyone said you'd be lucky to make it to your thirties, and now it's likely you can make it to forty, and who knows what advances next year or the year after will bring?'

'How do you know all this stuff?' I'd said.

'I keep up to date with things,' he said. 'I keep informed. If only you were a bit younger and a bit more terminal,' he'd said, wistfully. 'We could write to some Make-A-Wish foundation or some shit. The dying kids get all the best deals.'

I'd thought about Issy, and her chirpy headscarf, and how the whites of her eyes are yellow, and how swearing makes her laugh.

'That isn't exactly true, is it?' I'd said. 'I mean, they are dying.'

'I know, I'm sorry,' Ben had said, lowering his eyes, and I knew he was thinking about Issy at that moment too. 'You know how sometimes my efforts to be flippant tip over the edge into bad taste.'

'I am familiar with that, yes,' I'd replied. 'And anyway, you don't have to make it your mission to cheer me up, you know; I'm not your … charity case.'

'What?' He'd looked hurt and sat back in his chair like my words had shoved him there. He doesn't know I'd meant to say, 'I'm not your girlfriend,' but had changed tack at the last moment, because … well, just because.

'What I mean is, well, you are always hanging around being nice to me, but you shouldn't feel obliged. If you thought that, well, maybe we've outgrown each other, I'd get it. I mean, maybe a friendship formed when one of us wet their pants, and it wasn't me, isn't meant to last past, say, the age of ten. Although to be fair that *is* your mental age.'

'Hope Ellen Kingston.' Ben had looked horrified. 'We made a deal. We made a scared vow; we pretended to cut our palms and become blood brothers, but with a red biro. We're red-biro relatives. I'm in this for the long haul. You're my best friend; you know everything there is to know about me – I mean everything.' He didn't have to say out loud what he meant; the incident he was alluding to, which had involved me and him, a shatterproof ruler and me taking his

… er … exact measurements when we were twelve, is still indelibly printed on both of our minds.

'I'm just saying,' I'd told him. 'We made this deal when we were six, at around the same time you also vowed to become a striker for Arsenal and learn to fly, *using your arms*. It's not like some oath. You don't have to be my own personal cheerleader. You can … be free, you know.'

'That's not why I do it,' he'd said. 'Because I feel obliged. I do it because chicks really dig that I'm so kind to you. Having a cripple as a best friend gets me laid. And anyway, fate does not break up partnerships like ours; we're like Batman and Robin, or Romeo and Juliet.'

'You know they both die, Romeo and Juliet, right?' I'd asked him.

'Shit, I never got to the end. I was looking for the sex scene,' he'd said.

And I had made my usual heavy sigh, mature eye roll, and he'd done his usual schoolboy chuckle, and I'd thought, that's what I am. I'm his best friend, his side-kick, who he has no recollection of kissing. I'm a hanger-on, his best pet groupie, the girl that will always be there, telling him how great he is. I'm his straight (wo)man, and that is exactly the way I want it be, for ever.

And then he'd said, 'It's Open Mic Night at the Market Tavern every Saturday night, seven till nine. I've got an idea. To help you get back to full fitness, you should give your lungs a work out. Remember? That's why you took singing lessons in the first place – because it helps strengthen the lungs and get oxygen into them, open them up and shit? We were all shocked you could actually sing. Anyway, we'll work up one of your songs, you choose, just you and me. It's about time you started singing again – I can't remember the last time you let me hear you.'

'Oh, I don't really sing – you know that,' I'd said. 'Not for an audience.'

'But you should, you totally should. You have such a lovely voice: clear and pure and strong, and you've got range. Yes, that's what we'll do. You'll start singing and I'll help you, and we'll do a number at open mic night. You start singing next time I visit, I'll bring my guitar and we'll jam one of your songs together and make it really cool. Yeah. Because, you know, I like the band and everything, but they are at bit one-dimensional, with all the heavy rock and eyeliner. I fancy something a bit lighter, and a bit more poppy.'

'Are you saying that I write pop songs?' I'd asked.

'I'm saying you write tunes that people hum after they've heard them only once, and that is a good thing.' He'd looked so pleased with himself. 'Yes! This is brilliant. I'm a genius. And once you're ready to celebrate getting out, we'll go and sing your song at the Market Bar, together. I promise, I will be with you every step of the way, if you say yes. I will be, like, glued to your hip.'

And I'd found myself saying yes.

Shit.

*

I need a walk. It's quiet in the corridor. The nurses' station is empty, the lighting low. There's a sort of soft murmur – not voices, exactly, or machines, but a background hum, hushed in the darkness. It acts as a kind of reassurance that, despite the stillness, we are not alone: Marie Francis continues to operate all around us. Almost like it is not just a building full of people, but a sentient creature all of its own; this is somehow comforting.

I can hear someone boiling a kettle in the kitchen, and the rustle of a biscuit packet, which makes me think some sugar might be a good way of taking my mind off things. I stop by Issy's door, wondering if she is still up, reading, but the light is off and it's quiet. Her mum is in there with her, sleeping with Issy in her arms – the girl's head resting on her mother's breast. At least I thought they were both asleep but when I pause, Issy's mum opens her eyes and smiles at me. Of course she is constantly on edge and constantly alert to everything that is happening around her daughter, like any mother guarding her young, only now she is trying to defend her child against a foe that cannot be beaten. Even the small glimpse into a little of what she must be feeling is unbearable, and I think of my own mother, who will be at home now, still up but in her dressing gown and slippers, stirring a cup of tea with three sugars in it until it goes cold.

I suppose it will be a very long time before Issy's mum sleeps properly again.

'Would you like a cup of tea?' I whisper.

'Thank you, that's kind,' she whispers back, afraid to move in case she disturbs her daughter.

I pull the door shut and pad back down the corridor, the tiles feeling smooth and cool under my bare feet. The door to one of the rooms is ajar, and I try not to look inside, but I do, seeing an older lady who looks like there isn't much time left, and seeing her so very close to the end is frightening. I turn my face away and go back to the little kitchen, feeling the tightening in my chest, the pounding in my temples. My life, my body, reminding me how dependent I am on this faulty sack of bones and nerves to exist at all. It doesn't feel right; it doesn't feel fair. It feels like I should be able to fly out of this mass of biology and exist somewhere else, and it's hard, almost impossible, to accept that I can't. For a moment I just want to get away from it all, and I want my mum. My mum, who is standing in our kitchen in her slippers. I want my mum, like a little girl who isn't half as brave as Issy.

The person I find instead is Stella – her eyes closed as she leans against the counter. There are four empty tubes of sugar next to her. The shadows in the hollows under her cheekbones seem denser somehow and her eyes are tightly shut, as if against a bright light. I think she might have fallen asleep standing up.

I cough politely.

'Hello, night owl,' she says gently, opening her eyes. 'Come to make a drink?'

'Yes, and I'm making one for Issy's mum too, only I don't know how she takes her tea. Do you know?'

'Thea? Yes, decaff, milky and no sugar,' Stella tells me, blinking herself back into action. 'I'll make it. You can keep me company for a while. Hot chocolate for you, right?'

I nod and feel a bit foolish about my childish choice of drink. I always wanted to be the girl in the beret in the French café drinking *café noir*, *très*, *très* strong, but I don't like the taste and I don't need anything else to keep me up at night. Coughing my guts up and thinking at one hundred miles per hour does that for me. Mum in her slippers, and hot chocolate with little marshmallows on the top – that's what I need to feel safe again. But all I have to help me chase away the invisible demons that are stalking through the corridors is kind, tired, secretly sad Stella, which is good enough.

'Ben is going to help me start my vocal exercises again,' I blurt out. 'He came up with this madcap plan last night. I'm going to start singing, and we're writing a song together, apparently, which is crazy because he's already in a band. You can't be in a band and a duo. And I don't sing in public for people; that's not what I do. I don't like all that – the attention, people looking. "Oh, look at the poor CF girl. Nice little voice she's got. Isn't it a shame?"'

'Or maybe they'd just hear your voice and enjoy your music, and not think or even know about the CF,' Stella says thoughtfully. 'People probably aren't as curious about you as you think, you know? They've all got their own worries; no one really ever looks too deeply at someone else's life unless it affects them.'

'Do you really think that's true?' I ask. 'That's awful, if it is. I care. I care about other people, and other lives that don't affect mine.'

'I know.' She nods. 'And I didn't mean that. I mean that we all have to live and die alone, eventually, even if we surround ourselves with other people.'

'Bloody hell, you are depressing,' I tell her. 'Is that why you are always on night shift, because they're worried you might push the patients over the edge?'

She laughs then, and her face alters in every way. She looks younger, illuminated, alive.

'God, I'm sorry,' she says. 'I'm having a bad night. Didn't sleep very well today, and … well, it doesn't matter, but you are right. I need to snap out of it.'

'That's not what I said at all,' I tell her. 'Life isn't something you can just snap out of.'

She gives me a look that speaks volumes.

'I am being a tiny bit dramatic, I suppose,' I admit. 'It's easier, sometimes, than accepting that … well, that I don't have it as bad as Issy, for one. Or that poor woman opposite me. But if I accept that, then … I have to do something about this life that I am letting tick by, and I don't know what it is that I have to do.'

'Maybe all you have to do to begin with is get up on stage and agree to sing a song with your friend,' Stella says. 'Wouldn't it be wonderful if something so simple could be the key to being happy? Amazing – you're in a band. I always wanted to be in a band. Singing along to Bananarama into a hairbrush was the nearest I ever got.'

'I think it was the nearest they ever got, too,' I say, and she nearly smiles. I like to make her smile, to wipe away for a second or two that look of deep sadness she carries around with her. It's like her outside reflects my insides, somehow. Making her smile makes me feel less immature and selfish, more like the grown woman I am supposed to be.

Growing up with Ben by my side meant that my friend-ships with other girls my own age have always been sort of distant – friendly, fun, but never deep. There's never been a girlfriend that I've swapped secrets with, or talked about how I feel, like I just have with Stella. It feels nice.

'So you think it's a good idea, then?' I ask her. 'Because I said yes. I said I'd sing with him in public, and now I'm freaking out.'

'Yes, it was the right thing to do,' she says. 'You are very brave – I could never do that. The idea of all those people looking at me, noticing me. I used to like it, being seen. Being noticed, turning heads. But these days … I think life is easier if you're invisible. At least it is for someone who isn't as brave as you. I was brave once but, somehow, I think I've forgotten how to be.'

'I'm not brave,' I say. 'Ben keeps trying to make me as brave and as stupid and as certain as he is, but I'm not. I'm not like that.' She waits for me to say more, and suddenly the words just rush out, tumbling chaotically, barely sentences at all. 'It's like there is this unwritten law that if you're dying, or you have a "life limiting" disease – which, let's face it, is a polite way of saying that you are dying – then you have to be all chipper about it. You have to be brave and upbeat, you have to be inspiring and strong, you have to be defiant and embracing … and I'm not, Stella, I'm not like that; I'm not brave. I'm afraid all the time – terrified and sad, and *angry*, and I don't want to be inspirational. I want to be invisible, like you said. I don't want life to notice me, because if life does, then so will Death.'

There's a moment of silence, and then as I stand there watching her, her great big orange eyes fill up with tears.

'I know,' she says. 'I know exactly how you feel.'

I don't know what else to do, so I hug her, putting my arms around her slight body, and she hugs me back, presses me against her. And we both cry, there in the tiny kitchen, with the kettle bubbling and boiling away in the background. The button clicks off and Stella releases me, smoothing away tears with the tips of her fingers.

'What makes you so sad?' I ask her, as she turns her back to me and busies herself tearing open sachets of tea and hot chocolate.

'Honestly?' she says. 'I don't think my husband loves me any more. In fact, I think I make him hate himself.'

'Really? How do you know?'

'He can't bear to look at me,' she says simply, passing me first one mug of hot chocolate and then the tea for Issy's mum. 'And when the person you love stops loving you, stops seeing you, even, you might as well be a ghost anyway.'

Dear Reverend Peterson,

I am not a religious person, you should know that up front. I don't believe in God. I think it's a load of twaddle, but my husband likes the idea of a church service. He says it's more dignified than that humanist lot, and he's not in favour of a cremation while some bloody song by Barbara Streisand is playing in the background. He says he won't feel like I'm properly dead unless someone says a prayer over me, which you might think sounds a bit tactless, but that's the way we've always been, me and him. Say it how it is. No one gets hurt, or confused; no one expects anything other than exactly what they are going to get. Which wasn't a lot, to be honest, but it was enough for us.

You'll be standing up at my funeral and talking about me as if we've met, which we never have, and I thought you might like to know a bit about me, so as not to appear like the deluded charlatan you are. I'm fifty-nine now – I don't suppose I will see sixty. We never had children, me and him. I wanted them, and so did he, but we just weren't blessed that way. Truth be told, I like animals more than I like most people. I've volunteered for Cats Protection for fifteen years. You know where you are with a cat. Cats don't believe in God either, now I come to think of it. It's a good rule of life, I think, not to take anything seriously that a cat doesn't. Stops you fretting about all sorts of stuff and nonsense and keeps you focusing on what matters.

You know what? If there was a God, if he did exist, I'd like to grab him by the throat and throttle him for finishing me off this way – before I am ready. For making me leave my husband behind, when we both know he won't cope. If there was a God, I'd have a good old go at murdering him. But seeing as I don't believe in him anyway, maybe I kind of have. Ancient Egyptians worshipped cats, you know? That seems sensible.

If I have to have a hymn, I want 'The Lord is My Shepherd', and someone to do a reading – I don't mind about what, as long as it's tasteful. If he looks like he might cry, my husband that is, tell him not to be so soft. We knew it was coming. And remind him, he's only stood in a church so he can feel better.

We didn't make many friends – we didn't need them, not when we had each other. So, maybe you'll visit him from time to time. I wouldn't like to think of him being alone and missing me. That would seem like the Christian thing to do, and I have always liked that about your lot.

Yours sincerely,

Lottie Moorecroft

CHAPTER TEN

STELLA

'Hey, you,' I say to Issy in a low voice.

She is wide awake, staring at the moon out of her window, as Thea sleeps deeply on the guest bed, exhaustion temporarily excusing her from her vigil. A tired-looking soft octopus is tucked under Issy's arm, and a book open near the beginning is resting on her lap. This is where Shadow has been visiting tonight, I see – his long, lean body is stretched out along the length of her thigh. He lifts his head and looks at me sleepily for a moment before nuzzling it back against Issy's leg. 'How are you feeling?'

'Good, actually,' she whispers, turning her face, which shines softly in the moonlight, to look at me. 'Is that weird?'

'No,' I say, 'that's good, of course.' I take a seat next to the bed, and for a moment we both watch Thea sleeping – her mouth open, her face slack. Suddenly she snorts, a deep rumbling noise, and Issy smiles, reaching out and pulling her mum's blanket up over her bare arm. Once she is certain that Thea isn't about to wake, she speaks again.

'But it doesn't mean ... I mean, I'm not getting better or anything, am I?' She poses the question as if it worries her.

'Because when the doctors said that things were ... you know, nearly over, it was kind of a relief. I don't want to go through it all again: having more treatment, feeling so ill, trying to stay alive for Mum. And the reason ... the reason I asked to come here, instead of being at home, is because I didn't want home to be the place where Mum and Katy think of as the place where I died. If I go home again, then ... I feel OK now, but I don't want to do it all again.'

I sit down next to her and take her hand. 'There's this sort of phenomenon,' I say, 'that all nurses know about, but there's no evidence for it. But it's this thing we call a surge or a bloom. Just before the end, we often see our patients feeling so much better, as if their body is drawing up all of their energy for one last hurrah. I don't know what causes it or why it happens, but nurses see it all the time. There's more going on, you know, in our hearts and minds than those doctors know. Nurses see it every day. I don't think you need to worry.'

She regards me seriously for a while, and then she smiles.

'Would be it really naughty if you could take me for a spin out in the garden? I just want to feel the breeze on my face. Just for a little while; I don't want Mum to wake up and for me to not be here.'

'Of course,' I say, opening the patio doors, which each patient's room has, leading out to the grounds.

'And Stella,' she says. 'Would you write a letter for me? To Mum and Katy?'

Grace's room is lit very low, and no longer bare. Keris must have brought in the photo that is on her bedside table – maybe from her office, because at its heart is Grace wearing a lilac T-shirt, with the Marie Francis logo printed on, and a wide, wide smile, eyes disappearing into crinkles. Her arms are open but not quite encircling a large group of kids and teenagers – all ethnicities, girls and boys, grinning, their thumbs up, pulling faces, making signs behind each other's heads. A couple of them are holding one of those large outsized cheques that makes a presentation to charity. It looks like a snap that was taken in a moment of great fun. Sasha from the day team told me that there had been a constant stream of visitors by Grace's side all day, and the room is filled to the brim with cards, drawings, flowers, pastel-coloured teddy bears holding hearts – there's even a balloon gently bobbing in the corner.

She is sleeping, her face turned towards the darkest corner. I haven't had a chance to talk to her since she arrived, but I can see she has a gentle face, recently altered by pain. But it's a face that has a past, that has lived through difficult times. I can tell by the deep lines that are carved around her mouth and eyes. But for now at least she is relaxed. Pain-free. Her hands neatly folded on top of the bedspread.

Quietly I move around her, checking her pulse, her temperature, her blood pressure and oxygen saturation. I'm comforted by the routine, the certainty in numbers, the peace that fills every corner of the room.

'Where …?' Grace whispers the word as her eyes flicker open. Slowly she focuses on me. I take her hand and smile, reassuringly. Often a patient will forget where they are or why, for a few moments. You take their hand, and look them in the eyes, and help them to remember in the least frightening way that you can.

'It's OK,' I tell her. 'Grace, you're in a hospice, do you remember? My name is Stella. Keris brought you here, and we're looking after you now.'

I watch as her eyes glide around the room, taking a moment to focus, and I feel her fingers relax in mine.

'What time is it?' she says.

'Almost two in the morning.'

'Could I have a drink of water, please?'

'Of course.' I pour a cupful and offer it to her with a straw. She shakes her head, and I help her sit up, so she can drink from the cup herself. She's weak and she winces, but she can grip the cup and bring it to her lips.

'Are you in pain?' I ask her.

'No.' She shakes her head, but I suspect she is lying. Patients do that; they don't want you to know how much pain they are in, in case it means something. When you are here, facing the very end of your life, no one wants anything to mean anything.

'I'll get the on-call doctor to have a look at your meds, just to make sure.'

'I'm fine.'

'Did your family come in today?'

She sips the water. 'No, I don't have any family. Well, I did once, years ago. But I lost them.'

'But so many friends, though,' I say. 'Lots of people who love you. Just look at all the flowers and cards – it smells like summer in here. You know, you don't have to have all these visitors? If you find it too much, just say. Sometimes people don't really think what it can be like for you, having to keep on being brave.'

'No, I want them to come. I want them all to come, to keep me busy. I don't like it when it's quiet, when I can think and dream.' She rests her head back against the pillow, and I take the cup from her.

'Do you want to try and get in touch with your family again?' I ask her. 'I'm sure the day team told you, we can find people for you, track them down. It's at times like this when we often find that we want to reach out, resolve silly arguments, things that don't seem to matter all that much any more. We can try and get in touch with any one you like.'

'There's no one.' She leans back into the pillows, closing her eyes. 'Thankless job, the night shift.'

'I like it,' I say. 'It's peaceful, really.'

'When I was a young woman, I used to stay up all night, even after I was married. Stay up and go out dancing and drinking. Not all the time. Just sometimes. I got restless, you know. So I'd just grab my bag and head out the door. I loved dancing, and loud music and short skirts. The arguments we used to have, poor man. I was an alcoholic, you see. Addict is a better word. Addicted to feeling high, feeling excited. Couldn't bear normal life.'

'What happened to your husband?' I ask her.

'We didn't last, weren't likely to.' She smiles faintly. 'Oh, but he was the love of my life. Well, one of them, anyway.'

I smile. 'It's always the things you don't do that you regret,' I say.

'Never regret love,' she says. 'That's my motto. I don't ever regret having loved someone too much, only not loving someone enough.'

For a moment I think of the tears that came unbidden and unwelcome in the kitchen with Hope. Tears that came from love, but I'm not sure which kind. Do I love Vincent too much, or not enough?

'Rest,' I say. 'I'll be back soon.'

'I heard about you,' Grace says, before I can leave. 'Earlier today, from one of the day nurses. You write letters, don't you?'

I hesitate but she smiles sadly and says, 'Tell me more; I want to hear all about them.'

Her accent is pure north London, broad and flat, from the time before a kind of American slang slipped into usage. She sounds like my nan used to, and my mum too – before she and Dad sold up and retired.

'There's not much more to tell,' I say. 'I just write the words down, for people too tired or frail to write their own letters for their loved ones they're leaving behind. Things that people feel are important to say: ideas, thoughts, messages …'

'And post them when? Afterwards?' Grace watches me intently. Her hair is coarsely textured, still blonde at its tips and a wiry grey everywhere else. I recognise something urgent in her dark grey eyes. There's something she has to do, and it will keep her alive until it's done. We've all seen it: patients will keep going when everything medical and scientific says they should be gone; they will live until the person they are waiting for arrives, or until they've completed some task, or said something to someone that they must. To families it often feels like some kind of miracle, except that miracles never really happen, not in here. Or at least they're only temporary. And yet a nurse doesn't have to be religious to believe with total certainty in the human spirit. We see it, fighting until the very last, burning brightly in the eyes of people who are already dying. And after the moment, we honour it; it's rare to meet a nurse who doesn't open a window in the room of the recently deceased to help speed them, their soul, on their way.

'Yes,' I tell her. 'I make a promise to always post them after a patient has gone.'

'I've got a son,' Grace says suddenly. 'That husband I told you about, we had a child. He's thirty-five now. I'd like you to write to him for me, and you – you'll post the letter after I'm gone?'

'You've got a son, but …?'

Grace lowers her eyes. 'I haven't seen him for years … He'd not thank me now for getting in touch.'

I take her hand, between mine, leaning forward a little.

'Look, family feuds, falling out, it happens. People make bad decisions and tiny little spats turn sour. They get blown up out of all proportion and, before you know it, years have gone by. But I'm sure if he knew that you were here, that you were this ill, he'd want to come. I'm sure he would. For his sake as much as yours.'

Grace closes her eyes. Some unnamed pain closes down her face for a moment.

'It's not that simple, it's ... What I did to him is something that cannot be undone. I don't deserve the chance to even try, I just ... I want to make sure that he knows everything. I want to go knowing that I've told him the truth, because that's better, isn't it? To live with the truth. Would you write the letter to him, and promise not to post it until afterwards?' she repeats.

'Yes,' I say. 'If you are sure that's what you want?'

'And you never tell, you never tell anyone what's in it?'

No one has ever asked me that question before, and I take a moment to think. It's true, I never talk about what's in the letters, not to anyone.

'Well, as long as you're not confessing to a murder,' I say, with a small smile.

'Right, well, I need some time,' Grace says, and I can see sleep is washing over her once again. 'I need to think about it, think about what I want to say, and get it exactly right, because ... well, because some would say that confessing to a murder is exactly what I'm doing.'

My darlings,

The first thing and the last thing I want to say to you is that I am so sorry. Everything you read in this letter should be all the things I tell you as you grow up. I should be explaining why the sky turns black at night, telling you not to climb trees, or to look both ways when you cross the road. I should be telling you that those boys aren't worth the bother, and asking you what time you think this is – but I won't be there. I'm so sorry, my darlings, I won't be there.

My life has been so happy, but you two, you were the happiest part of it, and I know Daddy won't mind me saying that because he feels the same. Daddy and I love each other very much, and when we had you two that love was doubled.

There is so much I want to tell you, but these are the things that I can think of now. Be kind to people, just be kind. You never know what other people are going through, so whenever you can, however you can, be kind. Be true to yourself. When I say that, I mean just live life the best way that you can, honestly, decently. You won't be perfect; you'll make mistakes, maybe hurt people, and people will hurt you. But that's okay as long as you can know that everything you did, you did with the right intentions.

Don't wait to start your life. I know what I said about boys, but later on, a good few years from now, don't decide you are too young to fall in love, or settle down, or have children, or travel around the world, or become a rock star, or discover the cure for the common cold. Don't wait for anything – just do it. There is never a right time, except for now. The right time is always now.

Be kind to Daddy. After three years or so (not before), let him fall in love again. And if you have a stepmother, be nice to her, as long as she is nice to you.

But, my darlings, you are only one and three years old, my Milly, my Lucy. Don't forget me, please. Remember how I held you, how I kissed you, how I poured my love into you, into every pore, hoping that it would stick. Remember that, and feel it. Every day, for all the days that come, remember my love and feel it.

I will always be there.
Your Mummy

CHAPTER ELEVEN

* *

STELLA

I turn the key in the lock and open the front door very slowly. I know at once that Vincent is awake; I can feel it in the air, somehow it crackles with his energy.

Cold, invisible rain has soaked me through to the skin. In the dark, I felt it gathering force in my hair and dripping down the back of my neck. I am too wet for a five-minute walk from the bus stop, and I don't want to explain why. For a moment I don't know what to do, except he's heard the key in the lock now and I have to go in. I don't even know why I keep my running a secret from him, except that it used to be his, then it was ours, now it is mine. Even though he's started running again, even though quite soon he will be almost as strong and as fast as he was before, it will never be quite the same for him. The joy that he took from it, the addiction that he passed on to me, will never quite be his again, not the way it was. So I keep it secret.

'You're here,' he calls out from the living room.

'Where else would I be?' By the time I've hung up my coat, and slung my bag over the end of the bannister, he's in the kitchen, cooking eggs. He has a high-protein diet to help with his training. He looks good: washed, shaved. Perhaps last night he got some proper sleep. I reach for his face, and go to kiss him. Shuddering, he pulls away.

'You're freezing!'

There's a laugh in his voice and I smile, putting my cold hands on the back of his neck. He grabs me and pulls me into his arms. A spontaneous, familiar moment, an echo from a past where we were lovers, but then we remember who we are now, watching each other, like strangers who have somehow found themselves in a thigh-to-thigh embrace.

He's wearing his most basic leg – the model he uses for getting round the house – and shorts. If I look down I'll see a metal rod ending in a training shoe, but I don't look down; I know he doesn't like me to notice his differences. When he sees me watching him, something tenses in him, as if me looking reminds him of everything that has happened. And so I simply try not to look too closely.

'Good shift?' he asks me. He hasn't let me go yet, and I take that as a good sign. I hold my breath, heart racing, alert to his every movement, like some small mammal that happens to find itself in the path of Shadow's stalk. I nod and smile, carefully. Those beautiful blue eyes look clear and calm. Here, right now, in this close-cut frame, everything is the same as it was.

'Pretty good.' I think about Issy and Grace, but I don't say anything. I never talk about work.

'I dreamed about you,' he adds, almost talking to himself. 'It was nice.'

'If you dreamed, then you slept?'

'Same as usual,' he says. And just behind the scent of toothpaste, there is something else: his minty breath has a slight tang of alcohol. He was drinking quite recently. Perhaps that's why his eyes are bright and his smile is so relaxed. It doesn't matter, I tell myself. It doesn't matter how the smile comes, as long as it does.

'You look nice,' he adds. 'All wet and flushed. It must have really rained on you between the bus stop and here.'

'No umbrella again.' I roll my eyes, theatrically. 'I must have a dozen in the cupboard under the stairs, and yet never take one out with me. I don't feel pretty. I feel rank. I should have a shower …'

'Don't go … It's been a long time since we stood like this, hasn't it? I …' He shrugs. 'I miss it.'

I falter; he is trying. I think he is trying, or at least the last drink he had has melted away some of his reserve. This is new, at least in recent times. He is reaching for me, holding me, and, whatever the cause, I like it. I want it. It would be better if my heart would stop beating so furiously for a moment so that I can think, so I can take my time discovering the best way to react, but instead it insists on swelling with hope, because that's what we humans do.

Never have I been this nervous in the arms of a man, especially Vincent. I wasn't even this nervous before he kissed me for the first time. I didn't have time to be; we were so caught up in the maelstrom of our lust for each other. Perhaps it's that – the knowing that, once, everything physical was so easy for us – that terrifies me now. And there's something else: for Vincent to want me like this, he has to see me, and when Vincent sees me something inevitably happens that makes him angry. With every second that he draws me nearer, his hands travelling slowly over my ribs and hips, I'm waiting for that reaction to happen – for him to pull me close, only to let me go, as if touching me might scald him. We might still want each other, but we resist each other too. Two magnets pushing against the laws of attraction.

The planes of his cheeks graze mine, and his arms tighten around me. I breathe in the scent of him. My arms stray around his neck, and I feel him shift against me, balancing his weight on his natural leg as he bends to kiss my neck, just below the jaw.

'Vincent,' I whisper. We are closer than we have been in months. The frozen moment has happened, and still he goes on – his hands finding their way under my clothes, his mouth hot and searching against my neck. Maybe this is it: this is when our life together starts again, when all the stopped clocks start ticking and all the held breaths can be released. This is new, this is better than our first kiss, or any of the kisses after that when I got used to him reaching for me, and he got used to me being there. This is more important than our first kiss as husband and wife; this is our first kiss now, like this, since he came home from Headley

Court. And if it's a first, that must mean it's a beginning, and I let the hope soar within me as he slowly breaks the kiss to look into my eyes.

'I missed this.' I dare to smile, my lips curving against his, pulling back a little to have a look at him. 'What's brought this on?'

'Do I need a reason?' he says.

'No, I just ...'

He stops my words with his mouth, and I wonder if it can be this simple after all.

The kiss is a long, delirious, wonderful kiss. He nuzzles my neck. I hear him sigh. I feel his hands cupping my bottom, squeezing it, and dragging off my sweatshirt, and I am annoyed at my scrubs – so shapeless and sexless. I throw them aside and fling my arms around him, pressing my body hard against his, hungry for the feel of him. I'm not thinking about anything except how much I want him. And that's the problem. For one second I allow myself to forget who we are now, forcing him off-kilter. He loses his balance and stumbles, and in a foolish, confused moment, I try to steady him and make things worse, and he goes down, onto the kitchen tiles. His head bangs against the plastic bin with a dull thud.

'Oh, God, I'm so sorry.' I reach out, but he waves my hand away.

He's smiling, laughing even. A little uncertain, I smile too, kneeling down on the floor next to him. He picks up a carrot peeling from under the fridge and puts it in the bin. There's no anger or shame there – his eyes are bright, glittering almost. They make me feel less afraid to look at him.

'Well, as we're here,' I say, half smiling. Leaning over I kiss him teasingly.

'Go have your shower,' he says, and his voice is not cold, or cruel. I realise he just doesn't want me to be here when he gets up off the floor. 'I'll make you a bacon sandwich to take to bed.'

I hesitate. If I let this joyous, perfect moment go like this, unfulfilled, how do I know that another moment like this will come again, or that this one is even real?

'The shower can wait.' I smile, trying to remember that I am the girl he once stayed up all night to talk to, the girl that he said was his addiction. My hands run up under his shirt.

His hands close over mine, holding them still.

'Not now. Hey, you must be so tired,' he says. And his gaze drops from my face, as if something he had forgotten for a moment has suddenly come back to him. 'I need to get sorted for work. We can pick up where we left off another time.'

'Vincent ...' I try not make his name sound like a plea, and I fail. 'It's been so long, and ... I love you, you know. I don't care about ... anything. I just love you. Can't we just ... can't we just be us, for a little while, please?'

I hate myself for being so needy, for being so desperate, but I am. I am desperate and my need tumbles around before I can dam it.

He turns his face away from me, but not so fast that I can't see the tears standing in his eyes.

'I'm sorry.' I say. 'I don't mean to … crowd you? Rush you? I don't really know what it is that I'm doing wrong, but I do know that I don't mean to do it.'

'It's not anything that you do, it's …' He hesitates. 'It's me. I'm trying.'

Putting my arms around him, I press his torso close to mine. 'It doesn't matter. It's not important. I'm sorry. You were so happy a moment a go. Please, please don't let it be me that makes you sad. I can't bear it if it's me.'

I hear a sob, somewhere deep in his chest, and then, somehow, without either of us really knowing how, we're kissing. I can feel the passion building, the yearning and hunger, and something else too. The tears are still wet on his cheeks and I can feel his anger as he shifts his weight. Lying flat on the floor, he pulls me on top of him. We roll and suddenly it's his weight on me, pressing me into the cold tiles. Closing my eyes, I feel his hand tugging at the straps of my bra, pulling them off my shoulders. I feel his mouth close around my nipple and I want him so much. My fingers rake through his hair, my hips arch up to meet him, and I feel the emotion flowing out of him – the need, the want, the fury. And with my eyes closed I search and search for just a trace, just a glimmer of what is not there. The love.

I tug at the ties of my scrubs trousers, shimmying them off, and he fumbles with the zip of his jeans. His T-shirt, scented with stale alcohol, rubs against my breast as he struggles to find his balance. And then we are joined again. I feel the pleasure and the relief surge through me like a sigh, and, for a moment, I am myself again. I am his, moving beneath him, his fingers gripping my hair in handfuls.

He shudders as he climaxes, relaxing into my neck. Staying there, breathing heavily, I wrap my arms around him and hold him. This is important. This moment means something; it's a beginning after months, almost a year, of polite conversation and false starts. Now we are connected. We have begun again, taken our first step on the road back to each other. It's a victory, it's a chance – a chance I'd thought was long past. It's a start, here on the kitchen floor, with yesterday's or the day before's carrot peelings.

Rolling off me, Vincent rests with his back to me. I watch as he drags his jeans up onto his hips and then with some effort pulls himself into a sitting position, his back against the fridge, rubbing his hands over his face. I get up and sit next to him, leaning my shoulder into his.

'Cup of tea?' I ask him shyly. Once, long ago, this time – the time after we made love – was the most precious to me. The minutes when I would feel his need for me in every breath and word, in every gesture. The moments when his gaze would pour over me as if I were the most fascinating, wonderful creature that ever existed. He made me feel like being apart from me would be like snuffing out the sun. Now, he can barely look at me, but maybe it doesn't matter.

It's a long road, and we've only taken the first step, and first steps are always painful. Perhaps it's taking them that counts.

'Why don't you leave me?' he says, now. The words are so unexpected that I feel them physically hit me, heavy and sour, pushing me to my feet – my sudden ray of hope gone. 'Why don't you just go, because you know that I can't? I can't fucking go, I'm stuck here. Why don't you just run away?'

'Vincent, I love you.' I battle to wipe out those last few words, those last few seconds. 'I don't want to run away from you, I want to run to you, I always have. You are the end of my journey, my finish, more like. You are home and I love you.'

'Well, don't,' he says. 'Don't love me. I don't want you to.'

Dear Janey,

Yes, it was me. It was me in 1978: I took your Tiny Tears doll out of your room when you were out the front playing under the willow tree. I took it and I snuck out the back door, and crossed over the road, and chucked it face down in the canal. I threw stones at it until it sank.

When you came back in from playing, you couldn't find her and you cried and screamed and sobbed great big snotty sobs – do you remember? You said I must have done it, but I said I hadn't, I'd been reading all that time. I let Mum turn the house upside down, and you kept crying and crying until your eyes were like two fat red golf balls. I knew I couldn't admit to it, not even after I started to feel bad about it, because if I did, Dad would whack me into next week. But I did feel bad about it because you'd wanted that doll for such a long time, and they'd saved up to get it for you. And then I felt bad because Mum said that if I'd sworn I hadn't done a thing then she believed me because she trusted me. And she said that she expected the doll would turn up one of these days. Well, it never did. And you never got another doll like it.

I don't know why I did it. I think I was just jealous. You were three years younger than me, and sweeter and pretty. And Mum treated you like the baby instead of me. But I have felt bad about it ever since; even though we grew up to be good friends and you've been the best sister I could ever hope for, especially this last year. You've been like a rock for Lynn and the kids.

So this letter is coming to you with a new doll, a new Tiny Tears doll that the nurse went out and bought for me. This one wees, as well as cries – all the mod cons. Janey, I'm sorry, really sorry that I threw the last one in the canal. You didn't deserve that.

Cheers, sis. Love ya,
Jim xx

THE FOURTH
NIGHT

CHAPTER TWELVE

* *

HOPE

They say I need to build up my stamina, so I am pacing up and down the hall, wondering if taking a few steps will ever stop feeling like I'm climbing a mountain. When I pass Issy's room I see that she is alone, gazing out of the window – her pale big eyes full of the dark afternoon sky, her new best friend, the cat they call Shadow, on her lap.

'Hello,' I say. 'Mum getting a cup of tea?'

'She's gone for a shower in the relatives' apartment,' she says. 'I'm trying not to die till she gets back.'

'Shit, you won't, you're not going to, are you?'

She shrugs. 'They all seem to think it will be quite soon, but not so soon that she couldn't go and have a shower. The main thing is that I want to stay awake, which means that I have to feel pain. But I want to stay awake. I mean, I don't want to miss it, when it happens. Does that sound weird?'

I stand on the threshold of her room. There are posters lining the wall, her pink iPod is on the bed next to her and there's a column of books, all of them with cracked spines and pages that look like they've been well thumbed.

'Honestly?' I say. 'I don't know. I don't know if that is weird. I thought I was thinking about death every second, but I don't think I can be, because I've never thought about that.'

'Anyway, I'm just fighting the pain. I don't even mind it – I want to feel it. I want to be in it, right up until that moment when I am not.' She looks suddenly anxious. 'Don't tell anyone I said that, will you?'

'No,' I promise her, taking a few steps into the room. 'Of course not. You can tell me all your batshit-crazy, sick-girl stuff, and I will keep it secret for you. I swear.' I pick up the book I lent her. 'Did you manage to read any of this?'

'Mum's reading it to me. I was feeling better, but now that's gone again and it hurts a lot. But I'm afraid to sleep. Afraid not to open my eyes again; afraid of what will happen to Mum and Katy if I don't. I wish there were things I could do, things I could *know* so that I didn't have to worry about them.'

'What sort of things?' Tentatively, I sit on the edge of her chair, and I am ashamed to admit that I am nervous, frightened about being so close to her. Frightened that with Death so close by – it couldn't help but see me there too. But if it did, I would fight the bastard off again, and for me at least there was a chance I'd win. No such chance for Issy.

'Well, Mum needs a boyfriend,' she says a little crossly. 'She says she doesn't, but she does. She's not old at all, and

I think a boyfriend would be a good thing. Dad, our dad, left us when we were really little, and she's been alone ever since. She needs to think about herself a bit more. And they should get a dog. I'm a cat person, but Katy's been begging for a dog practically her whole life, and I read somewhere that dogs make you get out the house and meet people. I think Mum could easily meet someone dog walking, and Katy would be happy too. She used to sleep in my bed, before I got sick, if she was scared or something. If she had a dog to sleep in bed with her ... If I knew that these things were going to happen, then ... I'd really feel more ready. I don't feel ready.'

She stops talking, exhausted, and her eyes close for a long moment, her brow furrowed in concentration as a wave of pain hits her. After a long moment she opens her eyes again.

'Issy.' I sit down next to her. 'This fucking sucks.'

I'd hoped the swearing might make her smile again, but her face is set with frustration.

'It fucking does,' she agrees. 'But I am glad, for what it's worth. I'm glad that you get to go home. Maybe, would you just keep in touch with Mum? She's spent all of the last few years looking after me and my little sister, and there is no one else. Maybe after I'm gone, you could Facebook her sometimes, ask her how she's doing? I wouldn't ask but ... I don't know who else to ask.'

'Yeah,' I say. 'Sure, I'll Facebook your mum, I'll check in on her. Make sure she's OK.'

'You will do it, and not just say you'll do it to make a dying kid feel better?'

'I remember when you used to be shy,' I say. 'Yes, I promise. I'll do it. And now how about, until your mum gets back, I read a bit of this book to you? I can do all the voices and everything.'

'Hope,' she says, 'don't read me the book. Tell about you, and everything you've done from the age of fourteen to twenty-one. Tell me about the boys you've been out with, what was it like when you had sex. What was the first time you got drunk? Tell me that instead of the story.'

'My first kiss …' I take a breath. 'Well, I was old. I was eighteen, and it was at a free festival in Regent's Park that we all went to, the girls in my class, after our A levels. It's one of the few times I've done something without Ben. My group of girls got chatting to another group of boys, and once they'd all paired up it was just me, the lame chick, and this guy, the lame bloke. I was a crap flirt but luckily he didn't care much for flirting – he just snogged the face off me. It was sort of damp and intense, and I was worried about germs, but I liked it more than I didn't. That was also my first breast-squeezing experience, which I think was better for him than me.

'Sex. Well, look, this might disappoint you, but the one time I had sex, it was kind of boring and awkward and over really quickly, and I didn't know much about it, and afterwards it was sticky. But I was pleased I'd done it,' I refrain from telling her it was that same boy, the boy I met at the concert, and that for about three months after that first kiss, we'd gone out and kissed intently, mostly with his hand up my top. The sex had been a mistake, really; soon afterwards we stopped seeing each other, and my poor breasts were quite grateful. I don't tell her about the Ben kiss; it's hard to explain a kiss that you don't understand yourself.

'I kissed Jack Fletcher at our year-eight school disco,' she tells me, with a tiny little smile. 'It was like magic, like butterflies and rainbows, and there was music, and he was really sweet. We went out for a bit, but I chucked him when he went to Canada for the summer holidays.'

'Well, what are you asking me for, then?' I joke. 'You've had more experience than me.'

'Because I wondered what it's like to be in love,' she said. 'I thought you might have been. I read about it in books, of course, but I just wonder what it's like.'

'Like butterflies and rainbows, I think,' I say. 'And feeling crazy and exhilarated and high, and sometimes terrible and sad. But mostly feeling like you and the person you love are part of your own little universe that just the two of you have made, and everyone else doesn't really matter. I think it's probably like that.'

'Yes.' She reaches out and I hold her hand in mine, holding on tight to her, knowing that somehow all she wanted was an anchor to keep her in this life for a few minutes more, until her mother could hold her again. 'I think it's like that too. Hope, would you make me one other promise too? Before you start reading?'

'You don't want me to do all the voices?' I ask.

'When you get out of here,' she says, 'kiss as many boys as you can. Kiss them all, until you get butterflies and rainbows ... Kiss them all for me.'

'Yes,' I say, simply, because no other words will come.

'And read something from the end, I really want to know what happens in the end.' I open the book at a random page near the back, and start to read.

✦

Ben arrives at dinner time.

Ben likes arriving at meal times, because the nurses all fancy him, he says. I say they want to mother him, and *that's* why they sneak him pudding, which today is sticky toffee pudding. We don't worry about healthy eating in here; we are the condemned – we just get to eat what is delicious, even those of us who've had our sentences temporarily commuted. Whenever we can, we are encouraged to eat together. There's a long table in the dining room that we can sit at. There's not many of us here at the moment. Just me and Ben, and this bloke called Clive, who seems pretty chipper even though he is entirely yellow.

'Caravans, huh?' Ben has found out that Clive's passion in life is his mobile home. 'So you can just hit the open road, whenever you like? Wherever you lay your hat is your home?'

'Well, yes, but mostly we go to Margate,' Clive says. 'I'm trying to get Cilla to sell it now, while I'm still around to deal with chancers, but she won't do it; just keeps crying every time I mention it.'

'Well, maybe she wants to keep on caravanning,' Ben suggests, which is such a gigantic lapse of tact that I want to bury my head in my butternut squash mash.

'She can't drive,' Clive tells him thoughtfully, without turning a hair. 'I'm just in here while she goes to her sister's for the weekend. I could book her some lessons. Do you think she'd like driving lessons?'

'No,' I say out loud, when I really don't mean to.

'No?' Clive looks crestfallen, and I curse my mouth and its determination to talk.

'Well, I mean, I can't drive either, and the idea of trying, especially around here, in London, makes me feel a bit sick. And maybe your wife, maybe she wouldn't want something else to take on when she already has a lot on her plate.'

Clive and Ben watch me for a long moment.

'What?' I ask.

'Well, you know: learn to drive and stop being such a girl?' Ben suggests.

'This from the only one of us in this room that moisturises,' I retort.

'I think she might have a point, you know,' Clive says.

'Or,' Ben interjects, as I knew he would, 'or, maybe it would be something just for Cilla, you know, to take her mind off everything. Time for her, and also setting her for a little bit of independence. I actually think that's a very lovely and thoughtful idea, Clive.'

I watch Clive brighten and smile again, and look at Ben, who shrugs and steals the end of one of my sausages. 'Come on, eat up. Pud – it's pud time!'

It's an effort not to fork him in the eye.

＊

'We can go out again,' he says just after shift change.

I've pulled up the blind on the inside window to my room, and I was watching the corridor for any signs of activity around Issy's room. Her mum came back less than fifteen minutes after I started reading, her face scrubbed and shining, a smile pinned on.

'Your mum's here,' I said to Issy, who had allowed her eyes to close. 'She can read the last few pages to you.'

It had been quiet ever since – no more than routine activity in and out – but I can't take my mind off it. I can't stop thinking about Issy, and about how she will never know the ending of her own story.

'You are days away from being released.' Ben interrupts my thoughts. 'And the nice nurse, the one that fancies me, says I can take you out for a stroll down the market.'

The nice nurse who fancies him is how he refers to all of them, but I think it would probably be Stella.

'The market. Oh God, the market is full of people,' I say. 'And noise. And muggers. It's for tourists, not real people.'

'Hey, tourists are real people too.' Ben laughs. 'Come on, get your glad rags on.'

Stella arrives in the doorway before I can protest further.

'Tell him it's not good for me to go out,' I plead.

'Except it is quite good for you to go out,' she says, a little apologetically.

'But it's winter. I mean, what if I catch something else, right now, tonight? From a tourist? Ebola, anything. I nearly collapsed going to get a tea earlier!'

'It's more like autumn, and it's pretty mild out,' Stella says. 'And you did go to the pub the other night, and it brought the roses out in your cheeks.'

I give her my best 'don't you remember how we cried together' look, but she doesn't seem to want to see it.

She looks at Ben. 'Could we have a moment?'

'Oh sure, yeah. You have to do medical stuff, right?' I'll go hang out and wait for you on the comfy chairs.'

Once he is gone, Stella closes the door to my room.

'I'm sorry about last night,' she says. 'It was unprofessional of me to cry on your shoulder. I hope you accept my apology. You caught me at a ... very tired moment.'

A long moment of silence dwindles between us.

'It's OK,' I say, eventually. 'I suppose when you're in somewhere like this, all the patients are so caught up in their own struggles ... And to be honest, it made a sort of change, me feeling sorry for someone else, other than myself. I thought being in here was the worst kind of punishment, but … it put things in perspective. I mean, even the nurses are depressed.'

That wasn't quite how I meant it to come out, but, luckily, I don't seem to have offended her.

'Well, I shouldn't be bringing my problems to work,' Stella says, choosing her words carefully. 'And I shouldn't be letting them get to me, in front of you. It's not fair. You could make a complaint, if you like, and you would be completely within your rights.'

'That would also make me basically evil. I mean, what sort of person reports a nurse in a hospice for crying?'

Stella rewards me with a small smile. 'Thank you.'

I don't think our chat helped her at all. If anything, she looks worse – worn out with sadness, like it's rubbing away at the surface of her skin, blurring her features.

'Do you want to talk about it? The reason why you cried? You can talk to me … I talk to you. I mean, we can be friends, even though you're one of the nurses here, can't we?'

Stella thinks for a moment, and I see the shadows of secrets playing out in her expression.

'I can't burden you,' she says simply. 'It wouldn't be right. But you can. You can talk about whatever you like to me, anytime, OK?'

'It might not be allowed,' I say, 'but that doesn't mean it's not right. I mean … we all need someone. I've got my mum, who worries too much, but she loves me and I love her, and my dad, who is the only person left alive in the world who doesn't know the meaning of irony, and Ben, who is an idiot, but I can talk to him about things, when he lets me get a word in … I thought I didn't have anyone, but I do. And I am quite good at listening. I've learned to be.'

There it is again, that promise of a smile, just hovering there around the corners of her lips.

'I mean, probably you've got loads of friends and you don't need to be talking to some random sick girl in a cardigan, but just in case you don't have a person, you can talk to me. I don't mind.' I shrug. 'I like you. Even though you are full of bad ideas.'

'Bad ideas?' She half laughs. 'Like what?'

'Like saying it's OK for me to go for a walk with Ben. It's like someone gave me an enthusiastic puppy in human form as a guardian angel.'

'Sounds completely delightful,' Stella says. 'And I'm sorry, but you do need to get out and about. Build up your strength. A short walk will be a good start.'

I think for a moment, about how much a fourteen-year-old girl would like to knock around Camden market with a somewhat sexy guitar player, and what a kick she would get out of it. I suppose if you are going to start keeping promises, you have to start somewhere.

Dear Malcolm Sedgewick,

We've been neighbours for sixteen years, and I just wanted to tell you: you are a maddening, pompous, stupid, bigoted old fool. I've hated every polite conversation I've had to have with you over your ridiculous attempt at a topiary hedge, which looks more like a penis than a train, by the way.

Yours sincerely,

Mr David Davidson (from number 22)

CHAPTER THIRTEEN

HOPE

'I think the song is really getting there, don't you?' Ben says, his arm looped loosely through mine as we head towards the noise and throng of Camden market. Even now, at eight on a November evening, it's still wide open and full to the brim with a teaming mass of life. Considering I grew up down the road, I've never really liked it – never liked the press of people and the sort of underlying fakeness to it all. It's like a girl that tries too hard to be popular. You know the one – laughs even when nothing is funny. That's Camden all over.

Ben is wearing an ankle-length wool coat that flairs out behind him. His black hair is newly shaved around the back, long on top, and sweeps into his eyes. It's not just girls who watch him pass, but men too, straight and otherwise. He always looks so confident in his own skin, with me trailing behind. His old familiar.

'I think the song is actually really good,' I concede.

'And today, once you got over yourself, your vocals were really coming on.'

'Well, I can sing you under a table, any day of the week,' I remind him, and he chuckles. Damn, I fell into his trap.

'Of course you can. I can barely sing at all,' he says. 'It's all about attitude, dude.'

He picks up a bowler hat and drops it onto his head, waggling his eyebrows at me. 'What do you think?'

'I think it will flatten your hair,' I tell him, laughing as he whips it off again, speedily running his fingers through his carefully crafted do. My lungs creak when I laugh, and the pain is still there, but Stella and, yes, Ben were right. I feel better for being outside, under the lights and amongst the people.

'You need an outfit, for our debut at open mic,' he says. 'Maybe something PVC, lace-up? And thigh-length boots? And one of those corsets ...'

I ignore him and run my fingers down a rail of poorly made, overpriced dresses. Somehow I let him lead me deep into the labyrinth of the market, where the scent of patchouli hangs heavy in the air. Languages mingle all around me – peoples of the world looking to buy a little bit of hip in exactly the wrong place.

'Nothing here,' I say. 'Here is horrible.'

'I don't think so.' Ben picks up a sort of orange chiffon number. 'What about this, huh?'

Before I can reply, I am suddenly jerked back, and I realise that someone has pulled my bag off of my shoulder and down to my wrist. Looking up, I see a hooded figure tearing through the crowd. Hastily, I check my bag. My purse is there but my phone is gone.

'Oh God, my phone. It's not even worth anything,' I say, showing Ben my empty bag. 'It's ancient, but it's got all my music on it – it's got our recording of song … Ben! Ben, wait!'

Ben is off at full pelt, before I even finish saying his name, running somehow through the mass of people, leaving a small shocked furrow, parting in his wake, which I hurriedly thread my way through. 'Ben! Leave it, it doesn't matter … *Ben*!'

But he isn't slowing down, and I mutter curses out loud, keeping my eyes on him as I follow him down some steps and onto the canal towpath. I can see him running away from the noise and the lights of the lock, and into the darkness.

'God, bloody damn you, Ben, it's just a fucking phone,' I say, and I notice how lonely and loud my voice seems. I'm hurrying. I can feel my sore and exhausted lungs rub and scrape with every breath, and I can no longer see any sign of Ben ahead, or the guy that took my phone. No lights, no nothing. I stop and wait for a moment. I'm on my own on a canal towpath in north London in the dark. The only way to tell where the city ends and the sky starts is a few fiercely burning stars, bright enough to pierce the city's glare. Fuck.

It doesn't take long for the canal to take you out and away from the urban fantasy that is the streets of Camden and into an altogether darker and dirtier industrial world, bisected by the rumble of the trains and large empty-looking warehouses overhanging the water. The faint orange glow of the city is reflected in the murky water.

Ben has left me; he's left me, the dickhead. Or rather I followed him, like I always do. I am the dickhead.

And chances are he could be further along the towpath somewhere in the dark, bleeding to death, stabbed by the mugger, who is lying in wait for me, to do us both in together, then shove us in the canal, where we'd drown before we bled to death, choking on dirty water.

Dramatic, I am. Always have been.

I *could* turn around and walk back towards the lights of the market.

But it's Ben. And I still don't know if he remembers that the night he nearly killed me, he also kissed me. And I would really like to clear that up before one of us dies.

So, thinking of Issy, I say all the worst swears I can think of as I walk into the darkness to find him, and some more besides. I walk slowly and carefully, expecting to see his lifeless corpse sprawled across my way at any moment, but I see nothing, just lengths of the uneven path revealed and concealed by the night as I walk. If someone were watching me from the bridge, they'd have lost sight of me long ago. Unless they were following me, that is. I turn around, darkness behind me, darkness ahead. My heart thuds hard and heavy, my chest heaves, my lungs feel raw and my legs tremble. I'm far from the hospice and my fucking phone is missing. I could kill Ben. If I weren't almost certain that some crack-crazed knifeman hadn't killed him first, I would definitely kill him.

But there's something else; I'm out here. I'm doing it, experiencing life.

I knew it was overrated.

Far ahead of me, a match flares briefly in the dark, so that I know that someone else is there, lurking.

What if it's the murderer, smoking over Ben's body as the very life drains out of him? I should turn around and go back, but I don't. Very, very slowly I find myself walking towards the darkness.

Two people, neither of them Ben, are standing side by side. As I get nearer I see they have their arms around each other – lovers. Kissing and smoking with equal commitment.

'Excuse me,' I say, and the guy looks at me suspiciously. His girlfriend sighs.

'I've lost my friend, tall bloke, big coat – he ran this way? After this mugg—' I stop talking.

'No one been along here for twenty minutes,' the man, more of a boy, tells me, slightly warily, probably because he thinks I am a mugger.

'Oh, right … OK, thank you.' I turn on my heels and hurry back towards the light, expecting them to pounce on me at any second. Either Ben has already been murdered and tossed in the canal by the world's most lacklustre Bonnie and Clyde, or they are telling truth and I just scared myself to death for no reason. But it doesn't seem like a good idea to hang about and find out. The blare and glare of the lock seems surreal as I emerge into it once again, and I turn around and around, catching my breath, looking for Ben, knowing that he wouldn't just abandon me here. Finally, I hear something over the noise, something calibrated just for me, and turning towards the sound, I see him. He must be standing on something, bellowing out my name over the heavy bass.

'Where did you go?' I demand as soon as I reach him.

He leaps off a bench and presents my phone to me with a bow and a smug little smile.

'You twat!' I say, pushing him so hard that he drops my phone on the floor, where it skids under the bench.

'What? You'll break it, you idiot!' Ben bends down to retrieve the phone. 'What is your problem? I just got this back for you. I thought you'd be pleased!'

'You chased some mugger, who could have had a knife, who could have hurt you over a crappy phone – that's insured!' I punch him again, quite hard in the arm, and he yelps, backing away from me.

'He was only about nine, and I was fairly confident I could have taken him, but he just dropped it, anyway, after about three minutes of me chasing him. Where have you been?'

'Looking for you!' I holler at the top of my voice, so loudly that it seems that for a moment the music softens and everyone in the throng stops and looks at me. That doesn't happen, of course, but it feels that way, just for a second.

'I thought you'd gone off down the towpath after this potentially murderous killer …'

'Is there any other kind?' Ben asks me, and I punch him again.

'And I went after you, to protect you or drag your bleeding half-dead body out of danger, or die from multiple stab wounds to keep you company in the murky depths of the canal ... and it was dark, and scary, and you WEREN'T THERE.'

'Very rude of me not to be dead in a ditch,' Ben said, but a little less scandalised than before. He steps forward and catches my hand, pulling me out of the crowd and down the very steps I'd just emerged from, feeling lucky to be alive. 'You went down there, in the dark, to battle a knifeman, for me?'

'I thought about not going, but I didn't know how I'd explain it to your mother,' I told him. 'Yes, sorry Mrs D., it was too dark, and he bled to death whilst I was getting a policeman.'

Ben's smile is warm, and enticing, but not as all-engulfing as his embrace. Suddenly, I'm encased in his arms and his huge black coat, his chest against my cheek, and the smell of the women's perfume he insists on wearing ...

'You know my mum's been on tranks for most of my childhood. I'm pretty sure she wouldn't have noticed the difference, and my stepdad would have let my room out, first chance he got. He's been waiting for me to move out since he moved in.'

'Why don't you, then?' I ask him. 'Why don't you move out and get away from him?'

'Because even though my mum might not have got her act together enough to care whether or not I am alive or dead, I still love her,' he says. 'And she needs me. My stepdad can't take care of her; he can barely take care of himself. So as long as she needs me, and I've got you to rescue me from maniac knifemen, I'll be there.' He holds me even tighter for a moment, burying his face in the cloud of my hair. 'It matters a lot to me, you know. That you give a shit about me.'

'Are you sniffing my hair?' I ask him.

'A bit. I like it – it's sort of like Dettol and lavender, all mixed up.'

'Stop sniffing my hair and hugging me,' I say into his chest, thinking of the drunken kiss, and his drunken tongue inside my mouth. 'It's confusing.'

'How is a hug confusing?' he says, releasing me into the night air, with that familiar grin reinstated.

'You don't know how a hug is confusing?' We begin to walk slowly back towards Marie Francis, and I'm grateful to see the familiar dark wooden green door, set into the brick wall.

'No, I don't. A hug is one of the world's few unambiguous gestures. A hug says, you are awesome, I appreciate you. A hug is the one gesture of affection that comes without an agenda.'

'Unlike a kiss,' I say, as he opens the door for me to step through. The adrenaline from my not-actual-but-still-feels-like-it brush with death must still be pumping in my veins, because, after fully expecting to spend several years agonising over his drunken kiss and what it means, I've just gone and said something verging on the specific.

On the other side of the door, the world is peaceful again, still and calm, almost as if the high brick wall and the green painted door can keep out not only the noise of the city but also the sensation of the heavy press of humanity that rolls ever onward, crushing underfoot anything that gets in its way. Even the sky above seems clearer, and full of starlight.

'Well, a kiss is quite unambiguous,' he says. 'I mean, a kiss on the cheek, on the forehead, a massive great snog ...'

'What about that massive great snog you gave me, the night that I almost certainly caught the bacterial infection that nearly killed me?' I say. 'What did that mean?'

Ben stops dead and turns around very slowly to face me.

'Oh,' he says. 'I was rather hoping you'd forgotten about that.'

'And now you see perfectly clearly how a gesture of affection can be confusing,' I say, walking in through my patio door, which I left unlocked. My room door is open, and there's something wrong. I know it right away.

Ignoring Ben, I walk out into the corridor. It's almost too quiet here, and somewhere, from Issy's room, there is the sound of sobbing.

I stand there, unable to open her door, unable to move. I wait, with Ben at my shoulder, until the door opens and Stella comes out.

She looks at my questioning face and nods.

'She's gone,' she says.

I turn around and walk straight into Ben's arms, and everything else seems suddenly so unimportant.

Dear Mummy,

I know you will be sad, I know. But please don't be sad for ever. You aren't all that old. Forty is the new twenty, someone said on *This Morning* the other day. You've had so many years of being sad, and I don't want you to have any more. I want you and Katy to be really happy, all of the time.

Give my hats and scarves to the children's cancer ward at the hospital, and all of my toys and books too. Don't keep any of them, except for Octopus. I want you to give Octopus to Katy.

Will you tell Lucy, Jem and Alice that they are the best friends ever? They never got bored of me, even though I was too tired to be much fun most of the time. They always came to see me, made me those stupid videos that were so funny and that PowerPoint presentation on why they should be allowed to stay for a sleepover. I'm so glad you said yes – that was the funnest night ever. In my jewellery box, the one with the ballerina that goes round and round, there are three friendship bracelets. Will you give them one each? I used their favourite colours so I know they will know which one is which. There is one for that boy in my science set, Jack Fletcher, too.

I think you should get a dog, I really do. Katy wants one so much, and I know you thought it was too much bother to look after a dog and me and her, but people like dogs. And people with dogs always meet lots of people and makes lots of friends. I think you should get a really hairy dog, and call it Kitty, because that makes me laugh, thinking of you and Katy shouting, 'Here, Kitty, Kitty,' at a dog in the park.

I love you, Mummy. You are the best, most kind, most funny, most clever and most brave mummy ever. And you will always be my mummy, even afterwards. Don't be sad for ever, please. And don't be lonely.

Love you
   Issy x

CHAPTER FOURTEEN

HUGH

There's what looks like a tub of ice cream on my doorstep. It's hard to tell in the orange light cast by the street light, but I think that's what it is. I stand at the end of the garden path and look at it, sitting there on the red brick tiles. I approach it with caution and pick it up; something shifts inside. And I notice that, trapped between the lid and base of the tub, there are some sheets of kitchen roll, printed around the edge with blue flowers. The tub once held vanilla ice cream, what's left of the label tells me.

Just as I am opening my front door, I hear the neighbour's door open, and I wait, caught in indecision. Running inside now would be extremely obvious, not to mention ridiculous looking. And yet talking to her, well, that would involve talking. To her. I don't know why the thought unsettles me, because talking to women is something I'm good at, except that normally I don't care what they think of me – what I say and the way I say it doesn't matter. And yet it seems to with her. I think it's because I can see she leads a 'real' life – a life that isn't smooth and worry-free like mine. She tries hard, I can see that – not just at work or over the way she looks. She tries hard at life.

'You found the cakes, then?' She appears above the low brick wall that separates our narrow front gardens. Wearing a massive sweatshirt, which looks like it was built for some huge male specimen and hangs down below her knees. The hat is gone, her long hair is ruffled and her smile is anxious.

'Oh, you left them?' I say. 'And they're cakes, that's … nice. Thank you.'

Before I can escape, she hops easily over the wall and almost skips on to my front step, and I instinctively back up, one step closer to my door. What on earth it is about a tiny, slight little woman in a massive jumper that intimidates me, I don't know, but suddenly I feel gawkish and dumb.

'I was worried we'd got off to a bit of a bad start,' she says warmly. 'And the last thing I need is to fall out with my neighbour. I mean, we've only just arrived here.'

'It's fine, you apologised before, when you didn't have to,' I say. 'Don't worry at all, please.'

She doesn't move, which means I can't move. Several cars swish through the puddles on the road before I realise she wants to ask me something else.

'The thing is,' she says, weaving her fingers together anxiously, 'my boss just called and he wants me to cover a shift in the city, like now, and it would only be four hours, so I'd be back by one, but obviously I can't leave Mikey on his own. But then again, if I don't say yes, I think I might lose my job. If I can't find someone to take care of him, I can't go to work.'

'Um.' My key is in the front door.

'And I haven't got any friends round here, not yet, and no time to make any. And my mum ... well, we aren't talking. I'm really at a loss to know what to do, so ...'

'Mrs Catchpole over the road – she's got grandchildren. Maybe she might ...'

'But I don't know her and neither does Mikey. I know it's a lot to ask but, Hugh, please, would you come and sit in with Mikey? He won't be any bother, and I'll be as quick as I can.'

Hugh. She said my name out loud. Hugh. I must have heard it spoken recently. I must have heard it today, on the phone. Yesterday, perhaps, at work; in the last week, at least. And yet, to hear someone say it to my face, it's oddly affecting. Not quite enough to make me want to take on babysitting as a second career, though.

'I don't really know how to look after children,' I tell her, finally taking my hand off the key and taking a step back onto the path to face her. Her eyes look huge in her small face.

'You don't even have to look after him, just be in the house,' she says. 'I'll be as quick as I can be, I promise. Just sit with him. He'll take himself to bed and you can watch TV, kip on the sofa for a bit. Honestly, he won't be any bother ... and it's just we really need the cash.'

I think about offering her the cash not to go to work, but even I can see that would be exactly the wrong thing to do. She's working hard to keep her family going – some twat just waving money at her would be worse than insulting, it would be mocking her too. My dad would have said yes; my dad was a kind and gentle man, the sort of man that people instantly liked and trusted – with good reason. It's just that the idea of talking to a ten-year-old boy terrifies me.

'It's just, I haven't eaten …'

'Oh, right, well, um … You've got cakes now? And there's toast and beans at mine. You can help yourself.'

'OK,' I say, finally, because my dad would have. And I take my key out of the door and clamber over the wall after her, which isn't quite as low as it seems – or I'm not as nimble as my neighbour – and I scrape my inner thigh on the way. 'Just one thing: you still haven't told me your name.'

'Oh shit. I'm Sarah, Sarah Raynard.'

'Sarah. I'm Hugh.'

'Yeah, I know …' She falters when she sees me extend my hand, but after a moment she takes it and shakes it, quite clearly having to try pretty hard not to giggle.

'Now we've been properly introduced, let's get on with it.'

Inside Sarah's house I find a mirror image of my own house, and I realise that I have been in here before, although not for a long time. For a brief period in the late Nineties, a family lived here with a daughter who was in the same year as me in school, although we were eons apart in terms of sophistication. My dad and her parents kind of threw us together, in that way that parents have of assuming that friendships between young people of a similar age are automatic, and we spent a lot of one long summer holiday together. She was the first girl I kissed, the first girl I did a lot of things with, although she drew the line at sex because, although she liked me and said I was useful for gaining experience, she didn't actually find me attractive and thought her first time should be with a boy whom she at least fancied a bit. Funny how I remember her, sitting in this very room, delivering those very words, so clearly. I don't remember feeling upset or hurt by those remarks that I had forgotten for so many years. In fact, I think I thought, fair enough. Sadie Winters, that was her name. Pale ginger eyelashes and almost silver eyes. She smelt of biscuits.

'Well, Hugh's here, Mikey.' Sarah has already got her coat on, the huge hat pulled down on her head, a scarf looped around her neck.

'You'll be good, right?' she says, but Mikey does not reply, gazing steadfastly at the TV where he is obliterating what looks like an army of the undead with quite some gusto and aplomb.

'He's annoyed with me,' Sarah says as I follow her to the front door. 'Kids, they don't get what it takes to keep things going, do they?'

As she opens the front door, Jake slinks in and, seeing me, stops in his tracks. Then, realising that, as a cat, he is in no way obliged to suffer from social embarrassment, he walks past me as if we have never met.

'Oh, hello, Ninja!' Sarah bends down, and Jake, keeping one watchful eye on me, butts the palms of her hand with his head – something he used to do with Melanie. 'You come for your tea? I left it out for you.

'I don't know who the poor little bugger belongs to,' she tells me as she grabs her bag. 'But they can't love him enough; he comes round here all the time, begging for food, poor little kitty. I've started getting stuff in for him. Mikey loves him!'

'Right,' I say, looking at Jake, who is weaving himself in and out of Sarah's legs as if he hasn't got a care in the world, which he hasn't.

'Actually, there's a tin of cat food in the kitchen. Would you mind putting it out for him?'

'Not at all,' I say, staring pointedly at Jake, who really isn't bothered that he's been caught cheating on me, red pawed.

'Me, I understand,' I say to Jake as Sarah goes out. I watch her for a moment jogging up the street after a bus. 'But that you are so willing to trample on the memory of Melanie. Well, I'm shocked, Jake. Frankly, I'm shocked.'

Jake looks like he's wondering why on earth I would be talking to a cat. I suppose he does have a point. Bracing myself, I go back into the room where Mikey is still murdering zombies.

'She works hard, your mum,' I say, but Mikey doesn't respond.

'You're a bit pissed off that I'm here, aren't you?' I say, and he glances up at me, perhaps intrigued by my daring use of bad language. Well, if that's what it takes to get his attention, I haven't played all my cards yet. I've still got shit and fuck to show that I'm down with the kids. But, oh shit and fuck, who am I trying to kid? I wasn't interested in hanging out with children when I was a kid myself. What really is the point of trying now?

'I don't need an adult to look after me,' he says. 'All the doors are locked, I won't set fire to anything, I've got telly. You can go, I won't tell her.'

'How old are you?' I ask him. From what I've seen of him, he could be anywhere between seven and forty-six.

'I told you, I'm ten. Why, you pervert? Too old for you?'

'My mum died when I was ten,' I say.

'So?' He sounds harsh, but he puts his controller down, adding, 'That's crap, though, sorry.'

'Where's your dad?' I ask, thinking of that huge sweat-shirt his mum was wearing and what sort of a man it would take to fill it.

'Not dead, worst luck,' he says. And then after another moment, 'I don't know, I never met him. He was long gone before I was born. Mum says we don't need a dad to be a family.'

I stand there, he sits there – neither of us especially making eye contact or knowing what to say next. And I am the adult and he is the child, so I suppose it's up to me to make the effort.

'Well, I said I'd feed this cat,' I said.

'Ninja is back?' Mikey openly smiles for the first time since I've met him, and even looks like a ten-year-old for a moment. He scrambles to his feet, following me into the kitchen, which is clean and neat – much better ordered than mine. Jake is sitting on the table, waiting patiently. 'I want to keep him, but Mum says that he belongs to someone, and it wouldn't be right to, but he comes every night, and he's such a soppy cat. He loves cuddles, don't you, hey, Ninja? I call him Ninja because he's jet black and you never hear him coming.'

'Loves cuddles, does he?' I am not convinced, but sure enough, as Mikey sits at the table, Jake all but throws himself into his arms and wraps himself around the boy's neck, batting at his nose with his paw in a decidedly kittenish way. I squint a little, wondering for a second if this Ninja is actually another cat after all, but, no, it is definitely my black cat; there's that little, minuscule flash of white on his front left paw that makes him look like he's just brushed against some drying paint.

'So he does,' I say.

I put the ice-cream tub on the worktop and look through a few cupboards, which, although not overfull, are stocked carefully with rice, pasta, some potatoes marked down, and three tins of cat food.

'What did your mum die of?' Mikey asks me.

'Oh, I don't know, really,' I say, because I am pretty sure that, despite all his front and bravado, he probably doesn't want to know the details.

'How can you not know?' he says, and I think for a moment about how to answer.

'Well, I was a kid. No one really talked to me much; I think they wanted to protect me. Mum was ill, which I never realised until much later, and then she died. And even though Dad loved to talk about her while he was alive, he didn't like to talk about how it all happened. It made him too sad.'

'So you're an orphan now?' Mikey rocks Jake like a child, and his tough little face softens a little, revealing those baby edges that are just about still present.

'Well, technically, but I'm heading towards forty, so ... I'm not about to burst into "The sun will come out tomorrow".'

'What?' Mikey says, burying his face in Jake's soft tummy.

I'm not surprised that he hasn't heard of *Annie*, but I am surprised by how much his earlier statement has hit home, and the wave of sadness that wells up in my chest, taking me by surprise. I have to turn my back on him suddenly, sniffing as I search through drawers to find a can opener and blinking away a threatening tear as I spoon food into a bowl. This is stupid; this is not me. This is that stupid answerphone message and talking to kids about parents. I'm famously happy-go-lucky. I'm Mr Love Them and Leave Them if they get too keen. I don't weep in some stranger's kitchen. I take a breath and square my shoulders. Dad said a good cry never did anyone any harm – he'd cry at the drop of a hat, would Dad, the sentimental old bastard.

'So she just died. Did you go to the funeral?' Mikey asks. I take a second to compose myself. I am beginning to think children are like wild tigers: if you let them sense your weakness, they will pounce and rip your guts out.

'Why do you want to know? I ask.

'My granddad died, and Mum and my nan had this massive row, and we couldn't go to the funeral. Mum took me to his grave, afterwards, when everyone else was gone. But it was just a big pile of soil. I couldn't get my head around the fact that Granddad was somewhere under it.' He nuzzles his face against Jake's. 'I'm sorry. You don't have to tell me about your mum.'

'I did go,' I say. I remember the ice-cream tub and set it on the table, prising the lid off with a soft pop. Six delicious-looking chocolate cupcakes are nestled in the kitchen roll inside.

'My mum makes the best cakes,' Mikey says, waiting for me to take one before he does. 'What was it like?' he asks me. 'Did you ball your eyes out? Sometimes I try and pretend that my dad is dead, and I try really hard to make myself cry, but I never do. Did you cry?'

'Yes,' I say. 'I cried a lot about it, for a long time.' I consider attempting a little bit of male bonding. 'I still cry a little bit now, sometimes.'

'You are a sad case,' Mikey says, quite gently, though.

'Do you give your mother this attitude?' I ask him.

'Are you kidding me? You haven't seen her when she's mad.' He shakes his head and wipes crumbs away from around his mouth. 'The Incredible Hulk has got nothing on her.'

Dear Martin,

I've been thinking about it, and I've decided on Dawn for you. She's no me, but she's the best of a bad bunch. I know what you're thinking – you're thinking, bloody woman, trying to organise me from beyond the grave; will she never let me be? But, Martin, you and I both know you can't find your own nose on your face without help. And I shan't be resting in peace worrying about you wandering around with no good purpose. You are a man who needs to be managed, Martin, and I think Dawn's our best bet.

Now, obviously you can't just go round there and blurt it out, like you did when you asked me to marry you – face the colour of beetroot, stammering so hard it took you a minute and a half to get to the point.

There's got to be a period of mourning, Martin. I insist on it. The funeral, the wake. I want a proper, sad wake, everyone in black. No getting drunk, no turning it into a knees-up. Only tea to be served – <u>I mean it, Martin.</u>

Then I think six months on your own is sufficient. None of us are getting any younger, especially not you, and anyway a man in his prime, like you are, they'll be all over you like flies over honey. Especially that Oona Norman, waving her bust around like an open invitation. You'd think at her age she'd know better, but between you and me, I don't think there's hope for that one. You might be tempted, Martin. I don't doubt you will be, because you are a man, and men are very unimaginative when it comes to bedroom business and bosoms. But I know you, and I know that Oona won't make you happy the way you need to be made happy. Oona won't be hoovering under the sofas, Martin. There would be dustballs.

So once the six months is up, shave off that stupid beard, get your best suit out from the wardrobe – it's just been dry-cleaned and I put it away with mothballs so it will need an airing (and, while I think about it, you'd better stay away from those French Fancies you like so much – you don't want to be courting, bursting out of your trousers, do you?). Take yourself round to Dawn's and ask her out for a coffee. Don't take flowers or anything, and don't say dinner. Strikes me that dinner might be too much too soon. Coffee, cinema, walks in the park, maybe a historical society talk, but not one on war. After a month or so, ask her to marry you. She'll say yes – she's been giving you the glad eye ever since we did that French evening at the club and you impressed her with your French O level. And she makes a nice roast, does Dawn.

Well, Martin, it's been a good forty years, being married to you. You're a good man, a good husband and father. You never let me down or hurt me. You made me laugh more than you made me cry, and I don't suppose a woman can ask for much more, really.

Signing off now.

Yours,

Trudy

CHAPTER FIFTEEN

STELLA

The nearly full moon is shining brightly enough to battle away the perpetual orange haze, and the streets are very busy, still full of people who must have come out when the night was new. I don't know why – normally in the last hour before dawn it's quieter than this. There must be a big gig or a festival somewhere, where all the men have beards and the girls have hats.

I stop running ten minutes from home and slow to a walk – a dumb, stupid walk. It's been a long night. A long, hard night full of grief and loss, and sadness that is almost too hard to witness, and I am tired. I am so very tired.

I stayed with Issy and her mum for a very long time – just sat there, holding Thea's hand whilst she wept. The doctors came and went. Thea called the grandparents, who were looking after Issy's sister, and after a while I slipped the letter that Issy had asked me to write into the cover of the book that was still by the side of her bed. I left discreetly, as Issy's grandmother arrived, pausing to open a window before I left. Laurie was waiting for me by the desk, tears in her eyes. For a long time we hugged, keeping our own sadness contained between the two of us, because to let it slip out from the confines of our embrace would mean we weren't doing our job properly.

'We need to get on,' Laurie sniffed after a minute or two – the first to break the embrace and smooth down the front of her tunic, reminding us that no matter how much sadness we felt, this grief did not belong to us. I nodded.

'You'd better get some sleep,' I told Hope, who I found crying, though it was a trite and foolish thing to say. 'You know, the time you spent with her, it really helped. So don't feel sad. You made a difference to her life. That would have meant a lot to her and her mum. You should feel good about that.'

Grace was not asleep when I went to check on her. She watched me work for a while, in silence, and then, reaching out, stilled my hand.

'What happened?' she asked me. 'You look so sad. Sit down for a moment and talk to me.'

'I'm not sad,' I lied to her. 'But you're right, I'm tired. It's been a long day.' I tried to rise but she stopped me.

'Tell me,' she said.

'A patient, a young girl, she passed away today. I've known her family for a long time. It … it's always hard, but this time …'

'I don't know how you do it,' she said. 'How you let yourself care about people who you know will leave you. How it doesn't drive you to drink.' She smiles a little. 'Mind you, everything used to drive me to drink.'

'I do it because it feel like it matters,' I tell her. 'And I need something that I do in this world to matter. I feel sometimes as if … Well, here we are hurtling through space on a rock, and we're trying, all of us struggling, to make something count during our lifetimes, and … how can it possibly, really count? How can what one person does change anything at all?'

'Kindness changes everything,' Grace said. 'You can't worry about the rest of the world, never mind the rest of the universe. All you can do is look to your left and your right and try to be kind to whoever is there. When I stopped thinking only about myself, and started to see all the people in the world who didn't have anyone to make sure they mattered, that's when my life started to mean something. I wish I hadn't left it so long, but at least I got there in the end. I mattered. Have you still got my letter?'

I hesitated, not sure if tonight of all nights I had enough strength to bear witness to another person's secrets, their hopes and fears and final wishes. But then Grace has no less need, and certainly no more time than anyone else. I knew she'd want to talk about it, from the moment that I wrote her words down; I'd been hoping that she would. And also hoping she would change her mind.

'Yes,' I said. 'I promised I would keep it until it was time, although … maybe this is a letter that shouldn't wait.'

'You must think I am an awful person,' she said. It was hard to answer that.

'I know you are not an awful person,' I told her. 'I know you have given so much to so many people. An awful person doesn't try to make amends as much as you have. But, Grace, time is so short, and you could … you could tell the truth, make amends, face-to-face, and wouldn't that be better?'

'For who? For me? I don't deserve better, and I don't want it. When you've made the choices I have, there is no second chance, no going back.' She shifted uneasily in her bed, agitated.

'Not even for him? What about him? It seems too cruel. Perhaps it would be better not to send the letter at all.'

Grace's silver eyes seemed to travel over every inch of my face, taking in every detail, and I let her look at me, guessing she was making some assessment.

'When I'm gone I need to know he'll know the truth about me; I owe it to him. But not before I'm gone. You made me a promise. Can you keep it?'

'I'll try,' I said. 'It's in my bag. If you want to take it back, then you can.'

'Try hard. Let me pay for my mistakes now. I've been putting it off long enough. I need to pay.'

'I promise,' I said, seeing her distress rise. 'I promise.'

'You don't hate me?' she asked, tightening her squeeze on my fingers.

'Of course not.' I smiled sadly. 'What makes you think yours are the worst secrets I've written down?'

She eyed me suspiciously.

'Besides, does it matter to you that much, what I think?' I asked her.

'I suppose so,' she said. 'Because, even after all the good I've done, I still hate myself.'

And now I slow almost to a stop. Closing the last few metres between here and my front door is like pushing through a wall of dense, spongy fog; every step is an effort that I almost don't want to make.

Yesterday I lay in our bed and watched the daylight creep in through the gaps in the curtains and track its way across the green-painted wall. It was painted that colour when we moved in, and it was going to be my job to decorate it, change our bedroom into a sexy boudoir while Vincent was on his last tour. I'd bought the paint: a deep charcoal grey and a luscious deep pink; I'd even found a video on YouTube that was going to tell me how to paper my feature wall. I knew that I'd make a mess of it and that all the time I was painting and papering I'd compose funny stories in my head, for Vincent – to tell him when we spoke next, to make him laugh and shake his head and roll his eyes. But the paint sits in unopened tins at the bottom of the bed, next to four rolls of wallpaper printed with huge great chrysanthemums. The day after I bought the paper and paint, Vincent and his patrol were ambushed. And the walls stayed green.

As I lay there, I listened for any noise from downstairs, and hoped for a sound on the stairs that would tell me that Vincent was coming – coming to take back his words, and hold me and say he was sorry, that he loved me after all. But there was only silence, so I closed my eyes and made it dark, but I still didn't sleep. And I couldn't stop thinking about the letter, Grace's letter, and all the hurt and lies that it laid bare. Somehow, in the non-night, and the not-sleep, and the hours that stretched one after the other, punctuated only by the dull, constant ache in my lower back, her letter and Vincent's words became tangled up together, as if the decision she trusted me to make meant something else. As if whatever ever happened next would change everything. And yet, nothing was supposed to happen next, at least not until after Grace was gone. I'd promised her. I promised I wouldn't send the letter until she was gone, and everything after that is none of my business.

Except that by then it will be too late. Too late for Grace, too late for the man she wrote it to, and somehow – I don't know how or why I know or think this – too late for me as well.

Usually I can run through anything – sickness, exhaustion, injury – but not tonight. Sadness drags at my heels, slowing me almost to a stop. I stand at the top of the road leading to our house. This is usually my favourite part of the run, the part where gravity makes me fly and I plummet, almost free-fall, towards the quiet tranquil safety of my bed. But now I want nothing more than to sit down on the wet pavement and hope the rain will wash me away, layer by layer. And I think about what it would be like to slip down the drain, and to finally be lost at sea – to be nothing in a great expanse of never-ending water.

I really need to buck the hell up. I clamber to my feet, stretch my arms above my head and brace myself, and run.

Dear Maeve,

If only you knew how many times I've written this letter, again and again. Trying to find the right words for you and for Kip. I want to write the letter that will do him justice, that will show you what I know you already know – what a great bloke he was, what a brilliant dad and husband, what a top mate.

I'm no good with words, never have been. I didn't see the point in staying at school for exams, and so, when I joined up, I didn't really have much going for me. I always wanted to be good at talking, like Kip was, especially when I met Stella. I would practise things to say to her, to woo her, like, and Kip would help me. He never ribbed me over it, or nothing. He just knew; he knew that I had fallen hard for a girl, and he helped me. He understood how much it meant to tell someone that you love them; he understood long before I met Stella. He loved you and Casey, more than anything.

I think that was the best thing about Kip: he could make you laugh, and get you going, and you knew he always had your back. But the thing about him we all loved was how kind he was. I remember this stray little dog kept following us on patrol, yapping and barking, giving away our position. The other blokes wanted to put her down, but Kip said no. He fed her little bits of biscuit so that she followed him. And he took her back to base, and trained her up. Not like the bomb dogs, or anything, but just to keep still and as a sort of mate to us all. She'd sleep on a different bunk every night. Kip had always planned to bring her home to you. Silky, he called her, because she had these soft, soft ears that stood right up if she sensed something was coming.

The main thing that I have to tell you is that his death was quick; he didn't feel any fear or any pain. It happened on a routine patrol, one we'd done a number of times before, but no one was slacking off or not pulling their weight; that's not how it works. Every man in the unit was on point. It was an ambush, simple as that. We try to prepare for everything we can. We were vigilant, careful, expert, but sometimes ... you can't account for everything. Silky stopped and her ears went up, and we stopped, and then it just hit out of nowhere. There was no time to react, no time to ...

CHAPTER SIXTEEN

STELLA

I turn the key in the lock and open the door very slowly.

It's not raining but my hair is soaked with sweat. My muddy trainers are wet through; splashes of mud ricochet up my calves to my knees.

'Hey.' I walk into the living room. Vincent clearly hasn't slept; the room smells of beer. This time he hasn't tried to hide the drinking, and he is more than a little drunk.

'Hey, that's my girl.' He toasts me with an empty can. 'There she is!'

I have no idea what to say or how to say it.

He gets up, and then sits down again, rubbing at his leg.

'Man, I'm wasted. What time is it, anyway?'

'Coffee time?' I suggest, and he nods, watching me as I go into the kitchen and pile three heaped teaspoons of instant into the biggest mug I can find, topping it off with a lot of sugar.

'You came back, then,' he says, when I return and hand him a coffee.

His eyes are swollen and red. I can see that he's been crying, distressed, although I'll never mention it.

Whatever it is that keeps him up at night, that makes him hate me for not hating him, has made him cry and cry until his eyes are raw. I long to reach out and touch, take him in my arms and rock him, and let him cry some more, but I can't do that. I don't have permission to do that any more.

'Well, I do live here,' I say easily instead, sitting down next to him, sliding a couple of beer cans onto the floor to make a space. 'I don't have anywhere else to go.'

Our mutual weariness fizzes in the air between us. I wonder if there is any small part of him that, like me, would just like to curl up in bed, together, with our arms around each other, and just sleep, and for a few sweet hours not think about anything at all – just be two people, together, keeping the outside world at bay. Oh, how I long to lean against him, to rest my head on his shoulder, to fall asleep to the sound of his heart beating. I let myself lean against him, more of a brush, really.

Vincent holds himself carefully, with the self-conscious deliberation of a person who is trying not to seem as drunk as they are.

'I thought you might not come back, after what happened, what I said.' He cannot meet my gaze. He looks so hurt and so damaged by this vacuum of understanding that we have somehow created between us. I wait for him to say more; I wait for him to be kind, and gentle, to tell me that he didn't mean it. I wait for him to take it all back. With the greatest of effort, I lay down a building block, hoping he will follow suit.

'It's OK, you know. I understand,' I say, leaning forward a little. 'I know that you're angry, and there are things that still trouble you. Things you don't feel like you can say to me – I understand. But, Vincent, it's a long road to recovery. It takes a long time. If you just let me—'

'You have no idea what it takes,' he says, putting his mug down. 'You really don't. You can say the words they've taught you to say in training. You can say them over and over again, but that doesn't mean you're up here.' He taps his temple with two fingers. 'If you were ... You wouldn't like it, or me, any more. If you were up here, you'd change your mind about sticking by me. It's not just about getting used to this.' He moves the stump of his leg in a jerking motion that would have once have been a kick. 'Or learning to walk again, or looking in the mirror and seeing again and again the moment that my mates were killed imprinted on my skin for ever. It's not even about any of that. You can't understand. And you have no idea what it's like, so please, just stop trying so fucking hard. It's ... it's pointless.'

This is another moment, one of those moments that he's designed to get me to leave. One day, the time will come when I do, I suppose. When he gets what he wants, if that's really what he wants. But not today; today I am just too damned tired.

'The thing is,' I say carefully. 'I don't believe it is pointless. I don't believe that – because if it was, I wouldn't still want to try. Vincent, don't you think, if we just spent some time together, to get to know each other again, almost from scratch, that maybe I could understand what it is that keeps you from sleeping at night?'

He doesn't answer me, instead directing his gaze downwards. There isn't even a shrug to indicate that he's heard me.

'Somehow we let ourselves drift apart – no, that's wrong. Ever since you came home, we've been prising ourselves apart, moment by moment. Taking every little thing, every memory and emotion that bonded us together in the first place, and throwing it away. You can't sleep, so you never come to bed; I can't sleep without you, so I lay awake staring at the ceiling. You don't want me around at night, when you get drunk and listen to music so loud you can't hear yourself think.'

I pick up his beloved headphones, yanking the cord that runs to his record player out of the socket, in a bid to get him to look up. It works: he watches me as I wind the cord roughly around my fist, but still he doesn't speak. I don't know if it's losing Issy, or talking to Grace. I don't know if it's knowing that the closeness, that love we had, is still there somewhere, and he is choosing to withhold it. But I refuse to do this any more. I cannot go on being silent.

'So I only work nights,' I say, tossing his headphones back onto the coffee table, forcing him to keep eye contact with me. 'Walking out the door at exactly the moment when you start to fall apart. And suddenly it's like we have revolving door lives – I come in, you go out – and it's no wonder we don't know what to say to each other as we pass by, because we don't know anything about our lives now ... We keep secrets from each other, but I think ... do think that perhaps if we just let ourselves be side by side, then perhaps that might change. And if there's a chance for us to be together again, we should take it, shouldn't we?'

Vincent picks up his mug of coffee, drinking it down in a few deep gulps despite the steam that is still coming off it.

'Vincent, please – say something!'

He swallows, setting his mug down again.

'Do you remember the day I proposed to you?' he says, without looking at me. The memory leaps up at once, as bright as a new flame.

'Of course I remember.' I smile tentatively. 'It was the happiest moment of my life. It was a bright day, so sunny, dazzling, and we'd had a long night, out all night. You were making me a cup of tea, watching me in bed, looking at the mess of my bedsit, and you said, "You wouldn't last five minutes in the army – you never keep your kit in order."'

Vincent's smile is faint, but I know he remembers it exactly the way I do.

'And you said, "Well, I told you that about me from the very start; I told you that I am a terrible slattern,"' Vincent reminds me. 'You were lying there in bed, not a stitch on. You looked ... you were the most beautiful thing I had ever seen.'

It seems like an age ago that I felt so at ease in my body, and so certain of the way that Vincent saw me. When I think about it now, I can't believe I ever felt that confident in his love for me, but I did. I was immersed in it, utterly secure in his desire for my soft, round belly and doughy thighs, for my breasts, so diminished by all the weight I'd lost, and my long tangle of hair. When I think about it, it seems like a dream.

'"You are Mr Neat Freak," that's what I told you. And I said, "We are hardly compatible at all. I can't think what you see in me."'

The pressure of his shoulder against mine increases, just a little.

'And I said, "I really don't know except maybe that in bed we are the greatest. We make the best love that has ever been made anywhere, by anyone. We are sex champions of the world."'

We both laugh as we remember – soft shy chuckles, not at all like the raucous giggles we shared back then, back when he struggled to set the tea he had made me in the small space where my bedside table wasn't crowded with make-up and older tea cups and odd earrings, and where it was destined to go cold.

Now Vincent's hand reaches for mine, and although we don't speak, I know he is remembering everything I am, remembering what happened next. The touch of his fingers entwined in mine is spellbinding.

Sitting astride me, he'd taken my hands in his, bringing each set of fingers to his lips for kissing.

'I want to marry you,' he'd said.

'Yeah, sure,' I'd laughed. We'd been together for two years, but together in the same room for less than one of those.

'I do, I want to marry you. I love you, Stella. Shall we get married?'

I'd pushed him off me, feeling suddenly vulnerable, and pulled the covers up over my breasts. I knew in that moment how much I loved him and, because of that, exactly how capable of hurting me he was, and I didn't want him to joke about something that I hadn't known meant so much to me.

'Don't mess with me,' I'd said. 'Don't fuck about.'

'Don't you love me?'

'Of course I love you, you moron,' I'd told him. 'You know I do, more than … I expected to. But, why now?'

'I know blokes,' he'd said. 'Mates who have been killed, or fucked up. I'm going back, and before I go, I want to make sure that you'll be OK, you know, if anything happens …'

I'd fought my way out from under him, scrambled across the bed.

'Don't be crazy,' I'd said.

'Shut up,' I'd told him.

'Just shut up. Nothing will happen to you; you're invincible. And, anyway, you could just leave, just resign, and come home and get a different job, and we can get married when we are ready.'

'That's not exactly how it works.' He'd reached for me and pulled me into his arms. 'Besides, I want to go. It's my job; it's what I'm good at. But I don't want to go without marrying you.'

'Now, you mean, before you go back?'

He'd sat down and shrugged. 'Yes. I mean, how long do you need to choose a frock, invite your family, whoever they are, and your friends? I've looked into it: we can get married in about six weeks down the register office. Big booze up in the pub over the road afterwards. You and me, officially Mr and Mrs Carey.'

'You are so romantic,' I'd laughed. 'Except since I was a very little girl, I've had my heart set on the full fairy-princess job. I've made an album of ideas and everything. Great big puffy pink dress, six bridesmaids, a carriage that looks like a pumpkin ...'

I'd let the look of horror travel a little further down Vincent's face before I couldn't contain my guffaws any more.

'That's why we can't get married – you have no idea what I'm really like.' I'd thrown a pillow at him. 'You don't really know anything about me. We've been together a long time, but apart for most of it. You've not met my folks. I'm still your hot new girlfriend; this is still the honeymoon period.'

He'd leaned over me, his fingers finding their way under the sheets, trailing down my thighs and in between.

'I do know things about you,' he'd said. 'I know you like this.'

'Sex champions doesn't a great marriage make,' I'd murmured, closing my eyes and sinking back.

'Why not?' Vincent had whispered as his lips traced their way between my breasts. 'Why isn't it enough? All the other stuff we can do after. Because whatever it is I don't know about you yet, I know I'll get to love it, or just not even care about it, because *this* makes us perfect for each other. Say yes. Say, "Yes, I will marry you, Vincent Carey, in six weeks' time. I will be your Mrs."'

And I'd said, yes, yes, yes, yes, oh God, yes.

Realising I'd closed my eyes as I felt the echo of that delicious moment in the pit of my belly, I open them again, and find Vincent watching me. He looks into my eyes, and I swim into his – that brightest of blue, those two pure perfect pools, welcoming the chance to drown in them.

'The way I felt about you then, Stella,' he says. 'I didn't want to waste any time. I wanted you to be my wife, to be mine. I knew I was heading back to Helmand for another tour, and I wanted to know, before I went, that I had a wife at home. A proper family. I wanted it to be all right then. I wanted you, all of you, then. With your curly hair and your lovely hands, and your messy bedroom floor.'

'And you got me,' I say. 'You got me. I said yes, and we got married at the first chance we had. There was no pumpkin coach; just you and me, and your mates, and my parents, and some of the girls from work, a lot of confetti and the pub afterwards. We did it; we made our own family. We started it, anyway. We were so happy, Vincent, weren't we? We can be like that again, can't we? Are you really telling me that we can't be happy like that again?'

'Yes,' Vincent says, not unkindly. 'I am. I'm telling you that we can't ever be happy like that again, Stella, and that's what you don't get. We got married when we hardly knew each other. We've never really known each other. The man you married, the man you care for, he's gone. He won't come back. Not ever. I'm not him any more, Stella. I can learn to walk and run and ride a bike again. But the one thing I can't do is learn to love you, or any one. Not ever again. That part of me went in the incinerator along with my leg. If you stay here and try to love me, and try to make me happy or wait for me to make you happy, it won't happen. I can't ever be like I was. And you, you're not like you were, either. And I don't know if we can even live together, let alone be in love with each other, when we are two different people – two such different people from the ones we were when we first met.'

'Yes,' I insist, because I don't know how to stop insisting. 'Yes, we can. Because I still love you.'

He says nothing, but a noise, exasperated, raw and painful, sounds somewhere in his chest.

'Look, you haven't slept, you're barely sober. We both need some rest. We need some time out from this life. What if we take a walk down the road? Go to the Turkish place like we did every night for a week when we first bought this house? What if we have a drink and just talk – not about what's happened, not about anything. We can just talk about nothing, the way that we used to. Just be together. I'd really like that, Vincent. We could just take a break, couldn't we – from hurting each other – and just have a date, be together and see what that feels like?'

'You've been running,' he says, suddenly focusing on me.

'Yes.' For some reason I touch the toe of my trainer, as if for good luck. 'I run every day to work and back; it's why I've got so skinny. I don't know why I haven't told you before. It's not like you couldn't still run rings around me. I run, I run a lot. It … helps me cope with missing you.'

There's a moment of silence. I see the muscles in his jaw tighten – I'm not sure if it's grief or anger – and then a kind of exhaustion that sweeps through his body in one long continuous visible wave. For the moment, at least, he is defeated.

'I hate hurting you,' he sighs. 'I'm tired of hurting you. OK. We'll go out to that Turkish place tonight. We'll eat and have a glass of something. That sounds nice. I really fucking wish that I wasn't hurting you so much. I'd do anything not to.'

'I just wish I knew what to do.' I reach out and take his hands. 'I just wish I knew how to bring you back again.'

'You can't bring me back; I'm not here any more,' he says.

'But you are here, you are.' I lean my cheek against his knuckles. 'I can feel you.'

Vincent removes my hand from his face.

'I don't want to be here like this,' he says. 'I want to be the man that scooped you up and chucked you over his shoulder and took you upstairs. I want to be the man that was six inches taller than you, that you had to stand on your tiptoes to kiss.'

'But you still are …'

Vincent turns his face away from me.

'We can be happy again if we just try,' I tell him. 'You're still alive. We're both still alive, and we still have so much to be grateful for. We just have to try.'

'You don't get it,' he says. 'You shouldn't have to try to be happy.'

'Just come upstairs with me,' I say. 'Come to bed, and let me hold you while I sleep. Please, Vincent, please. If you can't do anything else for me, do this.'

I get up and hold a hand out to him. After a moment, he takes it and follows me.

Dear You,

It's hard sometimes not to let it get you all down, not to feel despair. Sometimes you feel like you are trying so hard, that you are always, always walking uphill and you never get to the top. I know you feel that way – you don't have to tell me. And I know you've been trying to keep it from me. You've been putting a brave face on for me, but you don't have to.

I know sometimes days weigh down heavily on your shoulders, and they seem cold and miserable, even in the hottest of summers. I know that sometimes you can't see the point of getting out of bed, that you only get out of bed for me. Because I need you.

Soon I will be gone, but you have to still keep getting out of bed. You have to. And you have to keep going to the shops, and going to work, and talking on the phone to your mum and taking the dog for a walk. You can't stop just because I have. You have to go on living. You have to live.

Ask for help. Tell people how you feel, how you are struggling. Say if you feel alone and you don't know what to do. Don't hide it if it feels as if just one heartbeat after another is too much to bear.

You love me, so live; that's the legacy I want most. I want you to live.

Not just to exist through all the days from now to the next time I see you.

But to live, and laugh, and be a thousand times happier than you ever have been, before. Live, my love. Live.

Me x

THE FIFTH
NIGHT

CHAPTER SEVENTEEN

* *

HOPE

'Let's go outside and play,' Ben says, and for a moment I thought he meant like we used to, when we were kids: inventing complicated games of pretend where he was a Premier League footballer and I was a warrior princess with a dragon. But he means let's go out in the dark and take our guitars and play them, which is even better. Except, except I don't feel like I should be happy, not today. A person, a person who I knew a little bit, who I read to, who I liked, is gone. I feel like I should stay inside and miss her.

'Let's go outside and play; play to the moon and the stars, for Issy,' he says.

I had thought he might not come back after yesterday's awkwardness over the kiss thing, and then the fact that I couldn't sleep, or stop crying or let go of him. He stayed for a long time, and let me cry. Stayed while I went through my physio, even though physio was the last thing I wanted, and stayed until sometime after I went to sleep. It all got a bit intense, and I know how much he doesn't like intense. So I thought he might not come back tonight. I thought he might go to the pub, or round a mate's, instead, and I would haven't blamed him, but here he was, right after work, still wearing his work shirt and his name badge.

I stare at the reflection of my room in the glass door, trying to picture myself sitting on this bed, trying to get a good look at who I really am. Who is this woman, this nothing person, who's done nothing, been nowhere, and sooner or later, but most likely sooner, will be in the ground without anything left behind to show for her life? I see myself, for just a moment: the ghost of living me. And I feel so disappointed in myself.

'It's November,' I remind him.

'It's warm, though,' he says. 'It's stupid warm – probably global warming or some shit. And last night, after you fell asleep, I couldn't face going home, so I went for a wander around the garden, and I've got something to show you …'

'That sounds like some sort of threat,' I say.

He picks up my guitar and throws a scarf at me. 'Put that on,' he says. 'In case there's suddenly a snowstorm or something. Come on. Something sad has happened; we owe it to Issy to mark the occasion, in the only way two outcast emo kids know how: with maudlin songs and introspection.'

He's right, of course.

It's oddly quiet outside as I follow him past the optimistically named patio and down a little path that slopes away towards where the canal is. I follow Ben down what quickly becomes a stony track, disappearing into the thick fringe of woodland that skirts the ground's borders. I pretend that the light that slants through them is generated by the moon, and not a thousand reflected street lights. Strange shadows give the path a magical feel, and it's a little surreal; perhaps if I keep following Ben, I will end up in Narnia or Wonderland.

Ben stops, and motions for me to wait. For some reason, we aren't talking, just absorbing the sounds of the night around us: the wind in the trees, the hum of the market beyond, and beyond that the thunder of the trains, and the greatness of the city, creaking with life. Ben messes about with something ahead, as I stand there waiting, listening, leaning into the quiet, straining to catch a fleeting note of something else. And then, quite suddenly, I see the glow of a lantern sitting on the stump of a tree, and then another and another. Eventually, a small circle of candlelight encompasses us, revealing a congregation of low benches made out of roughly cut logs, converging on a large carved wooden chair. I vaguely remember Stella telling my mum about story-telling events for the sick children at Marie Francis and for the kids who have lost someone close to them. Stories and role playing – ways to help them cope with layers of loss. This must be the special place she was talking about; this is the place where children come to try and understand death. I wonder if Issy came here.

Ben settles on one of the benches and takes out his guitar, easing it onto his knee.

For a moment it feels wrong to be here, in this place, like we are somehow trespassing. Not so much on the place itself, but on the feelings that have been faced here, the realities that have somehow been accepted, by people much smaller and braver than me. And yet I sit myself down and rest my own guitar on my lap. Through the trees I can see the lights of Marie Francis burning bright from the fourteen full-length windows. Issy's room is still dark tonight; tomorrow the lights will be switched on again.

Trains rattle by on the other side of the canal, and the eternal thud, thud, thud from the market persists. But I don't listen hard. I withdraw inside this little world and pretend that all there is to the whole existence is the candlelight, something like the moon, the stars and Ben.

He leads the singing again, on the song we are working on – the one I started and he picked up and made brilliant. I listen to his lone voice for a few bars before my fingers begin to move across the strings of my guitar – working, thinking, catching up – to make the song happen. And then, all at once, it comes just as it always does: the moment when I am not thinking about what I am doing any more. I'm just there in the moment, in the music, and it's part of me, running through my heart and to every nerve ending. Joy and purpose swell in my chest and I feel fit to bursting with certainty. I think of Issy, and how she loved it when Ben sang. And I sing not only for her but to her, because somehow, as foolish as it seems, just for a few moments I think I sense her somewhere near. It's so rare, it's so special, and then it's finished.

The woods are completely empty, except for Ben and me, and these empty children's chairs.

The background noise of London presses in, and Ben leans forward a little, and it seems to me that he is shouldering the intrusion away.

'I know you want to know why I kissed you and why I hoped you'd forget that I kissed you,' Ben says at last. 'I kissed you because you are very kissable, and I was very drunk – drunk enough to forget that you aren't on the list of people that it's OK to make a pass at.'

I open my mouth, but Ben gets there first.

'It felt like an out-of-body experience: I could see myself, but I couldn't hear myself telling me not to be a dick. And you were there, so beautiful and sad looking, and I wanted ...'

'To comfort me? Pity snog?'

'No, I didn't want to do anything,' Ben corrects himself. 'I just wanted. I wanted you. So I kissed you. And I am so sorry. I'm sorry because I know it was wrong. It was a moment that risks all the millions of other moments that mean so much to you and me. It was my loins talking; lust overtook me for a second or two. But then you pushed me off and the only thing I could think was, oh God, what have I done? Have I ruined everything?'

'It is very hard to know how to process this information,' I tell him, bowing my head.

'And then you got really sick and nearly died. Hope, you always think it's *you* who follows *me*, that I'm always the leader, but what you never understand is how much I need you. I need you here, in this world, alive, my friend, because … If it was me, if I made you sick, if I'd killed you, I'd never have forgiven myself. And I need you. Without you I'm just some twat who works in a phone shop.'

We don't talk for a minute or so. There's a breeze in the treetops and a siren, signalling some faraway tragedy, wailing in the distance. Somewhere a wind chime clangs.

'It might not have been you that made me sick,' I say. 'And, even if it was, what does it matter? It's not like it isn't a game of Russian roulette every time I stick my head out of the front door, is it? I got ill, and Death tried it on, and I told it to fuck off, actually. I thought about secretly blaming you for a bit, because you know how I like to get all doomy. But I don't blame you; I don't blame anyone for anything any more. I think I've kind of got it, the meaning of life … I think the whole point is that the only person who can make my life any better is me. And, you know, medical science, and charities and doctors and that, but mainly me. Because I can't cure myself, but I can choose to be happy. Like you can choose not to be some twat who works in a phone shop.'

'Bit profound, and also not totally sure it's true – after all, I have only got four GCSEs, and one of them is in theatre studies.'

'Look, let's just be us again,' I say. 'Ben and Hope, losers in it together. Because you might need me, but I need you too. So, we take the whole kiss debacle off the table. We acknowledged it and now ... we forget about it. We are young and alive, right now. We should be doing young person's stuff; that's what Issy told me to do. She said, do it all, do it all for me. And you know, I am hopeless at doing anything on my own, so you need to help me do it all for her. We get back to normal, and we never speak of the kiss again.'

'OK.' Ben nods. 'Speak of what?'

I laugh, and we wait for the moment to reset itself to a normality that we recognise.

'Well, we are going to rule open mic night,' Ben says finally. 'That should make your friend Issy proud.'

'Are we, though? There's a big difference between doing this, in a forest where no one can hear, and doing it in front of a load of other people who think they rule at open mic night.'

'So, what are you worried about? Making a fool of yourself?'

'No, I'm worried about ...' My mouth is full of words, so many troubles waiting to pour out, but I do what I always do and swallow them. 'Aren't you afraid of making a fool of yourself in a room full of hipsters?'

'Hmm.' Ben makes the noise, soft and low, but I still hear it.

'What does *that* mean?' I ask him.

'It doesn't exactly reflect your newfound philosophy of living life to the full,' he says. 'Remember when we were little kids? You stomped all over bullies to protect me. And I don't mean figuratively. You stood up to kids twice your size, this fury in your eyes, like a demon!' He chuckles, picturing that little girl. 'Nothing scared you. It was your idea, remember, when we were at primary school, to sneak out of the back garden and go for a picnic in Regent's Park with two packets of Wotsits and a can of Fanta. And it was you who did stand up at the school talent contest and told a series of terrible jokes. You got booed and hissed at, but you kept going so long that everyone started laughing anyway. What happened to that kid?'

'I realised what it means to be dead,' I say, my voice suddenly very small. 'I realised what it means to gone, to be nothing. To be dust. I started to see other people like me drop off the planet, to stop being present and start being past tense. I stopped thinking of CF as just this thing I had, and started thinking of it as the thing that had me. When you suddenly become aware of the clock ticking, it's the only thing you can hear. Honestly, I'm afraid of being nothing one day. I'm afraid of being ash and mud … I'm afraid of going out of my front door. I'm afraid of everything … except you.'

I look up to find his eyes, two tiny points of reflected candlelight, focused on me. 'Look up,' he says. 'Look up.'

He repeats it once again, and I comply. 'Keep looking for a moment, and wait, wait until your eyes adjust. The longer you look, the more you'll see the stars. If we had all night, and we were in the middle of the countryside, without any light pollution, we might be able to count about five thousand stars – if we were really good at not counting the same one twice. We don't know, of course, but experts think there are about seventy thousand million, million, million stars in the universe. That's a fuck of a lot of stars, little suns blazing away out there. When you feel afraid, go outside at night and look up, because when you do that, and you think about all those other stars out there, nothing on this earth is frightening any more. Nothing.'

'How do you know that stuff?' I ask him.

'Discovery Channel,' he says, smiling slightly. 'And, you know, my mum has had a steady stream of "dads" coming in and out of my life since I was a little kid. My granddad told me the millions upon millions of stars thing when I was little, before he died. It helped me. And also it's a great chat-up line with the ladies.'

I smile. That is so like Ben: one moment he is serious, and he'll show you just a little of what it is that makes him the man he is, and the next it's gone – hidden in some off-the-cuff remark. Our friends have always thought he plays the fool, and he does, but he's more than that. If you know him, if you look carefully, you can see the truth of him.

Sweet, brave, curious Ben, who wonders how many stars the universe might contain.

'You know how my mum never goes out?' he says. 'She stays in all day and drinks cider or pops pills, and watches telly and cleans the house. She's afraid. She's fifty-seven and afraid of her own shadow. That's how she'll end, in another ten or twenty years, if she keeps on drinking the way she does. She's afraid of everything, and she always looks down and never up. She's going to die looking at her feet.'

'What are you, a shit motivational speaker?'

He laughs, and I like to see him smile.

'What I'm saying is that … well, you should be doing everything you can to make your life last as long as it does. Stop skipping your physio because it's a bit boring, for one thing. Take care of yourself, not just that body but your head and your heart and your soul. You don't want it to be university all over again.'

'What the fuck does that mean? I had to come back from uni; I got really sick.'

'And then you got better, and you never went back.'

'It wasn't the right time. I'm just waiting …'

'For what?' he asks me. 'Seriously, for what? Because I'm the sort of bloke who will probably kick around Camden dressed as a rock star on weekends until I'm at least forty, and we all know I'll still be working in a phone shop …'

'Bullshit,' I say.

'No, it's true, and it's fine. I don't care. But you … you aren't that type of person, Hope. You are one of those annoying shiny, special people. People who achieve things, who change things. You're one of the people who matter. One of the ones that make life better for the rest of us. Not dust or ashes but one of the stars.'

I watch his face for a moment – the shadows constantly moving over his long nose, his eyes almost hidden.

'You think that about me?' I say eventually, scoffing so as to cover up the fact that suddenly my heart has swelled in my chest and I think I might want to hug him. 'No wonder you've only got four GCSEs.'

'Of course,' he says.

'Ben, you know the kiss?' I prise the words out of my mouth, making myself say them before the moment passes.

'What kiss?' he says, but his eyes never leave me.

'The reason I struggled and freaked out was … well, it made me feel things. Emotions and … urges.'

'Christ,' Ben says, holding his guitar just a little bit closer. 'And it wasn't even a very good kiss: it was all jaw bones and teeth.'

'And it wasn't even a good kiss,' I agree. 'But I liked it. I liked feeling things, and I think that's what rattled me so much. I don't want to be like this, Ben. I want to be well. Not like this, now, but more than I ever have been before. It sort of feels urgent that I get my act together and start to live whatever life I've got, but … I am just so scared. I'm shit scared.'

'Want to have another go – at the kiss, I mean?' Ben offers. 'Not out of lust, or anything, just in the interests of experimentation on the old urges front?'

I close my eyes and let my mouth fill up with words. I think of Issy: small, pale Issy, with no chance to have another first kiss – in fact, no chance for a lifetime of firsts beyond that – and I let her memory make me brave, reckless, alive. This time, I open my mouth and let the words come tumbling out.

'Ben, will you have sex with me? Let's just find a place, have sex. It won't matter if it's awful – you're my friend, the person I trust. I know you'll take care of me. And we love each other enough to be careful, without feelings and stuff getting in the way, and the only other time I have ever had sex it was over in less than two minutes and was frankly quite depressing … Please, will you do it, with me, for me? I want to feel that way again, the way I felt after the kiss. I want to feel alive.'

Ben looks in turn appalled and then terrified, and then he thinks for a long moment.

'Yes,' he says. 'Yes, OK, then.'

CHAPTER EIGHTEEN

* *

HUGH

Sarah opens her door as I walk up my front path, and I discover that I am pleased to see her – I've been thinking about her.

By the time she'd got in last night after I'd looked after Mikey, I'd dropped off in front of the TV, and Mikey had taken himself to bed. Suddenly, I was aware of her weight on the sofa, and forcing my eyes open I turned to look at her, collapsed into the all-engulfing cushions, her neat profile and small nose ending in a perfect ski slope. She'd smelt faintly of bleach, her jogging trousers were ripped at the knee, her boots worn down. Her hair was tousled, her hands looked chapped and cold, her sooty eyes were closed. She was too tired to talk; as I watched her, her breathing stopped and then slowed as she drifted into much-needed sleep in the very place she had been able to stop.

'How was it?' I'd asked her, because somehow it felt wrong to leave her sleeping there, her long day so unfinished.

Her eyes had fluttered open, and she sighed.

'You know, cleaning up other people's mess, it's always the same.' She'd reached out an exhausted hand and it landed heavily on my knee, with a soft thud. 'Cheers, though. You saved my life.'

Before I could reply, she'd used my leg as a prop to force herself into a weary standing position, and I'd followed her into the hallway, guessing how much she wanted to be in bed for a few short hours.

'Night,' she'd said, leaning on the front door as she opened it. And just before I left, she stood on tiptoes and kissed me on the cheek. That's the part that I have been thinking about.

'Hello, Hugh,' she says now.

'Hello, Sarah,' I reply. 'Everything OK?'

'I hope you don't mind: I wanted to say thank you for last night, for you sitting with Mikey and that, so I made you a casserole. It's nothing fancy, just cobbled together out of what I've got. You don't even have to eat it if you don't want to.'

'Well, that would be stupid,' I say. 'It smells lovely, better than the pizza I was thinking of ordering.'

'You probably think I'm weird.' She laughs as she holds out a casserole dish, encased in a tea towel. 'Last place I lived, no one talked to each other. We spent most of the time just trying to stay out of each other's way. But I remember my nan saying that she and her neighbour were always in and out of each other's houses, back in the day, and that … I always thought it must be nice to live that way.'

The look on my face must say a lot, because she laughs.

'Don't worry, I'm not eyeing you up for regular childcare. I just think if a person is nice, you should be nice back, right? I mean, that's what it's all about – I reckon, anyway.'

'Yes.' I find myself smiling, and I take her dish, noticing that it's quite hot, despite the tea towel, which is a little bit of an issue because she doesn't appear to be ready to go yet.

'Mikey told me you're an orphan?' she says, concerned.

'Well, both my parents are dead,' I say. 'But, you know, as I said to Mikey, I don't think it counts as orphanhood when you are over twenty-one.'

'And you live alone?' Sarah's dark, thickly fringed eyes elongate into a triangle of sympathy. She pities me, which is kind but disconcerting.

'Well, yes, but I don't mind. I'm living the bachelor life, you know.' She nods sympathetically, and I realise I have somehow made myself sound forlorn.

I shift the heft of the casserole dish from one burning palm to the other.

'But, you know, I actually like it.' Nope, no that sounded like I am protesting too much. Now she thinks I am a poor lonely man with only a cat to talk to – no, in fact she doesn't even know about Jake and our one-way conversations. She thinks I am more pathetic than a person who lives alone and does have a cat!

'Look, don't take that inside, bring it round mine. Come in, have dinner with me and Mikey? I've got more of that inside, plus potatoes, veg and that. I like to make sure Mikey gets his five a day. Let me make sure you've got yours today, too.'

'I can't,' I say, putting the dish down on the wall, feeling suddenly panicked at the prospect of her sweet, gentle face feeling sorry for me all night.

'Why not?' She looks at the dish, and I realise it looks a little bit like I'm returning it.

'It's work, my work. I've got this job; I curate this private collection, in a museum, and I'm working on a new exhibition, and I've got so much to do, and so ...'

'But you've got to eat, right?' she says. 'How can you work hard if you don't have the right food in your belly? Come on before this goes cold. Just to eat with us. It's nice for Mikey to have a bloke to talk to, every now and again, and you can leave right after pudding.'

'Pudding, you say?' I can't resist her kindness any more. 'Well, if you insist.'

Jake is curled up in Mikey's lap as I go in, and he doesn't even give me a fleeting glance that might signal some semblance of loyalty.

'Hello, Mikey,' I say, waving the flat of my hand at him in an oddly robotic way.

'Hello, Hugh,' he says back, mimicking my middle-class accent and mirroring the gesture. But he hasn't called me a pervert, so I'm taking the win.

I follow Sarah through to the kitchen, where she lays her table, which is small and square and only just about seats two comfortably, and yet I watch as she tries very hard to fit three sets of knives and forks around it. Her long hair is as dark as her eyes and perfectly straight, finishing in a ragged line just above the small of her back. She's wearing a pair of very tight jeans under another huge baggy sweatshirt. It's almost like she dresses to be invisible. I try not to imagine what her body looks like underneath the billowing top, but I think perhaps it might be like a dancer's body – light and wiry, subtle and mysterious. Correction: I try and fail not to imagine what her body might be like.

'I feel like I'm intruding,' I say, suddenly disconcerted by my own thoughts. 'Honestly, I can go. You don't need some stranger right in the middle of your family time.'

'Don't be stupid,' Sarah says, standing back from the rather precarious arrangement at the tiny table, brushing off my declaration as if it were an errant crumb. 'You don't have to be anything or any way with us. We are just eating dinner, not discussing politics or what's-his-face, Shakespeare. There, that's not bad, is it? Beer?'

Defeated by her utter disinterest in my declaration, I nod, and she hands me one of four cans that she has in the fridge.

'So, tell me about your job. This casserole will be heated through in a minute.' She opens a beer for herself.

'It's very dull to most people,' I assure her. 'But I love it.'

'Is it cleaning bogs in an office?'

I shake my head.

'Then you are already winning.'

'Very well.' I shrug. 'But I think I already told you the gist of it. I work in a private collection, a museum. I'm a historian, a curator of ...' I think about telling her exactly what the museum holds, but I hold back. I don't want to alarm her. 'Old Victorian relics. Me and a whole load of old stuff, all day long, and actually it's my dream job. And now the board wants me to put on our first exhibition open to the public, because they want a grant to help with upkeep next year, which is terribly trying, if I'm honest. But I suppose if I don't do what's expected, the museum might close down anyway.'

'Well, today,' she says, 'my vacuum got clogged up with something when I was hoovering under a desk, and when I unblocked it, I realised it was a used condom, so it could be worse.'

'Evidently it could be,' I agree, and I can't help but smile as she smashes some potatoes into smithereens.

'Do you always talk like that?' she asks, amused. 'Like Sherlock Holmes or something?'

'I have no idea,' I say. 'You'll have to tell me. I don't think I do. I don't think I do it on purpose, anyway. I always like to think I'm the hip, young cool dude out of all the academics I know.'

She glances up at me. 'You are wearing a bow tie.'

'It's ironic,' I protest, although I am starting to think Mikey might have been right about that. 'Is it hard? Managing on your own with Mikey?'

'It's hard not to give up, sometimes,' she says, turning the gas off underneath a pan of vegetables. 'It's hard to work at a crap job that is always going to be crap, and hard to have a son with no dad around. Hard to feed him proper food, bring him up to be decent. Hard to find the time or money to go out with my mates now and then; hard to not have anyone special, you know? But then, look at this place. Two bedrooms, nice area – I'm lucky I've got this. So it's hard, but not as hard as it is for some people. What about you? What do you find hard – apart from chatting?'

'Oh, my life isn't really hard,' I say. 'I've got enough money, and a house, and a job I love. Girlfriends now and then; it's cushy.'

'No kids, anyway?'

'No.'

'Mikey said your mum died when you were about his age? I think it must have got to him; he needed a proper hug that night.' She pauses, sipping her beer. 'It must be hard for him, you know, to think that he only has me and that's it. I worry about it. I mean, what if I get hit by a bus, what will happen to him?'

'I only had my dad for a long time,' I say. 'I never really thought about it. He was a really great man. I miss him.'

'And your mum? You must miss her too.'

I take a long drink of beer. One of the drawbacks of having an actual conversation that isn't just flirting, or work talk, is the moment when people ask about my mother. It's not like words turn to ashes in my mouth, because there are no words. There is no way you can say out loud that you can hate someone for dying as much as I hate her.

Dear Leigh,

There is something I wanted to say before I go. A thing that I can't really say to your face because if I try, you'll get that look again – that one when you think I'm interfering, that I don't really understand. I think you've forgotten that I did everything you did before you: fell in love, got married, had children. But I suppose, just like you, I never wanted to listen to my mum. I always thought she was interfering, that she didn't really understand. Which is why I am writing this letter, because I think if you see it written down, you might take it a bit more seriously.

I just want to talk about Lisa, just for a minute. You had a hard road to find her, Leigh. It took you a long time, a painful and difficult time to find the right woman for you. But Lisa is that woman; she's the one that welcomed you with open arms, that loved you, no matter what anyone else thought. She's the one that's given you a little boy, my darling grandson. She's made you into the person I always knew you could be: kind, gentle, the best parent in the world. She's taken all the anger that you had growing up and turned it into love. She succeeded where I failed. But sometimes I think you have forgotten everything you went through to be together. Sometimes, Leigh, I think you take her a little bit for granted. I'm not saying that you don't love her. I'm not saying that. But I am saying, make sure she knows it, every single day. Do something, say something, that will tell her how much you love her, and that without her you wouldn't be the wonderful, wonderful woman and daughter that I love so much now.

Dear, dear Leigh, no matter what happens next, just remember: always, always let the person you love know, every single day, how much you love them, and you will be just fine.

I love you,

Mum x

CHAPTER NINETEEN

STELLA

The house is dark when I wake up, silent and dark. The side of the bed where Vincent lay, for a little while, for the first time in ages, is empty and cold. I close my eyes for a moment, remembering the luxury of falling asleep in his arms, the beat of his heart under my cheek, the circle of his arms around me. I can't hear any noise downstairs or see any lights on under the bedroom door.

What if that was a goodbye? What if he left me while I was sleeping?

I sit up abruptly and, suddenly convinced that he is gone, turn on the lamp beside me.

'Hey?' He opens the door, and I see that he is dressed. Jeans, a shirt, open at the collar. He's shaved, which is hard for him because the stubble doesn't grow where the burn has healed but in all the places in between. I appreciate that he's made the effort, because I know it causes him pain. His hair is damp and there's a scent of soap. For the first time in months, it isn't masking the smell of alcohol.

'You're up?' he says. 'You were sleeping so peacefully, I didn't want to wake you.'

'Yes, I'm up.' I draw the duvet up under my chin, feeling suddenly vulnerable, visible. 'I slept well. Did you?'

'I did for a bit ...' He nods. 'I miss that, being near you, you know. It was good, to talk, to be near you. It felt good. Everything I said before ...'

'You don't have to talk about it, not now.' I climb out of bed, letting my arms drop by my sides. 'We don't have to talk about anything, do we, tonight? Tonight we are just a married couple going out for dinner. What time is it? Is there wine in the fridge? I wouldn't mind some?'

'It's not too early,' he says. 'You must have been exhausted. I'll bring you up a glass,' he says.

'No, it's OK. I'll only be a couple of minutes. I'll be down before you've poured it.' He hesitates and then after a moment more, he steps forward and kisses me on my cheek. It's just a brief gesture that's over almost before it has happened, and yet it fills me with this sense of quiet joy. After such a long time of feeling out in the cold, lost and alone, just that one simple kiss makes me feel like I am coming home.

An age has passed since I last looked in my wardrobe at the clothes I used to collect so avidly. It feels like I have lived in scrubs, jogging bottoms and T-shirts all my life. I go through the racks of skirts and tops with a kind of fascinated detachment. Who was this girl who had a bright pink mini skirt that barely hung beneath her bum? Who wore tight low tops and pencil dresses? Who had a taste for bold primary colours, because she knew they set off her hair? Right at the back I find what used to be my favourite dress – the dress I secretly always thought summed me up: my burnt-orange mini dress, made of a fine-knit light wool. I always thought it suited me down to the ground. It was the dress that I wore on my first date with Vincent because it fitted over my hips and breasts in just the right way, without making too much of a feature of my soft plump belly. Funny how much I used to hate that little pouch. I miss it now, because it signified something. It meant contentment.

The dress doesn't hang on me in quite the same way since I started to run every day. The places where it used to cling to curves are baggy and empty now, but my legs look pretty good with some thick tights and a pair of low rubber-wedged heels. I try a touch of lipstick, brush my hair and stop when I really catch sight of myself in the mirror.

A stranger is looking back at me. Some woman with short hair – hair she cut herself one night with a pair of nail scissors because it just kept getting in the way. Short dark curls that cling to a hollow-looking face. I never used to have cheekbones, my eyes never looked so big and I never looked so … hot. Not hot like a movie actress, but fevered. I touch my skin, which is moon-pale after weeks without sunshine, and it's cool to the touch. It's shocking to realise how rare it is these days for me to look at myself. I'm always leaving, running, rushing, keeping my head down, avoiding eye contact with everyone who isn't one of my patients, including myself. I vaguely notice the looseness of clothes that used to fit just right, or the rumble in my belly when I've forgotten to eat for the day. The dip in energy that sees me and Laurie standing in the kitchen, knocking back sachets of sugar, neat, like it's crack cocaine. But I don't stop to look at what the life I have accidentally slid into – no, run into – has done to me. It brings tears to my eyes. Vincent is not the man I fell in love with, and I am not the girl he first met. And perhaps he is right: perhaps it is too late to change that. And perhaps it is my fault because, as much as he has run from me, I ran away from her – from the woman he loved – and I'm not sure I left even a trace of her behind.

Something gnaws at my gut and I realise I am ravenous. It's been so long since I ate proper, cooked food, and suddenly I'm starving for sustenance. There is no way of knowing if there is one last hope for us, but we have to at least try. And eat, at least we can eat.

Vincent is waiting for me in the living room, a glass of wine on the table. He's turned on all the lights and is staring at the unlit fireplace.

'All set?' I ask him, picking the wine glass up and drinking it down in one. I don't drink much these days, and I can feel it fizzing through my bloodstream, going straight to my head. He has a glass of Coke in his hand, I notice – an implicit commitment to our evening together.

'Yes,' he says, and his smile is deliberate and carefully placed. I don't comment on it, because I know he is trying, and I know that to try he has to fight the many demons that

I don't understand. 'You look nice; I always liked that dress on you.'

Tonight he sees me. I exist.

✦

The restaurant is busy, and, dimly, I remember it's a Friday night. I lose track of the days of the week, in my job; there is rarely such a thing as a weekend off, and night after night seems the same. But Baki, the restaurant's owner, remembers us, and greets us like we are long-lost family.

'I saw your picture in the paper,' he tells Vincent, shaking him firmly by the hand for several seconds, not wanting to let go. 'You are a hero, a hero, my friend. So brave, a hero and a true man. For you and your wife, my finest table and free wine!'

His finest *free* table is more accurate; we sit at the back of the small dining room, near the kitchens and the loos, but it doesn't matter – it's the perfect spot for us. In a corner, two walls encroaching on our tiny table. We've barely hung our coats on the back of our chairs when a carafe of house red arrives.

I pour us both a large glass and smile at Vincent. I can tell he feels as uncertain and as shy as I do, but maybe that isn't a bad thing; we are trying to get to know each other again, after all. And in the candlelight we both look softer, younger – almost like the last year and a half didn't happen.

'So ...' I reach across the table and place my hand over his. 'How is it going at the gym? Are you enjoying it?'

'Not really.' He smiles wryly. 'I'm mean, the guys are nice enough, and the clients love me, you know, especially the women.' I smile at the trace of his old bravado. 'But it's boring: same old, same old, one person after another, and I'm … well, I'm a novelty.' He pats his bisected thigh.

'Well, it was only ever meant to be temporary,' I say. 'While you decided what you really want to do next.'

'Yeah,' he says, and the conversation peters away to nothing for a few moments. And then I remember something that always used to keep us talking – all night, sometimes.

'We talked about moving, didn't we? Once you'd left the army, remember? Going to Cornwall, becoming surfers, growing our hair out and wearing tie-dye?' I smile, and for a moment, just the briefest of moments, he looks unutterably sad and the joy of that old dream is lost. 'We talked about selling the house and just travelling around the world until we got old. And living on a canal boat. And you would grow a beard and I'd have long grey dreadlocks and we'd get a dog.'

'I remember,' he says.

'We could still do that,' I say. 'We can still do anything we want to; that hasn't changed.'

He regards me in the candlelight, his eyes searching my face, intensely, as if he's looking for something, anything that he might recognise.

'Let's just have dinner,' he says eventually. 'Tell me about work.'

I think of Grace's letter, in the pocket of my jacket. It's been at the back of my mind since I sealed the envelope, but I have no one to ask what to do with it. I can't ask Vincent, not with this fragile peace between us. One sheet of paper folded in half feels like a rock there, cold and heavy. Carrying someone else's secret is hard enough, but I made a promise to Grace. I made it twice.

And yet this letter. This is a letter that makes it seem impossible to keep that promise, especially when I know exactly where it will go one day, when I've walked past the house it is addressed to a hundred times or more.

If the address was in Scotland or France, or Ireland, or even just a city away, what would I do? Would I think about it twice, or just leave it with the other two letters in my backpack, waiting to be posted? I promised Grace I would wait until she is gone; I promised her, and yet … The address is just a few streets away. There is hardly a mile between Grace and the person named on the front of the envelope, and how many hours left for her I don't know.

Did she mean it, what she asked of me? Did she really mean it, or does she want me to ignore her instructions? Does she really want me to wait until it's too late to mean anything, to anyone? Is she asking something of me that she doesn't feel able to do herself? I just don't know.

I think of the letter, feel its cold heavy weight, and press it back down. This time is supposed to be about me and Vincent.

'We lost a patient yesterday,' I say. 'A young girl, only fourteen. Sort of puts it all into perspective, really – the things that are worth fighting for.' I glance up at him. 'It's a peaceful job, mostly. I know some of it is sad, but it's not all palliative care; we have respite patients too. And it's a place full of love, you know? Like all the love a person accrues over a lifetime is gathered up in those last few moments to cushion them on their way.'

'Best way to go, if you've got to,' Vincent says.

Baki arrives with a flourish, and we order what we always used to: lamb kofta, pitta bread, mezze including home-made hummus and stuffed vines leaves, and salad.

'Doesn't it get to you?' Vincent asks me. 'Getting to know someone and then seeing that person, that essence of a person, go? Don't you always feel sad? When I think about … the mates I lost … I never get used to it. I don't want to.'

I remember opening the window in Issy's room. Closing the door on her mum, as she wept in the arms of Issy's grandmother.

'It is hard, I suppose, but I know why I am there, and what I am doing it for – to make the final stages as easy as possible for the patient and their family. To help them. Before, when I worked in trauma, I used to think it was all about beating death, giving people back their lives, but sometimes, it's a game you can't win, and helping people make that last journey, that transition, it's just as important.'

'Transition.' Vincent picks up on the word. 'But there isn't anything else afterwards, is there? It's not a transition, it's an ending.'

I don't know how to answer or to explain how I feel or what I see, so I don't. Only I feel sure somehow that once that essence of life leaves a person, it changes what's left behind so completely that it must be some kind of entity, some kind of force that goes somewhere – even if it's just out amongst the stars.

'Well, as I said, it's not always all about dying, anyway,' I tell him, trying to lift the mood. 'We have patients who are recuperating too. Recently we've had a young woman with cystic fibrosis recovering from a very serious infection. She'll be leaving in the next day or so. It's not all about opening windows at a hospice, you know; it's mostly about life, living, enjoying, loving people, finding ... purpose.'

'Opening windows?' Vincent asks me.

'Just a nurse's thing,' I say.

Our food arrives and we eat for a few minutes in silence, and I drink a lot of wine very quickly. Vincent doesn't touch his, but I see him looking at the glass every few seconds with naked longing. He's as nervous as I am. I wasn't this nervous and uncertain on our very first date. I remember it. I remember walking into the pub, where Vincent was leaning against the bar already, black T-shirt, tan, his eyes on some football match, and how I'd felt lust for him at once – physical and deep. Just looking at him made me need him, and I think I would have run over the edge of a cliff to get to him. Maybe that is exactly what I did. I felt consumed, obsessed, thirsty, hungry for him from the moment I saw him, but not nervous, not self-conscious or afraid, like I feel now. I suppose, perhaps, it's because at our beginning nothing was particularly at stake, except for our pride. Now everything is at stake, everything we gambled on. The wheel of our choices is about to come to a standstill, or the dice are about to fall. This is where we find out if our luck will hold.

'Look.' He speaks first, setting his fork down on the plate, pushing it into a perfectly vertical line. 'Since I came out of Headley Court, I've been … Well, you know how I've been. Struggling with civvie street. Struggling with what happened to me, to my mates. With what happened to Kip. I wanted to come back alive. I wanted it so badly, and I have. And now …'

'Now you don't know why?'

'Now I don't know what, or who I am. Surviving has taken that away from me,' he says. He shrugs. 'I don't know. I'm sorry.'

He stretches his prosthetic leg out – most likely a sudden cramp in his thigh muscle – which inadvertently forms a barrier across the narrow gangway between tables, stopping a man on his way to the loo in his tracks.

'All right, mate,' the man says, affably enough. 'You don't own the place.'

'Sorry.' Vincent retracts his leg with some difficulty, wincing. A flash of the metal shows under his trouser leg.

'Shit, sorry,' the man says. 'I didn't know you were … disabled.'

'It's fine,' Vincent says, looking at the tabletop.

'Still, these days it's nothing, it is? I mean, look at the Paralympics, super humans and all that, hey?'

'Yep,' Vincent says, but the man doesn't move on.

'How'd it happen?' the man asks, any natural reserve he might have had stripped away by wine. This time Vincent looks up at him, actively wanting to see the person who is tactless enough, drunk enough, stupid enough, to want to intrude on someone else's privacy this way. I see a dangerous new edge to the set of his jaw.

'Afghanistan,' he says. 'Ambush. One dead, two injured,' he says, and his matter-of-fact voice breaks my heart.

'Fuck, can I shake your hand?' The man holds his hand out, and I notice that the people on the tables around us are all watching now. Vincent looks at me, and I give the slightest of shrugs.

'Sure,' he says, taking the man's hand. He shakes it once.

'I think you guys are heroes.' The man will not let go of Vincent's hand. 'I think what you've done is amazing – the sacrifices you've made. I mean, Jesus, no one knows why you were out there for so long, or what difference it will make in the end. None, probably – it's all politics, isn't it? You go out there to keep the terrorists at bay, but how long for, really? And does anything change, really? Lads like you, coming home in bits or in boxes, and what was it all for … really? Nothing. It's all a waste.'

Vincent is still holding the man's hand as he surges up out of his chair and punches him so hard that he flies across the narrow gangway and careers into a table, sending a woman sprawling to the floor, with a crash of plates and crockery. There are screams all around.

The look on Vincent's face is pure fury, and if he could kneel easily, I know he'd have grabbed the bleeding man by his ripped shirt and punched him again and again, and I'm not sure that he'd be able to stop.

'Get up.' He spits out the words in quiet, cold fury. 'Get up and tell me again that my mates died and I lost my leg for *nothing*. Get up, go on.'

'I'm calling the police,' a woman behind me says, her voiced laced with genuine fear.

The man scrambles to his feet, backing away terrified without taking his eyes off Vincent. He holds his hands out in supplication.

'I'm sorry,' he says. 'I didn't mean anything. I wasn't thinking.'

'No, you weren't.' Vincent takes a step towards him.

'Vincent.' I reach out and touch his tense arm, and in one sharp movement he turns and pushes me away. It is not a hard push but I am caught off balance and knocked back against the wall, my head following on a second later with the sharp whip of my neck. I'm not hurt so much as shocked. Leaning against the wall, I stare at him. He stares at me, and then, taking a deep shuddering breath, he steps over the man and leaves.

'I've called the police,' the frightened woman says. 'They're on their way.'

Grabbing my jacket, I put all the cash I have on the table and follow Vincent out into the busy street. Looking both ways, I can see his head, his determined gait, already far ahead of me, swallowed up in the crowd, heading towards Regent's Park. I break into a jog to follow him, catching up with him as the street gives away to parkland and the path disappears into a hazy darkness.

'Vincent!' I call his name, but he marches on, his fists still clenched at his side. 'Vincent.'

Eventually I catch up with him, standing in front of him, challenging him to push me out of the way again.

'Stella, go away,' he says. 'Go away. I don't want you to see this. I don't want you to see me like this.'

'Too late, I've seen you,' I say, touching my bruised shoulder. 'I've felt you.'

'I'm sorry.' He covers his face with his hands. 'I didn't mean … I didn't mean to. I just wanted to get away, and so I pushed you. I didn't meant to; it just happened. I'm not the sort of man who hurts a woman, not any woman. I just … I'm not coping, Stella. I'm not coping. And I don't know how to ask for help.'

'Vincent.' I press my hands against his chest; I feel his heart fiercely pumping. 'Tell me. Tell me what it is. Let me help you. If you tell me, it will be a start and together we can go back and ask for whatever help you need. Just tell me, because you can't go on like this.'

'You can't help me,' he says. 'How can you help when you're the reason that I wish I had died out there?'

'What?' His words make no sense. 'What are you saying?'

He sidesteps me and walks – no, marches – on.

'Vincent, what did I do? You have to tell me what I did. You can't say that and walk away. Where are you even going?'

'I'm trying to get away from you,' he says, his eyes locked forward.

'Vincent!' I howl his name, so loudly it echoes in the damp air. 'Tell me what you mean.'

At last he stops. He bows his head, dragging breaths out of his chest, closing his eyes; he trembles, fighting tears, fighting fury.

'I should have died, the day of the ambush,' he says. 'It should have been me and not Kip. Or, at least, not just Kip.'

'A lot of soldiers feel that way, remember?' I say. 'The counsellor said …'

'Oh, for fuck's sake, Stella, I'm not your patient! I'm your husband! Will you let me talk to you like a man, for once in my life?'

'I'm sorry.' My voice is small, frightened. I'm not scared of Vincent, but of what he is about to say and how whatever it is will change everything. The park is not empty – groups of people and couples stand in their own little pools of darkness, but I know they are all straining towards us now.

'I've been over and over it, again and again,' Vincent says. 'And every time it's the same, it's exactly the same, but it didn't have to be. It could have been different. We were out on the road – routine patrol, all the precautions taken – looking for IEDs; everything was as it should be. Kip's little dog was trotting at his side. We got used to her stopping every few metres. We paid attention to her – she heard things we didn't, sensed stuff. But that day she was relaxed, happy. You should never relax, they tell you that; you should never let your guard down. But it was hot, and me and Kip, we were laughing about this YouTube video we'd seen – a cat and a photocopier. So fucking stupid; the sort of bollocks that Kip loved. And the dog was chilled. I looked up at the trees on the horizon, scrubs, really. And then I saw it: this flash, this reflection in the foliage, sunlight bouncing off metal where there shouldn't have been any. And I knew that, whatever it was, it was aimed at us.'

As I watch him talk, I realise Vincent isn't standing with me in soggy Regent's Park any more – he's thousands of miles away, back on that dirt road again, in the final seconds before his whole life was torn apart.

'I had a second, one second. Kip was right next to me, oblivious. He didn't see it; he didn't know it was coming. I should have warned him, grabbed him, pulled him out. I should have told him to run, to dive with me. I had one second, you see, Stella, one second, maybe less, and I knew if I used it to try and warn Kip, I knew it would be one second too late for both of us. And I saw your face, Stella. I felt your skin. And I wanted to come home to *you*. I ran for cover.

I didn't get far, a few feet at most. The rocket hit us square, hit Kip dead on. Took my leg off. And I saw it: I saw it go up in the sky in an arc, like it was a dream, and then there was this pink mist raining down on us, all of us. And it was a second or two before I could hear again – the thud of my leg in the dirt and the screams. My screams. And pain – pain that I had no idea was possible. I remember my squad facing sniper bullets to drag me to shelter, and realising the pink mist, the pink mist that was slicking my face and my hands, that was what was left of Kip.'

For several long seconds I can't say anything; there are no words. Before, I just knew the bare bones of what had happened to him, but now the images he has conjured up, the secrets that he's kept to himself all this time and the nightmare that keeps him awake, are all too vivid for me as well.

'But Vincent, you couldn't have done anything … There wasn't time. You didn't know …'

'Now, see that is where you're wrong.' Vincent takes a step towards me. 'I could have done one thing very differently. I could have been a mate, I could have been a soldier, I could have been a *man* – and reached for him, warned him, taken him with me. We might have both died, but we *might* have both made it. It was a risk, a risk that I didn't want to take. I had to choose, Stella. I had to choose between being the man I always thought I was and coming home to you. And I chose you.'

The air smells of distant smoke. There are shrieks and howls somewhere in the distance, and it feels as if the world outside the pool of lamplight we are standing in doesn't exist.

'And I thank God every day that you did,' I whisper.

'Well, I don't.' His shoulders heave with the effort it takes him to speak in a level tone, fighting to keep his voice calm. 'I'm not glad. Every night, every time I close my eyes, I feel that mist, the rain of my best mate, sticky on my skin; I smell it. I see the photo of his wife and kid that he kept taped above his bed. I know that I failed him; I failed my unit, my regiment, myself. I know that I am not the man I always thought I was. The man who when the moment came would step up, would do what he was trained to do. I didn't think it would ever be in doubt, because that is who I am. Who I thought I was. But the moment came and I failed. I'm weak, I'm useless. Broken body, broken mind. Not a soldier any more, not anything …'

'You're still my husband,' I say. My hand hovers towards him, hesitating.

'You just don't get it,' Vincent says. 'I try to make it go away, Stella, but it won't. Sometimes there are moments, seconds, when I think perhaps it will be OK again, but they hardly ever happen and, when they do, they don't last. I didn't get out of bed today because I didn't want to disturb you. I got up because I couldn't be near you. Because when I look at you, all I see is the person that I am not. I see the reason why I failed.'

I run.

CHAPTER TWENTY

* *

HUGH

Mikey is really very good at shooting zombies.

I've never been much of a video gamer, or in fact any sort of gamer, so when he handed me the controller for the game he was allowed to play for thirty minutes after dinner, I was reticent. I really should have been leaving. I had planned a whole evening of research on Victorian funeral practices, but Jake was stretched out along the back of the sofa and he gave me this look that said, let the good times roll, loser. And Sarah's living room, exactly the same in dimensions as my own, was somehow a hundred times warmer and more inviting that mine, which is really just its own little museum of my life so far. So I took the controller and flailed about miserably, dying repeatedly, while Mikey showed me the ropes, clearly laughing at me but with a surprising amount of good nature and patience. An hour later and now I can stay alive for almost five minutes.

'Bed time, *now*.' Sarah turns off the TV, clearly not prepared to be conned into letting us play for yet another 'just ten more minutes'.

'Ohhhh,' Mikey and I chorus as one, and she laughs. 'You're as bad as each other. I already let you have twice as long as you need.'

'But he's just getting good,' Mikey says. 'If we stop now, he'll be crap again by the next time we play. I've spent all this time training him.'

'My heart bleeds,' Sarah says, pointing at the door. Mikey throws me a look of defeat and scoops Jake up into his arms. My treacherous cat lies there like a rag doll, about as soft as an animal can be. It really is hard not to be offended.

'Can I take Ninja?' Mikey asks.

'Yeah, go on,' she says. 'But he'll want to go home later, so make sure you leave the window open.'

She turns back to me as Mikey disappears to his bedroom, chatting to the cat as he goes.

'He likes to pretend he's tough, but he loves it when Ninja is here at bedtime. I think he lets Ninja sleep on his pillow to protect him from zombies,' she says. 'I wonder whose cat he is. I feel bad about it sometimes. Still, he does always leave before I go to bed, so he's probably going home, right? Maybe he gets a better breakfast there, than dinner.'

I think about my two bits of bacon that I cook every morning, and how I always feed one half of a rasher to Jake. Sarah has certainly got his number.

'He's my cat,' I confess, and Sarah laughs and then bites her lip when she sees my deadpan expression.

'Seriously? What, you're not joking?'

'Yes,' I say. 'Well, sort of mine. A girlfriend bought him – for me, ostensibly, as a present – and got tired of me soon after, leaving me behind. I don't think I'm Jake's idea of a dream owner. I thought he was out all night, killing things and having sex with lots of lady cats, but it turns out that he's just starved of the love of a little boy who is more scared of zombies than he lets on. I can't really hold that against him, so if you want to share him, that seems OK to me. Although you must let me pay for all the food he eats here.'

'Oh, God, we've nicked your cat!' Sarah seems genuinely mortified.

'No, you haven't. You are sharing him, like I said, and you know what? He's a nice cat round here. Round my house he's just … disappointed.'

Sarah presses her lips together in a clear attempt not to laugh. 'But he's clearly special to you, right?'

'Well, he's very nice for a cat,' I say. 'And really it would be very unfair to hold any of his cat behaviour against him. I mean, you know, being emotionally rejected by a cat, it's not my finest hour, but it's not the worst, either. When I was about Mikey's age I had a hamster. It actually killed itself. Got out of its cage and jumped out of my open bedroom window. So a cat that seems to tolerate me is definitely a step up, you see …'

Sarah guffaws, covering her mouth with her hands, although it does little to stop the laughter from coming.

'Oh, my God, you are a sad case!' she tells me sweetly. 'You are an epic loser. Still, I'm a loser too. Knocked up at fifteen, no man, no family, barely two pennies to rub together. What a pair we make.'

Curiously I rather like being in a pair with her. Making her smile is giving me a strange sense of satisfaction. What I don't really understand is why the next question escapes from my mouth before I can stop it.

'Do you mind ... I hope I am not intruding if I ask about ...' I shift from one foot to the other.'

'Mikey's dad?' Sarah says the words for me. 'Where is the fucker?'

'Well, those weren't the exact words I was going to use. Mikey says he's never met him.'

'I think that's the way he'd like it to be,' Sarah says sadly. 'That's what he tells people ... the other kids at school. But it's not true. Mikey's dad lived with us for a long time. He was an all right bloke, just had this temper on him, and he was ... easily led. Fell in with the wrong people, ended up in the nick more than once – in and out. Stupid petty stuff, you know. But he kept going back, and then he got involved with drugs and ... It wasn't like he ever hit me, or I was scared of him. I just realised one day that if I stayed with him, my life would always be the same. Me waiting. Waiting for him to get back from whatever he was doing, waiting for him to get nicked, waiting for him to come out. And Mikey was getting bigger and seeing all this going on, and

I wanted something different for him. I want him to grow up decent, you know what I mean? I want him to try hard to make something of himself in the world.'

I nod. 'Yes. I do know what you mean. My dad wanted that for me. My dad was my hero. Every day I think about him and think about how lucky I am that I had him in my life. We did so much together, you know. We were such good friends, and in the final years before he died, we took up fly fishing together. We'd make our own flies and stand up to our thighs in freezing water, and never say a word to each other. And yet, when I look back at those times, I think they were the times I felt the closest to him, the times I learned the most from him. The times I learned just to be still.' I pause for a moment. It's a very long time since I talked about my father at all, let alone at some length, and I realise how good it feels to remember, this way, out loud in the world.

'I'm sorry Mikey hasn't got that, hasn't got a dad, like mine,' I say. 'But he's got you, and you are pretty special.'

Sarah's eyes widen for a moment, and she drops her gaze from me, blushing under her make-up.

'Oh, God,' I say, mortified that I have made her feel so uncomfortable. 'I wasn't ... Did you think I was flirting with you, or trying to come on to you? I wasn't, I swear. I wouldn't even try, not with you, which sounds really rude and not at all what I mean, and—'

'It's fine.' Sarah stops me in my tracks with a brush of her hand. 'Don't worry about it; it's nice. You said a nice thing.

I just … I'm not used to hearing nice things, I suppose. I liked it, though, OK?'

'You did?'

There's a sudden shift in the atmosphere, and I don't feel relaxed any more but tense and confused, uncertain of what is expected of me and how I am supposed to deliver it. Only I think that, whatever it is I do, I want to say more nice things to Sarah; I want to see her laugh again. It's a terrifying prospect. I put down my almost-full beer on the table.

'Well, I'd better get going,' I say cheerfully. 'I've still got work to do.'

'You never did tell me what exactly it is you do at the museum,' she says, smiling tentatively. Is that a welcoming look in her velvet brown eyes? I don't know, and I don't want to be wrong, so I choose not to dwell on this.

'Not much to tell,' I say. 'It's just boring, boring academic stuff – you'd be bored rigid by it,' I say.

'Because I haven't got any GCSEs so I must be thick?' she asks, and now somehow I've offended her.

'No, no, not at all. Even well-educated people get bored by my job. It is unutterably dull. Like me.'

I'm hoping the self-deprecating remark will raise another smile, but this time her eyes are doleful and sad.

'See you, then,' she says, turning her back on me and heading into the kitchen, starting to fill the sink with warm water. I hover for a few moments, at a loss how to leave on a better note.

'Good night,' I say. 'And thank you.'

As I step out of the front door and pull it shut, venturing out into a wet and rainy evening, I feel my world contracting back to its usual few square feet again – a tiny world, one that for the first time ever since I have been an adult feels unsatisfactory.

And then I see a stranger standing outside my house, staring at my front door, holding a letter in her hand.

Dear Adam,

I hoped and I waited and I prayed, but the letter from you never came. I don't blame you for that, not at all. In a way I am pleased. I think it means that you are happy, content. It means you didn't feel a hole where I was not.

I called you Adam. I don't know what your adoptive parents called you, but for the afternoon that I was your mum, you were my Adam. That afternoon, that one short afternoon that I was a mother, I held you in my arms and watched you. And you watched me back. The feeling of how much I loved you almost drowned me – it was like I couldn't catch my breath. I had to let you go, though, Adam, because I was very young, seventeen. I didn't have a choice. It was the right thing to do, for me and for you. But that didn't stop me hoping that one day you might write to me, so that I could tell you that in that one afternoon I loved you more than I have ever loved anyone since. You were my only son, my precious child.

So if one day you do decide to find out more about me, this letter will be waiting for you. It seems funny to say that I am proud of a man I have never met, but I am because I have all the faith that the tiny little person I cradled all those years ago grew up to be wise and kind and clever. I know it, somehow, as if they never really did cut that cord that joined us, as if it spins all around the world, keeping us linked, just a little, no matter what.

With all my love,
Your mum, Lucy

CHAPTER TWENTY-ONE

STELLA

I run. I don't have plan.

It's busy. It's Friday, so of course it's busy.

I run, weaving in and out and always in between, sidestepping other people's lives with expert deftness and fleetness of foot.

It's started to rain quite heavily now, but that doesn't stop girls in short skirts, arm in arm, racing through the showers to the next bar and pub, and lads gathering on street corners in short sleeves. I dart in and out of them, and none of them really notice me. They simply step out of my way, then occupy the space I pass through a moment after I have been in it. I know the way to the address on the letter; it's a couple of streets down from the flat I used to have – the place I lived in when I first met Vincent.

I stop at the top of the road where I once lived and catch my breath, looking down the street, wondering who now lives behind those curtains above the chippy. I wait until I have almost caught my breath, and then I start again. I can't let my body think that it's time to rest; I have to trick it into wanting to keep going, even though I'm wearing completely the wrong shoes for running.

The address on the letter is a quiet, suburban street: houses either side, trees spaced out neatly, residents-only parking. Ten or fifteen years ago it would have been lived in by normal local London people, but now at least half of the houses are lived in by people with money. It's easy to tell: doors painted matt green, loft conversions, glass extensions in the side return. It's been a long time, a very long time, since Grace walked up this street. Chances are the person she has written to isn't here any more, so I walk down the street, watching the numbers fall away until I get to number eight. There is a door painted black, chipped to reveal that once it was red. The glass is bobbled and textured, with a crack in the corner. The front garden is caked in concrete, and there are a few abandoned pots, with nothing growing in them. There's a light on upstairs. This little house has not been gentrified. It could be a rental; it could be anyone living here now.

I take the letter out of my pocket.

I don't even know if Grace is still alive. Maybe after everything she poured into that letter, words tumbling out quicker than I could write them, maybe she has let go, like so many do if they feel that they have done everything they need to, or have nothing left to hold on for. She might be gone by now, and I won't know until I clock in next, because I am supposed to be professional enough to keep a distance between myself and my patients. So I could post the letter now, through this letterbox, and perhaps I would be keeping my promise. And perhaps I would be changing everything.

'Can I help you?'

I start. A man stands behind me.

'Who lives here?' I ask him. I'm surely not a threat to him, slight as I am, but he frowns and takes a step back. I frighten him.

'Who wants to know?' He is well spoken, confident.

'I am looking for someone for a friend. This was their last known address.'

'Well, this is my address,' he says, slipping a bag off his shoulder – one of those bags you see media-type men wearing on the tube, a canvas satchel. He's wearing something that looks like an anorak, maybe a fishing jacket – khaki with a lot of pockets – and a grey scarf around his neck, which doesn't quite conceal a bow tie. 'And I've lived here all of my life, so who's your friend?'

It's him. The letter is for him.

A door slams over the road. A guy rides past on his bike. A dog barks somewhere. Time moves slowly, perhaps even stops for a second, as I hand him Grace's letter.

'This is for you,' I say. 'There might still be time.'

I hope that is still true, as I turn on my heel, walking fast down his path. As I reach the street I break into a jog and then a run, finally kicking off the wrong shoes and sprinting as fast as I can in and out of the Friday-night crowd on the high street until my lungs scream and my legs tremble and I feel my heart pumping hard. I run, and, because I feel almost like I can't stop, I run right into a wall, hard, skinning the palms of my hands. I stop dead.

Perhaps I kept my promise, and maybe I didn't.

Dear Mrs W.,

I just want to write and say thank you for everything you did over the last few weeks. Funny, isn't it, how you don't know who your friends are, or who the good people really are, until push comes to shove? And we never even found out each other's first names, and I still find your Polish surname impossible to pronounce, let alone spell.

I always thought I had so many friends, what with ballroom on a Thursday and the Cancer Research quiz night every other Sunday in the pub. But when I got ill, they all fell away, one by one. I suppose some of them just didn't care, and some of them found it too hard. Well, it is hard, trying to make small talk with a man who looks like a walking mummy. But you came in, every day. First of all I was rude, and I told you not to bother. I was angry, I think. But you still came, and that's a kindness that, although I don't deserve it, I will always be grateful for. You'd make us something to eat together; you'd just be there when the drugs made me sick, or the pain got so bad. I came to rely on you and your gentle ways. I never found out if you used to be a nurse, but if not you would be a very good one.

I'm writing this knowing that, when it comes to it, you will be here at my side. And you will hold my hand. I don't suppose it's the done thing to fall in love with a woman whose first name you still don't know, and who you only got to know when it was all too late anyway, but that's what happened. Dear Mrs W., I love you. You have given my final days a great deal of joy.

My name is Noel Kincade.

CHAPTER TWENTY-TWO

* *

STELLA

I have run and now walked very far in my tights. My feet are wet through and numb now. I walked until the crowds around the tube station thinned to nothing – around and around, until the little Turkish place closed and the damp air was as near to silent as it ever is in London. I have thought about what happened, and about what I've done.

About Vincent, about everything he said and the way he looked at me.

About that poor man, who will have read that letter by now.

And I wonder about the fallout, and I wonder about falling to pieces. And I wonder if I am unravelling into streams of thread so thin they are caught in the air and will be blown away into nothing.

I don't think I realised before now that it wasn't only Vincent who came back from war with pieces missing; it was me too. I have lost so much of what made me the woman I was, and I don't know where to begin looking for her, because I'm not exactly sure who I was in the first place.

These last few months, I have simply been a woman waiting be loved once again, loved in a way that I let define me. But I existed before Vincent loved me. I existed before he became lodged in my heart. And if I have lost him, I must still be able to exist. What choice is there when a man stops loving you? You can't really just let yourself be blown away on the wind, can you?

As I turn into our road I wonder what it is that I have lost. I know that I have lost myself – the strong, funny, capable woman I used to be. The woman who knew what to do in a crisis. The woman who never failed. I think I must have left her by the roadside one night, concentrating so hard on running away that I stopped running after what I wanted, or to the people I love.

I stop in front of the windows of the corner shop and look at my reflection in the glass. I'm soaked through to the bone; my feet are shoeless and wet. I'm exhausted and pale. I'm a half-person, living a half-life, surrounded by death. I'm a ghost, a shadow.

I hear the long sound coming before I realise that I am making it. Low like a moan, it is grief and it is mine. Slowly it builds into one wrenching sob after another, and I realise I am mourning. I am mourning for the life I had once. The exciting job that made a difference, that brought people back from the brink of death. The strong, handsome, brave husband who adored me. I am grieving for the girl who always knew what she wanted and knew how to be alive in this terrifying world. That girl is gone; she is lying in pieces somewhere, and I miss her. I miss her and I want her back.

I put the key in the lock, let myself in and listen to the house. It's quiet.

I go up the stairs. A sound startles me and I realise that it's my phone, vibrating against the bedside table where I must have left it all night. I pick it up. Thirty-seven missed calls in total: a dozen from Vincent and the rest from my message service. He must have been worried about me, out most of the night. I've been so thoughtless, so selfish and stupid. I need to tell him I'm fine. I need to tell him I know what I need to do, to make it better.

I call his number. It rings once and then goes to voicemail.

I hear the front door open, and I go to the top of the stairs. Vincent walks in and closes the door behind him very quietly, as if he doesn't want to be heard. Because he doesn't want to wake me up. Because he's been out all night too.

He leans against the hall wall for a moment, and I see the briefest moment of pain pass across his face. He looks tired.

'Hello,' I say, sitting down on the top stair. He's startled to see me.

'Where have you been?' he asks. 'You didn't come home. I waited and waited, called and called. Nothing. And then I realised what I'd done, that I'd lost it. I went to the nick to turn myself in – thought it was better than waiting for the Old Bill to come here. That bloke, he's not pressing charges, though; he said he was drunk, and his wife said he was an idiot. They let me off with a warning, but that doesn't matter. I crossed a line, Stella. I crossed a line with you that I don't want to go back over again. I know now, I've got to go back to the army. I've got to ask for more help coping.' He stares up at me, my head and shoulders in shadow. 'I got home, and you weren't here, and you weren't answering your phone, so I've been out, looking for you.'

'Why?' I sit there on the top stair and wonder about going down, about going to my husband and putting my arms around him, and resting my cheek against his chest and listening to the beat of his heart until mine slows and synchronises with his. That's what I want to do, so much, but that ease of intimacy is long gone. 'Why look for me, when I make your life such a misery?'

'I didn't … The way things came out …' He looks up at me. 'Come down here. I can't see your face.' He stands up straight, watching.

I get up and descend one, two stairs and sit again; this time my face is exposed under the harsh hallway light.

'You blame me,' I said. 'Is that it? You blame loving me for your friend's death.'

'It's not that simple. I said stuff when I was angry and hurt, and so tired. You've got to understand, Stella. On the day I first saw you walking through the park, I knew who I was. On the day I first talked to you and asked you for coffee, I knew who I was. On the day we first kissed, and I fell for you before the kiss was even over, I knew who I was.

I knew what I was offering you. I was an honourable man, a man who would lay down his life for his mates. I was brave, strong and certain. That's the man I was when I met you; that was the man that fell in love with you. The man you fell in love with. But he's dead now.'

'And it was me, me that is to blame for that, for this?' I nod at his leg and gesture around at our cold, neglected house.

'No, not you.' Vincent leans against the wall again. 'Not you, but me. I thought that in that moment, when it came, in that life-or-death moment, I thought that I would be selfless, be a hero, fight for my mates. But I didn't. I ran. I ran because ... I wanted to see your face again. And now ... I've been trying to write a letter to Kip's wife ever since, and I don't know how to tell her that I failed him, I failed her and her kid. I failed me.'

'Doesn't it count for anything that you didn't fail me?' I am surprised by how calm I feel, how still. 'Doesn't that matter?'

'But if I can't love you any more, then what's it for?' Vincent asks me. 'If I can't forgive myself for choosing to live, if I can't love you any more, then why did my best mate die? Why did my leg get blown off? Why am I covered in burns? What for? Because when I look at you, I can't feel what I want to feel, and I know I've failed you anyway, and that guy that I hit, he becomes right – it has all been for nothing.'

There is a long silence. Each moment that passes pulls us further and further apart; much more and we will be out of sight of each other.

'We're broken, aren't we?' Vincent says finally. 'I'm broken, body and soul. And you can't fix me. Only I can do that. Only I can find a way to forgive myself. All this time that you've been trying, been so loyal, so sweet, so … hopeful, you've been falling apart too, and I've let you. We're in a bubble, two little unhappy bubbles bouncing off each other. You can't help me, I can't help you … we just keep hurting each other from a distance.'

Slowly I get up and walk down the rest of the stairs until I am standing in front of him.

'What's going to happen?' I ask him.

'I'm going away for a bit. Frenchie – you remember, Frenchie from training? – he's got a spare bedroom in Vauxhall. He says I can go there for a few days. I'm going to go and crash there for a bit. We both of us need to figure it out. I need to find a way to tell Kip's wife what happened, to look her in the eye and tell her what I did. I need to find a way to live with myself. And you … you need to be free of me.'

He leans forward and kisses me lightly on the forehead. It's only then I see he's packed his kit bag, and it's leaning by the door. He heads to the door and pauses for a moment, his hand on the latch, his back to me. I see him turn his head very slightly towards me. And then he opens the door and is gone.

Sitting down on the bottom stair of my empty house, I close my eyes, and in that moment something shifts inside me and resets.

I'm done with feeling like this.

Girls,

I'm off, and this is just a quick note to say bye!

I've been thinking about that cruise we went on, after my divorce. Jen, you said, fuck him, let's go on a cruise; and Sue and May, you were on board at once. Well, all I can say is, it was a good job that it was an all-inclusive cruise, because between us we nearly drank that boat dry.

When Barry fucked off, I thought life was over – that I'd spend the next forty years miserable and lonely. I didn't even get half of the next forty years, but what I did have was the best years of my life because of you, my friends.

You lot, you make me laugh till I can't speak. You make me adventurous and brave. If it hadn't been for you, I wouldn't have opened the shop, I wouldn't have dyed my hair the same colour as a postbox or had my nose pierced. I wouldn't have had the guts to have that eighteen-month, pure-sex affair with lovely young Fernando, who of course was really called Dan, but how we loved to call him Fernando.

Cancer is shit, and it hurts like a fuck, but I would have missed out on many months of my life if it hadn't been for you lot, keeping me fighting. Well, I've lost this battle, but you go and win the war for me. I expect you all to be in every fundraiser in pink tutus and wigs – I'll come and haunt you if you don't!

Cheers, birds.

Have a large glass of wine for me, and then have three more.

Cheryl xxxx

THE SIXTH
NIGHT

CHAPTER TWENTY-THREE

· ·

HOPE

I had a shower, and then I paced.

I took my meds, then paced, then did my physio behind a closed curtain, and paced. Then I looked at my underwear and panicked. For reasons unknown, I didn't bring any sexy underwear with me to Marie Francis. What's wrong with me? Why didn't I plan to have sex with my best friend during my stay here? I am so short-sighted. All I have is plain white bras, now slightly grey, and no matching pants at all – nothing at all to stand between me and the fact that I am about to embark on something very foolhardy indeed. In the end I go black vest top, black pants and jeans. And then I wonder if jeans might be a bit awkward to take off, so leggings, for easy slip-downage, but then I take them off again and put the jeans back on because what has ever been alluring about an elastic waistband? I find a loose T-shirt; I'm not wearing a bra and that's a bit awkward – I don't want him to notice that my breasts are free-range until, you know, he notices. I try to think about what it will be like for Ben to see me naked, and for me to see him naked. I should just calm down; after all, it's not the first time we've gone au naturel together. Of course, the last time we were seven and sharing a bath. Oh God, oh God, oh God. I need to pull myself together.

Shadow appears outside my patio door and stares at me through the gap in the curtain, with his huge mournful eyes. Hastily, I go over to the door and let him in. He hops up onto my chair and nestles into a pile of discarded-as-too-vile pants.

'The trick,' I say to him, 'is to think of ways to make the act as easy as possible. After all, it's not like we are going for any awards for style or technique. No one has to actually enjoy it. All we need to do is get it done. In. Out. In and out again, maybe. Then, done. No, wait. Everyone has to enjoy it – that's why we are doing it. Why are we doing it? I can't remember. What was I thinking, Shadow?'

Shadow's luminous green eyes say, 'Fuck me if I know.'

'What do you think Ben is thinking?' I ask the cat, who seems to be pretty good at listening. 'Is Ben thinking about what pants to wear? I bet Ben isn't thinking about it at all. He's so lucky, that Ben – the way he just sails through his crazy life, never knowing or caring what comes next, or whether it's going to be good or bad. And me, I just think all the time. I think of everything, every permutation, every scenario, every outcome. I try to think of a contingency plan for every possibility. But then usually my plan is to just stay inside, because that covers everything.'

I pick up clothes, fold and refold them, and then drop them back on the floor. Then I sit down on the bed, suddenly exhausted. The effort of trying to get dressed in order to get undressed has wiped me out for a moment, and I need a second to rest. Shadow stretches out, his claws becoming entangled in a pair of tights, which he vigorously tries to shake off his claws before becoming beguiled with the whiplash of tights and rolling over to try and kill them.

'And now I'm thinking, what am I thinking?' I tell him as he rips great holes in my tights. 'What are *we* thinking? We can't possibly go through with this, based on a whim and the death of a very young girl who had even less time than me to make stupid mistakes. It's just silly. It was a moment; he was all worried about me with his germs, and I was all worried about not living life to the full, and thinking about Issy, and wishing I'd had better sex stories to tell, and that sounds really wrong!' I pause, and Shadow rolls off the chair, engulfed in nylon.

'We both let it get to us, in the moonlight, under the trees: the moment, my mortality. We are *such* a pair of planks. He's going to turn up in a minute and give me that sheepish grin, and I'm going to give him my 'who knows?' shrug and we'll laugh and get back to doing whatever it is that we do. Singing songs and teasing each other. Won't we? Won't we? Are you evening listening to me, Shadow?'

As the young cat rolls over and over again, shredding my tights with his extended claws, I think I can safely say the answer is no. Still, maybe if Shadow doesn't give a shit about my problems, then neither should I.

Stella is having some time off, which is most inconsiderate of her. If Stella were here, she'd listen to me. Better than a stray cat with murderous tendencies towards hosiery listens, anyway.

A warm, tight feeling knots in my gut when I think about the things that Ben and I do, the friendship we have. That's what it's like to be with Ben; in every moment there's this distant drum of longing always beating – always wanting more of him, just a little more. Perhaps I am like a vampire, a life vampire, stalking the night, sucking experience out of other people, out of Ben, who is always so fearless and brave. Ben, who never flinches from what the world has to offer. But I can't take this from him. This is just … I can't take his metaphorical life force via his penis.

We can't have sex, we simply can't. Because afterwards there would be nowhere to go. No singing and teasing any more – not after I'd seen his boy bits and he'd … Oh God, it doesn't bear thinking about.

Oh, I wish Stella were here. If she were, I would tell her. Stella would *get* a sex plan, I know that. Stella has the look of someone who is used to desperate measures.

A coughing fit comes suddenly, but not out of nowhere; I realise I've been breathless for the last few minutes and probably ignoring it. The explosion of noise sends Shadow careering for the door as it opens, a trail of tights flapping crazily behind him.

Tonight's night nurse, a well-meaning older lady called Mandy, who has certainly never needed a sex plan, pops her head round the door and then, seeing me sitting on the bed, comes in.

'Choke up, chicken; it might be a gold watch,' she says, patting me firmly on the back. I feel a nodule of mucus loosen sharply and then evacuate into my mouth. She hands me a box of tissues. Once it's gone, I take a few deep breaths and wait for my eyes to stop watering, while she rubs my back.

'A gold watch?' I say.

She tips her head to one side and looks at me.

'Something my nan used to say. So I hear your young man is taking you for a trip out? They reckon you'll be discharged soon.'

'Just a drink, and he's not mine, as such.'

'You look nice. That lipstick suits you.' Her smile is benign.

'Like Ben would even notice if I was wearing lipstick,' I say. 'I could get up in full clown make-up and he wouldn't turn a hair. He only has eyes for himself.'

For a moment I wonder if full clown make-up would make inappropriate sex more manageable, but just the thought alone makes me want to book therapy.

'You say that as if he's no good, but from what I hear he comes every day to see you, and he makes everyone laugh while he's here. He's a rare sort of man – a man who keeps his word and brings happiness. You should keep him.'

'I don't think I'd be allowed to. I think that would be unlawful imprisonment,' I say.

'Well, anyway,' Mandy says. 'They are chucking you out soon, you know. Maybe even tomorrow.'

'Really?' I thought I'd feel happy, elated even, but I don't. As soon as she says the words, there's this little buzz of panic and a foreboding, because while I've been at Marie Francis, I've been in the holding pattern, this limbo. Now I have to make choices, or really just one choice, the same choice that I've been making over and over again since I was a little girl: whether to go out there and say hello to the world, or stay indoors with Mum. I know what Issy would want me to do.

'I'm here,' Ben proclaims as he opens the door, ushering in with him a miasma of Lynx.

'No kidding.' Mandy wrinkles her nose. 'I'll leave you two to it. Oxygen's on the wall if you need it.'

'Or you could stay,' I say, catching at her sleeve, a little desperately. 'We could have a chat. All three of us, together. In a group.'

'Darling,' she says. 'I've got work to do. And remember what I said, and think on.'

'What did she say?' Ben asks me.

'Something about a gold watch,' I say.

It's fair to say that in the seconds after Mandy left the room, no two people have ever wanted to die more. And that's saying something in a hospice.

'So, let's do this thing.' Ben is stoic, in typical Ben fashion – never backing down from a challenge once he's agreed to it. Like that time he ate a spider when we were eleven. 'I've booked us a room in this hotel up the road. It's not exactly The Ritz, it's bordering on being a dive, in fact, but there's no nurse's button that we could accidentally push whilst in the throes of ...' He looks at me anxiously. 'Doing sex stuff.'

Stay indoors with my mum, that's the choice I make. I make the choice to stay indoors with my mum.

'This is madness.' Standing up, I notice that Ben takes two steps back. 'Look, don't panic. Don't look like you are about to be led to your doom, because it's fine, it's OK. You've been granted a reprieve, OK? I've been thinking about it, and it was a silly plan, stupid and impulsive, and maybe we were both a bit drunk on the moment. But a stupid plan is a stupid plan, and just because we came up with it, it doesn't mean we have to do it. It's only one of many of our stupid plans through history, and let's look at how those turned out. Like that plan you had to motorise a shopping trolley, or that time I thought I'd stand up to Jessie Sinclair because all bullies are cowards, and she punched me in the stomach and then you for good measure. It was a silly idea, and you are a sweet, good friend for offering to go through with it, but really. It's fine, stand down. Stand your ... bits down.'

I am not getting the reaction of relief that I was expecting from Ben. Instead his frown deepens, and his expression is complicated and closed.

'If that's what you want,' he says eventually. 'Whatever you want.'

'Well, isn't that what you want?' I ask him, confused.

He sits down opposite me, his long skinny legs folded inwards. He looks like some kind of bird – a rook or a crow, a portent of doom.

'I want to keep you safe,' he says. 'And you want to have sex. And, well, if you are going to have sex with someone, I want it to be with someone who will care for and respect you and take care of you, and not be a dick, like pretty much all guys my age are, including me at times. I want it to be nice, and warm, and kind and friendly, and full of love. And even if it's not lust-type love, actual real love for this person you are doing this amazingly intimate thing with.' He leans forward. There's a gravitas about his expression I'm not used to seeing – something that makes me sit up and listen. 'When you first asked me, I thought, fuck that's weird, and I went home thinking, shit we can't do that. I'll turn up tomorrow and she'll say "what a joke" and everything will be fine. But then, I was awake all night thinking, thinking about the sex that I've had ...'

'Ben, really ...' I don't want to know.

'No, just listen.' Ben shifts in his chair. 'I've been with a few girls. Not that many, actually. Fewer than ten ...'

'Ten is loads!'

'I didn't say ten, I said fewer than ten.' Ben looks exasperated.

'Fewer than five?' I feel that clarification is important.

'Oh God! Six, I've had sex with six girls,' he says.

'Well, why not just say six? What's this whole "fewer than" thing about? Because six is sixty per cent of ten.'

'Hope,' he says. 'Do you think you are maybe getting off the point on purpose?'

'Six,' I say. 'Sex with six girls.'

A sharp rip of disapproval and jealousy tears through me, though I'm not sure if it's the six anonymous girls or him I am jealous of.

'Yes,' he says. 'Yes. And it's nice, it's great, sex with girls. You know. It's fun, and they are mysterious and fit, and they all look different naked, and it's great. All the sex I've had in my life has been great, but it's never been ...' He hesitates, struggling to express himself, which is most unlike Ben. One thing Ben is usually very good at is talking.

'It's never felt safe, or kind, or caring, or special,' he says. 'And I've never felt ... cared for. Worshipped, sure, but not cared for.'

I look at him. Here is where I would normally laugh out loud, or tease, or insult him fondly, but I can see what it's cost him to tell me that. And I know how his life has been so often absent of care. There's his mum, who drinks cider in front of the TV all day and takes pills, and his stepdad, who blames everyone but himself for everything he's ever done wrong. Ben was the kid in the unwashed shirt, the scuffed, too-tight shoes. The boy who had beans on toast every night for a week, unless I took him home for tea. I know how he has longed all his life to feel cared for, except I thought he'd grown out of that now – that now he is so vibrant, so present in every moment, that he would never need anybody. But now he's saying that if we do what we said we'd do, it wouldn't just be for me, it would be for him too. Shit.

'Is this an elaborate plan to make me feel better about emotionally blackmailing you?' I ask him. 'Because it's sort of working.'

'It's your call,' Ben says.

'Well, if we are mainly doing it for you,' I say. 'It's worth a try.'

With that he reaches out and takes my hand, and though my heart is pounding, I let him lead me out of the door.

CHAPTER TWENTY-FOUR

STELLA

No rain, no moon.

After Vincent left, I slept like I haven't in months. Deep, dreamless, certain sleep. I woke to the sound of a bus creaking pass. It's troubling, this sense of peace. And I wonder, why now? Is it simply because the man I love, the man whose happiness and well-being I've worried about and obsessed over for so long, isn't here any more? Did I exchange my marriage for deep, dreamless sleep?

Perhaps it's the relief. The pain of living a life that is less than you always imagined, hoped it would be, is excruciating. It's so restful to stop trying to make things right. To make life smaller.

I'm not due at work tonight, but I go anyway. I have no idea what happened while I slept so soundly – if my delivery has had any consequences yet. Hugh, that was the name of the son, the poor man whose life I dropped a hand grenade into yesterday, he's probably been to Marie Francis by now. I need to find out what's happened, to apologise. To make amends for letting the tragedy of my life mix and mingle with something that had nothing to do with me. I need to make amends, as much as I can. I need to start again, reset, restore factory settings.

So the first thing I have to do is find Grace and tell her what I did, explain. Apologise. It might be too late; she might already be gone. The battery in my phone is dead, and I didn't have time to charge it before I left. What happens, whatever is waiting for me inside the walls of Marie Francis, on the other side of the green-painted door, I won't know until I am there.

As I run, falling into that easy comforting rhythm, it occurs to me I could just not go in and not face the consequences. I could just keep running now, and there would be no reason to turn back. I could run and run on to the next town, perhaps somewhere by the sea, and start again, start fresh. Like the night I packed up my rucksack. It's a thought that won't let me go, as I plod through the chilled night. There's a lure to it, a deep, abiding attraction to simply sweeping all of my mistakes away and starting again. And yet, deep down, I know I can't do that. I have to face them; I know that much. I just don't know how or what will happen next.

It's a quiet evening. The streets are empty of people, cars sweep by infrequently, as I make my way steadily towards Marie Francis. Across the street I see the fluorescent lights of the bakers flicker off. Two more minutes and I slow, ready to walk. In the next moment I become aware of a stranger's hand on my arm, stopping, holding me, attempting to control me. Adrenaline kicks in and my legs move faster, but he accelerates with me, pulling me backwards. It's happening so quickly there's no time to think, except to decide that my charmed life as a woman alone in the night is over; I've been seen. I do not know if he intends robbery or worse, but I try to shake him off. He stops me, holds me. I flail at his shins with my soft running shoes, and he lets go. I career off, shouldering a wall, feeling the stab of pain shoot inwards, using the impact as a launching point to run again.

'Stop. Wait!' he calls after me, his voice echoing in the almost-empty street. Once I get up on to the high street, well past the entrance to Marie Francis, there will be more people, who may very well be indifferent to what happens to me, but still somehow I think a crowd will deter him. I can find a place to go inside, ring the police. I just keep running, and so does he. I am sprinting, and I'm fit, and I realise with an unexpected thrill that I will lose him. He's further behind me but still calling after me, and I am yards from the busy high road. And then it hits me: what mugger or would-be rapist asks his victim to slow down so that he can catch up?

I turn around and look. He's stopped a little further down the street to catch his breath. I recognise the bag and the shoes, the scarf, the fishing jacket. It's him. The man I gave Grace's letter to. Hugh.

I just stand there, in the dark, and wait for him to reach me.

'I'm sorry,' he wheezes. 'I didn't really think that through – pouncing on a woman alone in the dark. You're very quick, though.'

'What are you doing?' I ask him. 'Why are you here?'

He laughs, and it's full of anger. 'You deliver that letter to me and you don't *know*?'

'I'm sorry, I ...' I don't know what to say. 'I shouldn't have.'

'I didn't know what to do,' he said, his gaze falling away from me. 'You gave it to me, and I didn't know what to do or think. Whether to laugh or cry or ... what? And I can't ... I can't *see* her. This woman who says she is my mother. I can't just go and see her. So there is only one other person I can talk to, and that's you.'

'I don't have any answers,' I tell him. There are a few feet of pavement between us. Passers-by walk in and out of our conversation, oblivious to this moment that means so much, just within this few square yards of grubby street.

'I have to talk to someone, and I can't talk to her, you see. She's a ghost. She's a dream. She's ... a monster.'

'She isn't.' I shake my head. 'I can tell you that; she isn't. She has been broken. Life's broken her, and it's hurt you. But she isn't a monster. She just wanted to leave a clean slate.'

His laugh is bitter, cold, and I take a step back. I don't blame him, I can't blame him, for the way he feels. I can only blame myself for bringing him the news.

'She wants to leave a clean slate.' He shakes his head. 'No matter what pain she leaves behind. Well, yes, I suppose that is her MO.'

'Hugh.' I hesitate. 'May I call you Hugh? I understand how you must feel. When I wrote the letter for her, I was shocked, but ... Grace is your mother.'

'My mother.' His smile is so wretched as he says the word, pregnant with meaning. 'The mother who left me a suicide note and vanished into thin air. The mother I've thought was dead since I was ten years old.'

Dear Son,

The last letter I wrote to you was supposed to be just that. It's important that you know that. It wasn't a trick, or a lie. It wasn't an excuse or a get-out clause. I meant to do it. I meant to die.

I wanted to love you so much, my little boy. So much. And you poured all of your love into me, no matter what a terrible mother I was. No matter how many afternoons I was passed out drunk on the sofa, or not there to collect you from school. Or the days that you didn't eat until your father got in. I'd fail you, day by day, year on year, and yet still you greeted me with shining eyes. You deserved so much more than me – than my selfish, capricious, cold-hearted self. No, it's not even that. I wasn't cold-hearted. I knew what a sweet, funny, clever, lovable little boy you were, but I couldn't <u>feel</u> it. I couldn't feel anything but the dragging down of this great sadness like a millstone around my neck, and I thought, I thought what a relief it would be to let it take me, to not have to fight to come up for air any more.

And I thought about you without me there any more, and I was certain life would be better for you, and for your father, without having to battle my black cloud that covered us all.

But I am a coward, darling boy. I'm a coward and I always have been. I didn't want to live but I was too scared to die, so I ran away. And I did have a sort of death for a long time. Day after day, drunk, lonely, I let life use me up. Sleeping rough, doing things … things I am ashamed of.

One day, years and years after I left, I found a friend, or rather she found me. A stranger, a passer-by. She lifted me up from the gutter and took me somewhere where I could wash and be warm, and eat food and feel safe. And she let me stay there. Every day I thought I would leave, but every day I stayed. And first one, then two, then three days went by without a drink, and the days turned into weeks, and months. It wasn't as easy as that: I cried, I beat my fists, I threatened her and myself, but I could have left at any time. Only I didn't. I stayed. And one day I got up, and the black cloud, it hadn't gone, but it had lifted – enough for me to see a far horizon. That's when I cried for you, my darling boy, for you and your father. That's when I cried and grieved over what I'd done to you. That's when I fell in love with you, when I wanted you, adored you, longed to hold you. At the exact moment I knew it was too late. I knew that I could not come back. That you were both better off without me.

Well now, my son, I am dying, and I am still a coward. I don't want to go. I don't want to leave this world that I feel like I have only just learned how to live in. But I have to pay the price; there is no choice.

When you read this letter, I will already be dead. You will hate me. You will be angry, and bitter and outraged; you will not understand why. I don't ask you to forgive me, or to even care that I am gone. But dear, dear boy, please know you had a mother who loved you – not for long enough, and from afar, but she loved you with every waking moment, and in every sleeping moment dreamed of you.

Your mother,

Grace

CHAPTER TWENTY-FIVE

STELLA

Looking at him across the table is a curious experience. It's the first time I've seen him in full light. The chase must have taxed him; his face is waxy with sweat, his dark hair turned wavy with damp. He has a sort of sweet softness to him – the polar opposite of Vincent's rugged good looks. He has a face that has read a lot of books. There was nothing to do but to cross the road with him to the twenty-four-hour café next to the taxi rank and buy him a cup of milky white, strong and sweet.

I smiled at Hussein behind the counter. He knows all of us from Marie Francis; we come in a lot throughout the night, and sometimes he'll bring us over a tray of doughnuts as a treat.

'I'm sorry,' I say to Hugh. It seems like the only sensible thing to say. He's lost so much, and even the things he's found, he's going to lose again. 'Perhaps, though … Perhaps this might be for the best …?'

'Because everything happens for a reason?' he says wearily. 'Sounds like one of the posters you see with kittens on, pinned up in an office. Not everything happens for a reason. Most things happen for no reason at all.'

'Believe me, I know that,' I say. 'You must have had a very long time of missing her. Life must have been hard for you.'

He shakes his head once. It's a tight, tense movement, guarding so much pain. I feel it radiate from him. I recognise it: it's anger.

'Not at all. I had a wonderful father; I never wanted for anything. She was right, what she wrote in the letter. Life was better without her.'

I don't respond; there is no response. Looking out of the window, I watch the empty street, existing beyond the reflected lights of the café, and I wait.

'She doesn't know that you gave me the letter?' he says finally.

I shake my head. 'I was on my way to tell her, when you stopped me. I broke my promise to her. I've betrayed her, and I don't know why, really, except that last night … I was hurt and angry, and tired of life never being the way I think it should be. So I made a gesture. I thought that you both deserved a chance to say things to each other's faces before it was too late. But that wasn't my choice to make. It was foolish and selfish. And I'm sorry.'

Once again he is silent, and I let him be.

'I think … well, I think perhaps my marriage fell apart last night. And I'm not offering that as an excuse, or even a reason. It's just … fate has this way of throwing a bomb into our lives and standing back as everything we thought was certain is scattered to the four winds. I came here tonight because I knew I had to see Grace. But after that ... I really have no idea what is happening next. I've come to this point in my life – thirty-two years old – and I believe that from today I have to start again completely. I have to start from zero. So what I'm trying to say is, it feels shit right now, but eventually, knowing everything, knowing it all, as bad as it is, means you can start from zero again. You can build your life on the truth instead of lies.'

'You like to talk, don't you?' he says wearily, and somehow I know it's an effort for him to keep from resting his head on the tabletop. I know, because it's an effort for me too.

'I'm sorry.' I shrug. 'You know, I think that's partly my problem; I always want to fix everyone, everything, whether they want it or not. I think that's why I became a nurse in the first place. I trained to be a trauma nurse, and that was simple. I mean, it wasn't *simple*, it was hard, but we knew what we were trying to do; we were trying to fix bones, hearts, heads – people. After my husband got his leg blown off in Afghanistan, I couldn't face it any more, going to work to fix other people when I couldn't fix him. And I needed a job out of his way, so when I saw this job, I thought it would work well for me. No fighting against anything any more, just caring. I thought that would be good. I don't know. Maybe I'm not cut out to be a nurse after all.'

'You could retrain to do a job in talking the hind leg off a donkey,' Hugh mutters. 'Sorry, that was rude. And I'm sorry to hear about your husband. And actually it's not you that I'm angry with. It's just, it took Dad and me a long time to get our act together, but we did it. And now I'm at a point in my life that is settled, even optimistic – a point where I find myself thinking about a life with someone else in it. It felt nice, and now this. Now I have this to deal with.'

'So all this time you thought she had killed herself?' I ask him.

He nods, hunching his shoulders against some cold that only he feels.

'When I was ten years old, I came downstairs one morning, and there was Mum's letter on the table, written on a piece of lined paper ripped out from my exercise book – my homework was on the back. Her watch, a cheap gold watch Dad had given her when they were married, was weighing it down, along with her rings.'

He stares at the tabletop as he talks, reliving that moment, watching it play out on the Formica.

'Dad was still asleep. It was Saturday, and my dad always had a lie in on a Saturday. I always got up and came down and had toast with Mum. She'd be wearing her nightie, we'd sit and eat and talk, and she'd tell me jokes and make me laugh, she'd ruffle my hair. Sometimes I helped her sort socks or iron pillowcases. It was this small amount of time we used to spend together, before my mates came to knock and I was gone for the day. It was a certain thing. My mum, for all of my childhood, was a certain thing, until the day

I found the letter.' He pushes his cup of coffee away, as if tracing the outline of a long-lost letter on the surface of the table with his forefinger.

'I read her letter. It said, "Frank, I'm so sorry. I can't go on. I thought when I met you I could change for the better, and I've tried, I have. But nothing changes. I love you, and the boy. Don't blame yourself. Take care of him, Frank. He'll be so upset. Grace."'

There was a pause, and I thought of the letter I had pushed into Hugh's hands just hours earlier.

'She couldn't even bring herself to say my name,' he said, unable to meet my gaze. 'I didn't really know what the letter meant, and it was Dad's lie in, so I waited until it was eleven and I made him a tea, like she always did on a Saturday. And when he asked where she was, I said, "There's a letter downstairs on the table. Mum says she's sorry, but I don't know what for."

'I've never seen him move so fast. He tore down the stairs, picked up the rings and the letter and ran out into the street. I went after him, and I told him it had been there when I'd got up, that it had been there a long time.

'And he grabbed me, and shook me, and asked me why I didn't wake him. And he kept shaking me and crying, and shaking and crying. When he let me go, he went into the house and called the police. She hadn't taken anything. No clothes, no money. Her purse was on the sideboard. No door key. Later that day they found a pair of shoes on the beach in Clacton. They were Mum's shoes. That was all we knew about what happened next: a pair of shoes on a beach.

'There was an inquest, more than a year after she disappeared. It was an open verdict, but we got a death certificate. We had a funeral. There was an empty coffin, even. Dad was a fisherman; this is his jacket. He taught me to love fishing too. He'd take me on weekends, after she'd gone, deep into the countryside, to fish. It was wonderful *and* awful, because ... after she'd gone, there was this kind of peace, this tranquillity that wasn't there before. It was after she was gone that I realised I was like my dad; that we liked the same things: reading and fishing, history and ghost stories. Life with just the two of us, it was gentle and kind. On Sundays he'd drive us out of the city, to posh parts of the Thames, and we'd fish. And sometimes I couldn't help being glad that she wasn't there, and I couldn't help but wonder if, somewhere under the surface of the water, she was watching us – angry that we didn't miss her more.'

He pauses and shudders, closing his eyes for a moment. I reach for the sugar bowl, picking up a sachet of sugar, just for something to do, something to look at, because looking at him now feels too intrusive.

'When I was about sixteen, I went to look for something in the shed – I was building something. I wanted to make a table, that was it, for Dad's birthday, so I went to look for some tools. Right at the back of the garage there was something covered up with ground sheets. I pulled them back and there were stacks and stacks of boxes. Forty-four boxes. Each one filled with six empty vodka bottles. Dad kept her empties, for years. He went around the house and collected them, poured what he could down the sink and put the bottles in the garage. I guess it was before the days of recycling. He never wanted me to know that she drank, and I didn't know until that moment. I had no idea. I was this happy little kid, with this happy mum who'd take me out in the middle of the night to look at stars that we couldn't really see, or get me up at five a.m. to come with her and watch the sunrise, and I loved it. I loved that I had a mum that took me on adventures, and a Dad that slept in on Saturdays. And then … it all changed and she was gone. She was gone and she couldn't even write my name in her suicide note. And for the last twenty-five years, I've woken up every morning knowing that my mum didn't love me enough to stay alive. Until this morning. Now I know she didn't love me enough to die.'

There is nothing to say, so neither of us speak. Instead we just sit in the café, sipping cold coffee. Taxi drivers come in and out. Conversation and laughter, life, going on around us, everywhere except for the four square feet where we are. Here, life is standing still, and there's a kind of bond between us – a survivor's bond, perhaps. Or just the bond of the broken-hearted. But I feel it; it's comforting.

Meeting Hugh's eyes, I notice that behind his glasses he has hazel eyes that seem kind and warm. He doesn't hate me, the way that I thought he might, the way that he perhaps has a right to. He sees me. He sees why I did what I did, and he understands.

'I thought that if I delivered the letter to you before your mum died, I could be a hero, at least in your lives if not in my own. I had an idea that I could at least save *something* – save you, save Grace. Make something that was terrible, better, but it was a stupid idea. A thoughtless one. I shouldn't have given you the letter at all. I should never have written it. I just wanted to feel important, somehow, to someone. To feel that I mattered. It was selfish, and I am so, so sorry.'

Hugh sighs, shakes his head. 'Would it have been any better if you hadn't delivered the letter?'

'Well, you've moved on. You had grieved, and now I've dragged you back into pain that I imagine took you years to recover from. So yes, yes, I think it would have been better.'

I glance across the road at Marie Francis. At this time of night, it looks dark and closed, but that's just because you can't see the ground floor from behind the wall.

'Are you late for work?' he asks me.

'I'm not due in. I was only going in to tell Grace what I'd done.'

'How long has she got?' he asks.

I remember my dead phone and hope it's not too late, that the choice hasn't been taken out of our hands.

'I'm not sure,' I say. 'I can find out, if you give me a moment?'

He nods. 'I need to know if I have time to think, or if there is anything to think about.'

Mandy, the night nurse on duty whenever I am not, is surprised to see me.

'What are you doing here?' she asks. 'Surely you've got something better to be doing with that lovely strapping husband of yours?'

'I wanted to check in on Grace. I've been thinking about her; how is she?'

Mandy checks her notes.

'Stable, comfortable. Keris is visiting with her now. She's peaceful. Why?'

'Why what?' I lean against the desk, wondering if this is the news that Hugh will want to hear.

'Why have you come all this way to ask about Grace? Why not call?'

'You know, sometimes a patient just gets under your skin,' I say.

It's clear that Mandy doesn't believe me, and she knows that I know that, but she doesn't question me further.

'Well, she's stable for now, pain-free.'

'How long do you think?' I ask her.

'We never answer that question. You know that,' she says, bemused. 'Stella, what's going on?'

I glance at Grace's closed door; the low light that radiates from it seems so comforting and secure. Am I bringing a whirlwind into her life? Am I bringing the chill of anger and regret into what should be a peaceful death?

'Grace asked me to do something for her, and I … I'm not sure if I have enough time to do it. That's all. I got sidetracked and I forgot, and I'm hoping that I'm not too late. I couldn't rest. You know how it is.'

Mandy gives me a decidedly sceptical look. 'All I can tell you is she's comfortable. It could be another day or two, it could be hours. You know how it is.'

'OK, thank you.' I attempt a reassuring smile.

'What is it?' She reaches across the desk, taking my hand in hers; her fingers feel so warm and strong. 'You're freezing! At least have a cuppa as you're here, and talk to me. You seem like you might need someone to talk to about something.'

I squeeze her fingers back and let them go.

'Thank you,' I say. 'But I'm fine, honestly. I can't stay for a tea. Vincent is waiting for me.'

'OK.' She accepts my explanation, but I see her face is full of concern. 'Stella … you look … just tell me, are you OK?'

I think for a moment. My fragile life, constructed of matchsticks, has disintegrated around me. And yet, I do feel OK. I feel somehow free. Sometime in the last twenty-four hours, I reached the very bottom. I'm here, I've arrived, and it's survivable. Now all I have to do is find a way to surface again and the courage to take another breath of air.

'Everything will be OK, one way or another,' I tell Mandy, and I walk back into the night.

Dear Deborah,

I hope this letter finds you better than it does me. I must admit I've wondered how you will take the news of my demise; if it will be with ill-concealed glee or something a little more sober. I hope you're not completely delighted to hear of my passing. I hope you remember some of those twenty years we were married to each other as happy.

Deborah, I want to apologise for the way that I treated you, over the matter of our divorce. I thought that I had fallen out of love with you, and in love with another woman. But the truth is, it wasn't love, or even lust, that drove me to end what had been a very satisfactory marriage; it was fear. Suddenly I felt old and afraid. I think I thought that having a new wife, a wife twenty years younger than me, might make me somehow immortal.

The truth is, Deborah, I think she probably drove me to the very edge of this early grave I am about to find myself in. It took about a year for me to wake up and come to my senses, and perhaps you will be glad to know that the last eight years have been wrought with regret. How I have missed you. Your quiet passion for life, your grace, your scent. The smooth plane of your cheek, the way your hair fell against the back of your neck. Your familiarity, your calm.

Of course you will say that I am just a stupid old man who always wants the opposite of what he has, and you are right, I expect. You remarried, of course. I always knew Kevin carried a torch for you. I do hope that you are happy.

In the divorce settlement, I got the fisherman's cottage in Devon that I know you always loved, but now I am bequeathing it to back to you, in the hope that sometimes you will remember our first summer there, when we did nothing but make love and laugh all day.

Your first husband,

George

CHAPTER TWENTY-SIX

· ·

HOPE

'Right, then.' Ben takes the key from the receptionist, and we head towards a tiny and suspect-looking lift.

When it opens, it looks like a small, mirrored, upended coffin, with barely enough room for one. Panicking, I look around for some nice reliable stairs to idle up, but if there are any stairs, they aren't around here. There's no emergency exit – that just about sums up my entire life.

'After you,' Ben says. Without an escape route, I see no alternative but to step inside the tiny box, and Ben follows me.

At once we are thrown into uncomfortably close proximity, and I am excruciatingly aware of every inch of Ben that I already, at least in theory, know so well. His hair, blacker than black, thanks to semi-permanent gloss, which he doesn't know I know he applies (but is fairly obvious due to the blue tide marks behind his ears). The scar on the back of his neck from when he fell off his Chopper bike doing wheelies when we were nine. His arms, mostly bare; the curve of his forearm; the small of his back. I've never thought about … about what's under his trousers before. And how can it take so many seconds for a lift to go up two tiny floors. He raises an eyebrow at me, as if he's somehow sensed my mental skimming over his genitalia, and I close my eyes. Is he thinking about me naked? Am I thinking about me naked? I don't know when I last shaved. Will he expect me to be bare down there like an adult film star, when I am entirely as nature intended me? Perhaps we can turn out all the lights.

The relief is palpable as the lift door slides open and we tumble out of it.

The corridor is narrow and long, with an odd-angled curve at the end, following the unorthodox cutting and shutting together of a row of crumbling terraces.

'Room thirty-two...' Ben says, tapping the key card against his chin as we follow the trail of numbers. Finally we stop in front of a white-painted door bearing our number. Ben jiggles the key card in and out of the lock several times before finally the red light flashes green and it releases the lock. He pushes the door open and stands back to let me in first. I keep expecting him to laugh and change his mind, to point and guffaw and say something like, 'I really had you going. Christ!' But he doesn't; he's very quiet. And so am I. This feels more like a condemned man's last walk to the electric chair than a lovers' tryst.

The room is not nice, *exactly*. It might have been, once – about fifteen years ago – but if you squint, and don't notice the threadbare curtains, the coffee stains on the carpet, the shadow of an iron burn on the carpet next to the bathroom, or the greying nets, then, yes, it's OK. It beats a hospital room, any day of the week. It's clean, at least, and with the bedside lamps turned on, it's pretty cosy. It's not a terrible place to have sex.

The trouble is, now we are in the room, I have no idea what to do. I look at Ben, at a loss.

'Well, you're the one with the six lovers,' I tell him. 'You start.'

'Not six lovers all at once,' he says. 'Shit, I don't know. Shall we have a drink?'

'Did you bring anything?'

He looks crestfallen then nods at the mini kettle in the corner.

'Cup of tea?'

I can't help but cover my mouth with my hand, and he smiles. He takes a step closer to me.

'We should kiss,' he says. 'The last time I kissed you, I wasn't at the top of my game. But I'm sober now, and also germ-free.'

'Have you got a certificate to prove that?' I ask him. This time his smile is shy, nervous. It's nice. I like the fact that he isn't treating this like a joke. If he did, I'm sure I would lose my courage much sooner.

'About those six girls,' he says. 'There were only three of them. And I'm not sure one counted.'

He takes another step closer to me and places his hands carefully on my hips. I gaze resolutely downwards.

'It's going to be hard to make out with the top of your head,' he says.

'I was just thinking about other stuff, you know. Practical stuff like … like condems. I mean condoms.'

'I've got it covered,' he says. 'Well, it's not covered yet, but it will be.'

It's a terrible joke, but we both have to repress a snigger.

'I think let's stop with the talking and try the kissing again,' Ben says.

Taking a breath, I look up and see him, his face right there. That dear face that I've always known, that sweet mouth. We slowly move together, our lips meeting hesitantly. It feels weird and strange. I close my eyes and concentrate on the faint pulsing of blood under his skin. His tongue tests my mouth, and I remember the last kiss, when I had resisted, and teeth and gums and saliva were in all the wrong places at all the wrong times. This time I let him lead me into the kiss; I let him explore my mouth, and then I reciprocate. It's almost like writing a song, a balancing act of discovery, each of us sensing the other as we look for harmony. Pretty soon, much sooner than I feared, it starts to feel right, this kiss. If my eyes are closed and I don't let myself think too much about who I am kissing, it starts to feel really good. My arms snake upward around his neck, and I'm pulling him closer to me, enjoying the resistance of his firm body against my soft one, and then he moans with what I imagine is desire. Ben moans, and because it's Ben, I freak out and let him go.

'What?' he says, taking a breath. 'I thought it was going quite well.'

'Nothing, nothing,' I say. 'It was just you made a noise, and you know. It was like you were getting into it.'

'I was getting into it. Weren't you?' he asks me. 'I mean, there isn't a rule that says we can't get into it, is there?'

'Yes, I mean no,' I say. 'I was enjoying it. But ... look, I haven't been with even three women ... I mean men ... so cut me some slack. Let's just be a little less ... into it. At least out loud.'

Ben grins, and I pick up a cushion and throw it at him.

'So what next?' he asks me. And the way he looks at me, it's different from any way he's ever looked at me before. The atmosphere has changed between us; it's charged with something that I didn't expect at all: anticipation, expectation, even desire. I realise that we both want whatever it is that is going to happen next, and it's a revelation that's both exciting and terrifying. I need to be in this moment, and I need to be brave. I liked the way he wanted me just then. I liked the way my kisses made him moan with desire; it makes me feel bold. I grab the hem of my shirt and pull it off over my head, revealing my black vest, which shows pretty clearly that I am not wearing a bra.

'Shit,' Ben says, staring at my breasts. 'You look good in that.'

'Your turn,' I say, tossing my shirt over my shoulder, warming to my role as sexual siren. He hesitates, and my confidence ebbs a little. 'Come on, fair's fair.'

Still his hands remain at his sides, and I think, well, I'm in this deep, so I attempt a sort of a flirty swagger over to him and start to unbutton his shirt, my fingers fumbling with the stupid little buttons.

'Press studs would be easier,' I mutter. 'Didn't you have anything with Velcro?'

His hands still mine, and finally he pulls the shirt off over his head.

'That works,' I say. Well, I more sort of squeak. It's odd to look at him this way, to see the curves of his muscles, the flat surface of his stomach.

'Relax,' he says. 'Can we just go back to kissing again? We aren't in a rush. And you look so good, I want to kiss all of you.'

'You're sure that it isn't that I look disgusting with my shirt off?' I ask him.

He shakes his head. 'You really don't.'

Hesitantly, he reaches out. The tips of his fingers graze my breasts in a downward stroke, and I hold my breath, unprepared for the jolt of lust that it sends coursing through me. He grabs me, tighter this time, and I hear myself sigh as his lips find their way onto my neck. I don't know how it happens, just that we are clinging to each other, kissing again. Only this time it's different: not searching or hesitant, but passionate, needful. We stumble onto the bed and I don't need to worry if he finds me attractive; I know that he wants me. I can feel his hardness against my hips and thighs. His lips are on my neck. His hand drags my vest top up, revealing my breasts to his eyes, his mouth. And I close my eyes and think, if I die now then that will be OK, actually – this is the most wonderful feeling I have ever had in life. Except, except that now I want more than ever to know what it feels like to have him inside me; I don't want to wait a second longer. I want to feel his skin against mine, now. But as I feel my desire for him build, he is suddenly still and backs away.

I stop.

'What? What did I do?' I ask him. 'Too much… enthusiasm?'

'Nope, nothing. It's fine,' he says, smiling at me so sweetly. 'I just got a bit, you know, too into it. As you were.'

'Too into it? What do you mean? You mean like, you know, about to pop your cork, sort of thing?'

'Are you seriously asking me this question now?' Ben asks me, moving away from me.

'Um … well, I suppose I am,' I say. 'Sorry, I'm just nervous. And that's what we do, isn't it? We take the piss out of each other; that's what mates do.'

He looks at me for seconds, and I'm aware of him retreating rapidly from the moment.

'This is a mistake,' he says. 'It's not your fault, it's mine. I don't really know what I was thinking.' He picks up my vest top and hands it to me, turning his face from my nudity, and hastily I drag it back on.

'Ben, I'm sorry. I wasn't trying to take the piss out of your sexual prowess. Please, Ben, don't be pissed off with me. You know what an inept person I am.'

'I'm fine,' he says, although he is clearly not. 'So ... are we back to the way things were before tonight?'

'Ben.' I sit down on the bed as he starts to gather his things together. 'What just happened?'

'Nothing happened, and that's for the best. Everything is fine,' he says, but his shoulders are tense, his jaw clenched. Nothing is fine.

'Tell me,' I say.

'Shit, Hope. If you don't know, then you will never know,' he blurts out angrily. 'And fuck you for making me talk like a woman!'

'What? What?' I stare up at him, bewildered, and he turns to stare at me.

'You're so caught up in your own tragedy,' he says. 'And who can blame you? Anybody would be. Anybody would be angry and hurt and frightened if they had to live with what you have to live with. And so ... everything is fine. There is nothing to worry about. I should never have let it get as far as it did; I'm a fool for even ...'

'I've made you really angry, and for once I don't know why,' I say.

He presses his lips together as he stares at me, and I'm frightened to see tears standing his eyes. I can tell he's trying hard not to blink, afraid that they might fall.

'I am in love with you, you idiot,' he says. 'I love you, Hope. I don't know when it changed from being platonic to an all-consuming, unbearable passion, but it did. I am in love with you; that's what I meant when I said I was getting too into it. I was afraid that I was going to blurt it out. I've been waiting like a goddamned girl for years for you to notice that I am in love with you, and you never do.'

'Wait … what?' I ask him, and for a moment it's almost as if he's talking another language.

'I thought that one day you would notice me, that you would suddenly realise that the guy that hangs around you all the time is actually the guy for you, but you haven't, not ever. And then you nearly fucking *died*, and even then – nothing. No epiphany, nothing. And no thinking that maybe I kissed you because I fucking love you, Hope. No, it had to be something all weird and doomy and Hope-like, because you live in your own little psychodrama and you don't notice or care that there are other people in this world who need you to be alive. And now, now you've made me do a stupid girl speech. Next you'll be forcing me into some kind of prom-dress makeover situation. But no – no more. I'm not being your pathetic little hanger-on any more. I'm getting a life.'

'Ben.' I stand up. 'Ben, you are crazy. Stop it. You aren't my pathetic little hanger-on – I'm yours!'

'You are not mine,' he says. 'You mean, you seriously haven't noticed that I am your entourage? It's fine. I get how you wouldn't feel the same about me. I mean, I am a kid off an estate, who still lives with his mum – who ignores him – and who works in a phone shop. I'm not a catch; I get that. But you know … you know what? You could at least try being a bit more gracious, a bit more polite about the fact that I fell in love with you. You could at least say … thank you.'

'But …'

He leaves, bowls out of the room at a furious rate, the door slamming against the corner of the desk as he goes.

'Thank you,' I say to an empty room.

What the hell just happened? What was that? Was that an elaborate ruse to get out of the sex pact … Was it a joke? I think about everything he said, and the way that he said it, and it sounded like a joke. Ben doesn't love me, does he? I mean, not in that way, does he?

I mean … how could he possibly? I mean, does he?

My phone rings and I see his name and a photo of him appear on my phone. I answer the call.

'I'm really sorry,' he says. 'You'll need walking back.'

'I'm OK to walk back,' I say. 'It's just down the road.'

'You're sure?'

'Ben.' I go to the window and see his tall figure ranging from under a street light across the road. 'I am really very stupid and self-obsessed, you know.'

'I know.' Our eyes meet – even though I can't see his face, I just know it. I sense our connection. I press my palm against the glass.

'I'm a fucking loser, anyway,' he says.

'You aren't,' I tell him. 'You're the best person I know.'

'But you have literally no friends, apart from me,' he says. And I laugh; it's not exactly true, but almost.

'I'm waiting for you to come down, and then I'll walk you back,' he says.

'Ben, about what you said … it's not that I don't …'

'Stop talking now,' he said. 'I'll see you in five.'

CHAPTER TWENTY-SEVEN

VINCENT

'Vincent?' She opens the door in a dressing gown, and I salute her. I didn't plan it that way, that's just the way that it happens. She gives me a little nod, a signal that I can stand at ease.

'Maeve,' I say. 'It's been too long. I'm sorry about that.'

'How are you?' she says, putting her arms around me. I don't think I should hug her back, so I don't, but she leans into me, just for a moment, resting her head on my shoulder. 'Oh, but it's good to see you. I don't know, somehow hugging you, it's a bit like hugging Kip, in a way.'

She presses her cool palms against my face, as if she is checking I am real.

'I'm sorry I wasn't at the funeral.'

'Don't be so silly,' she says, standing back to invite me into her home.

Hesitantly, I take a step over the threshold; I feel like an intruder.

'You were fighting for your life,' she says. 'Of course you couldn't be there. But I'm so glad, for you and for Stella, that you pulled through. And for Kip, too; he'd be so pleased that you did. Do you want a coffee or a tea, or I have beer? I don't normally keep it in, these days, but I saw some of Kip's favourite on special offer and just picked it up – didn't even think about it until I got home and unpacked the shopping. She smiles at me, but it's a smile fringed with tears. 'Hey, maybe he knew you were coming. Kip always did like to be the host with the most.'

'Mama, who is it?' I hear a small voice from upstairs, and a moment later this little girl, so small, with curly strawberry-blonde hair and a chin just like Kip's, comes running into the kitchen in her pyjamas.

'Casey, you should be in bed, you tinker!' Maeve scoops the little girl up and sits her on her hip. 'This is Uncle Vinnie. He was Daddy's very best friend.'

I swallow. 'Maeve, me and Kip, we made a promise to each other. We said that if the worst ever happened, we'd be there, you know, for who was left behind. We said we'd do what the bigwigs never do and tell you what it was like at the end, what it was really like. Because we knew how it drove families mad, the not knowing. How the not knowing is so much worse than anything.'

Maeve nods but doesn't speak. There's a deep slot of worry in the centre of her brows, extending down to the top of her nose, making her look so much older than she is, which can't be much more than thirty.

'Vincent,' she says, gently, offering me an open bottle of beer. 'I know you've come across London with something to say, and I know it's important you say it, but will you wait a moment, till this wee one is settled?'

'Of course,' I say, smiling at Casey.

'Would you like Uncle Vinnie to read you your stories tonight?' Maeve asks the little girl, who laughs with delight at the idea, and for a moment she looks even more like her dad. I'm not sure if I can do it and keep my shit together, but I don't know how to say no, so I carry the kid upstairs, and she finds me a book and then another one and clambers into bed.

'I just read it out to you, do I?' I say.

'Yes, silly,' Casey says. 'And do all the funny voices. Daddy did all the funny voices, and Mummy tries but she's not as good at it as Daddy is. Are you good at funny voices?'

'I'll give it a go,' I say.

I sit on the edge of her bed and open the book and read to her about some bears. After a page, she nudges me in the ribs, so I try it in a deep growly bear voice, and she giggles. So I do it again, and again, a different voice for every bear: a deep one, a high one and a squeaky one, which is the one she likes the best. And she laughs and laughs, and I find myself smiling back at her, aping around like a fool just to get that giggle once again.

'Again!' she demands as soon as we reach the end, and so we read the story again and again, until we are both laughing and she is bouncing up and down on the bed, like it's a trampoline. Maeve is in the doorway, arms folded, pretending to be cross with us.

'Well, Uncle Vinnie knows how to settle you down,' she chides me, with a wink. 'Come on now, chicken, time to go to sleep. Love you. Sleep tight. See you in the morning.'

She turns off most of the lights until just a night light glows in the corner, right next to a photo of Casey's dad in dress uniform.

'Kiss, Uncle Vinnie,' Casey demands, in one last-ditch attempt to stay awake a moment longer. I bend down and kiss the top of her head; she rolls over and is asleep at once.

'Amazing, isn't it?' Maeve whispers beside me. 'I wish I could turn off my head like that.'

Downstairs, I sit, upright, back straight, on Kip's sofa, in Kip's living room, drinking what should have been Kip's beer.

'You'd better say what you want to say,' Maeve says, a little anxiously. 'I can see it's killing you, keeping it in.'

'I wrote you a letter,' I tell her. 'I've written you a lot of letters, but I've never quite managed to finish them. But this time, I think I might have got it right. It took me a long time to get the courage together, to say what had to be said, and then when I did, when I finally did, it felt wrong to just post it. So I brought it with me.' I hand her the letter, expecting her to take it and read it, but she shakes her head.

'You read it to me, Vincent,' she says softly. 'You've come a long way to tell me what's in it.'

Her face is tense and quiet as she watches me stand up. I don't know why, but I feel like I should be standing up, to honour him, to salute him.

I take the folded square of paper out of my jeans pocket and put the beer bottle down. I see the quiet look of worry on her face, and I see how much she's had to bear in the last year and a half, and how much sadness and loss there is still to process, but I know I have to tell her the truth. I look at the letter; it reveals the tremor in my hand. I begin to read.

'*Dear Maeve,*

I wanted to write to you to let you know what a very fine man, and a very fine soldier, Kip Butler was. He was my mate, my brother, in life as well as in arms. He could be the most idiotic man I ever knew – stubborn as a mule, and soppy when he'd had too many. He was kind too: knew when a bloke was having a rough day somehow, and always knew how to give them a lift. I remember how he rescued this little stray pup, starving on the roadside, and brought her into camp. He fed her up, trained her. She was a proper little hero, always brought a smile to the lads' faces. But he wasn't just a decent bloke, he was the best kind of soldier too.

The day that we got hit ...'

I hesitate and take a breath.

'*He did everything right, the whole patrol did. It was an ambush, and we didn't have time to react. Except ... there was a second, one second that plays over and over again in my head, when I think I could have grabbed him. I could have tried to take him out of harm's way. But I didn't; I lost my nerve and I went the other way when the shell hit. He died right away – he wouldn't have known about it. There wouldn't have been even a second of fear or pain. And afterwards, the evac team took care of him, right away. He was never left alone, not for a second, not until we were all safe. I wake up some days and I wish I was dead alongside him, or instead of him, because I think he had so much to live for, and so many people that he loved and who loved him back. I only had one person who really loved me in my life, and all I wanted was to be back by her side. Now I don't even deserve her love, because loving her just makes me feel guilty. For months and months, I've known that I've had to tell you that there is a chance, just a small chance, that I might have been able to save him, and I was too scared to take it. And I want to say, to your face, how sorry I am that I failed him, and you. I failed myself.'*

I swallow and stop reading and look at Maeve. She says nothing for a moment, burying her face in her hands. Her shoulders shake. I wonder if I should go to her, but I don't know how. I just stand there, the letter in my hand; hopeless, helpless.

Eventually, her shoulders rise and fall as she takes a deep breath, and she uncovers her face and looks at me. Her expression is kind, gentle.

The sting of tears threatens at the back of my eyes, but I won't let them show.

'I'm so grateful, Vinnie, that you came; that you told me that. It's such a … relief. To hear from you that he didn't suffer. It means so much to me.'

I shrug. I can't speak; words are thick in my mouth. She stands and takes a step towards me.

'You don't know if you could have saved him,' she says softly. 'We'll never know. But if it had been Kip who'd had that second, I would have wanted him to save himself for me. I would have hoped and prayed that he would have done everything so that he could have come back to me and Casey. Vincent, you can't change what was inevitable, not in one second. And you did the right thing; you made the right choice. The choice I'd have wanted Kip to make. He knew what he was doing. We knew there was a chance this could happen – we talked about it. And he said that if I asked him to, he'd leave the army, because loving me and loving Casey meant more to him than anything. But I didn't ask him to leave, Vincent. He died doing the job he loved, protecting the rights and freedom of a people he came to care about and respect. And if he had been the one with that second, I know he would have chosen me and Casey. I know, because he made me that promise before he went back.' After a moment, she steps closer and puts her arms around me.

'It means so much to me to know that it was quick and painless,' she tells me, holding me very, very tight.

After a moment, I return her hug. And for the first time in what feels like months, I let go of the breath I have been holding.

Dear Simon,

I hope this letter reaches you in time, and that you aren't waiting for me, wondering where I am. It seems ridiculous that we've never exchanged phone numbers or addresses. But that wasn't the way it worked, was it? Just one meeting, once a year. One night together, away from our lives, that no one in the whole world knew about but us. Except when you go to the railway station café in Penzance on December 6th this time, I won't be there. I'd hoped to be, I'd prayed to be; I just wanted the chance to say goodbye.

Ours was not a torrid affair, was it? It was hardly an affair at all – more just a deep and abiding love that lasted thirty years. Thirty nights, one each year. Two single bedrooms side by side in that nice little B&B. A walk on the beach, dinner where perhaps we might hold hands, and then the next day, after a pleasant breakfast, you'd walk me to the station and kiss me on the cheek. And you'd say, 'Goodbye. I'll see you again, my dear.'

I had no idea, the last time you said that, that it would be the last.

I love my husband, and my children, my family, and my life. I've loved them all, but those thirty walks on the beach, dinners on the front, sleeps with only a wall between us. Those thirty goodbye kisses on the cheek were some of the happiest moments of my life. And I thank you for them.

Goodbye, Simon. I'll see you again, my dear.

    Frances

CHAPTER TWENTY-EIGHT

STELLA

The walk from the café into Euston isn't long – although it's taking us a little longer than it has to because Hugh insists on taking the less direct routes, which he claims are shortcuts.

'I've lived round here all my life,' he says, as we walk down house-lined streets, passing tall concrete blocks of flats that are bulging with life and drama, losses and loves, all contained, tonight, at least, behind tiny little squares of light.

'And does that mean you can defy the physics of basically walking in a straight line getting you anywhere quicker?' I ask.

He laughs, thrusting his hands deep into his pockets.

'My dad was an engineer. He worked out all the routes everywhere – to the nearest millimetre. I watched him do it. I promise you, we are getting where we are going by the fastest possible route.'

'And where is that, exactly?' I ask him. 'I know you said you wanted to show me where you work, but what do you do for a living? Is it something scary like butcher or serial killer?'

It feels a little surreal, that this complete stranger and I have fallen into this excursion together. Odd, but oddly natural. As if our paths crossing at exactly this moment in our lives is for a reason – perhaps this reason, even if the reason is just to walk and talk and not think about the pieces of our separate lives that are disintegrating around us. I see something in him that he also recognises in me. He is lost. I am lost. And both of us just want to find a way back to somewhere we recognise.

Hugh leads me past the smell and bustle of Euston Station and into the quiet elegance of Bloomsbury, the crowds on the streets thinning as the evening turns slowly towards midnight.

So when he had asked me, in the twenty-four-hour café, what I was doing now, I'd said, 'Nothing.'

I'd expected an invitation to the pub to catch last orders or something. Something that I'd planned on refusing, although I wanted to know what it would be.

'Would you like to see where I work?' he'd said.

'Where do you work?' I'd asked him. 'I mean, it's really late …'

'Up the road, sort of. In Bloomsbury. In a museum.'

'The British Museum?'

'No, not there.' He'd smiled, as if he was used to people making that assumption. 'The Liston James museum. When I first worked there, it was soon after my dad died. I found it really hard losing him. He was my anchor. I'd spend long, long hours in the museum, in the rooms when it was quiet and empty, and dark, looking at the relics of other people's lives and thinking. I worked out of lot of my problems there. You've got problems, I've got problems. We'll go there and work them out.'

'We've only just met,' I'd said.

He'd shrugged. 'Good – fresh perspective.'

And that's how we started this walk: two strangers in a city of strangers, looking for a way to be found.

It is becoming increasingly cold. We walk quickly, and in companionable silence, trusting Hugh's dad's route, keeping our heads down, tucking our chins into our coats, to keep the chill from biting at our cheeks.

Our pace doesn't slow until we draw up opposite the British Museum – floodlit, stately and magnificent. As I look at it, standing sentinel over the city, I realise what a small life I've been living recently. The little dark triangular world I live in: home and Vincent and work – three points that I keep on running away from, one after the other. No wonder I am so tired.

'My museum is not as grand as that one,' Hugh says, almost apologetically, as we cross the road.

I follow him down a narrow road I've never noticed called Willoughby Street, and towards the end of that, tucked away behind a Japanese restaurant, is one of the secret little spaces that, even in a city like London, you would never stumble across by accident. Hugh leads me through a small alleyway, barely shoulder-width, into a tiny mews made up of five perfect Georgian houses, two either side and one at the end. It's lit with wrought-iron street lamps, casting dramatic shadows across the cobbles.

'I had no idea this was here.' I whisper because somehow it feels appropriate, like we have stepped back in time. Every window in every house is shuttered and dark. The sound of the city has drifted away, and even the dark sky seems more dense – as if this is a world of its own.

'No, most people don't; it is not exactly a tourist attraction. Liston James House is the one at the end, and the others are owned by rich Russians, an actress, a polictican, I think. Rarely occupied. It's a scandal, really. Sometimes I think about crowbarring open the shutters and inviting in all the men and women sleeping in doorways at the end of the road. But I suppose I was brought up too politely to be much of a revolutionary, so every Friday night I buy whoever is there fish and chips and a cuppa, instead.'

We stop at the unnaturally large, black-painted door at the front of the end house, and Hugh fishes out a selection of keys from his jeans.

'Before we go in, I just want to say – the collection, it's very unique, and a difficult one for a lot of people to stomach, these days. I think you will be fine with it, but if for any reason you don't like it, just say and we will go.'

I do waver; on paper it feels a little bit like I am volunteering to go down into a cellar when there is a maniac on the loose, but there is nothing about this situation that frightens me – no sixth sense or hairs standing up on the back of my neck. In fact, being with Hugh is unexpectedly calming. Like being with a friend or my brother.

'Well, we're here now,' I say.

He unlocks the door and punches a code into an alarm system. As I walk into a grand and vaulted hallway, built around an elegantly sweeping marble staircase, lights come on all around me, glittering against crystal chandeliers. I stand for a moment and let myself understand that this is a real place, and I'm not in a dream. It has all the traditional hallmarks of a grand mews mansion – everything you'd assume when you see one of these houses from the outside: ornate plaster work, high ceilings, a sense of space and symmetry – but it's like no other room I have ever seen. The walls of the vast room are painted a dense, light-absorbing black and are covered from floor to ceiling in white masks, spaced only an inch or so apart. It's like suddenly finding yourself on stage in a pocket theatre, with the house lights up. Propelled by curiosity, I walk over to one wall and examine the masks. They're faces, all kinds of people's faces: men, women, children, mostly with their eyes closed, expressions dormant, but some lids remain open, white blank globes gazing at nothing.

I turn to look at Hugh, who is also examining the display on the walls, as if he is trying to remember what it's like to see it for the first time.

'Is it a welcoming committee?' I ask, stopping at the face of a chubby toddler, positioned at eye level.

'They're death masks,' Hugh tells me. 'These are casts taken from corpses, all collected by Liston, until his death. He lost his own family, you see: wife, children, six of them, all before him. It devastated him; he felt bereft. He never recovered. His life became an obsession with commemorating those who had died. Those he knew, those he didn't. When he died, the collection went to a nephew, who carried on the tradition, which he then passed to his son.

'Victorians were desperate to have something of their loved ones to treasure when they were gone. It's not that they weren't afraid of death, but more that they weren't afraid of acknowledging it.'

I can't take my eyes off the sleeping baby's face – the full lips, the softly closed lids. I am familiar with death, and yet somehow this image fills me with emotion that I can't understand: a pain, deep and tangible, so strong it takes my breath away for a moment. I'm grieving for the loss of an infant who was gone almost 100 years ago and also something more: a loss of something I have never had.

I turn my face away, closing my eyes, waiting until the unexpected wave of emotion subsides.

'Don't worry,' Hugh says gently. 'It gets a lot of people that way.'

'It's funny,' I say. 'Looking at that mask just made me realise how much I want a baby, Vincent's baby; how much I've always believed that we would have a family together, and be parents. And now … that feels like it's slipping away from me.'

He watches me thoughtfully, his face still and calm.

'Maybe knowing what it is that you want, the future that you have been fighting for, is what it will take to make it happen. It's easy to admit defeat and let go of people you love, or dreams you have, because it's difficult. Fighting for them is what takes courage. Fighting for them is what matters.'

'But you can't force a person to stay with you,' I say. 'Sometimes you have to accept defeat.'

I follow Hugh through a drawing room, lined with portraits, past a piano topped with photographs, into another room, which lights up as we walk into it.

'Motion-sensor lighting,' Hugh tells me. 'It saves on the bills, but it can be a little alarming if you're doing some research and suddenly all the lights go off. And, yes, you are right, sometimes you do have to accept defeat; sometimes, but not until you've fought with your very last breath. My mum, she gave in too soon. She stopped trying too soon. Stopped trying to get better, to let my dad help, to stay in our family, to be a mother. She waved the white flag on our lives when another battle could have changed everything. She is even getting ready to die without one more fight. And it's hard to forgive her for that. So I am saying, just make sure you have fought to your dying breath for the man that you love, the children you want, the future you thought was yours.'

This room is lined with glass cabinets filled with all kinds of jewellery: rings, pendants, watches, earrings.

'It wasn't just the Victorians that kept memento mori jewellery,' Hugh tells me, as I stray to his side and peer into one of the cabinets. 'This collection dates back to the fifteen hundreds, but it was the Victorians who liked to incorporate relics into the design. See this watch?' Slipping on pair of white cotton gloves, he removes a simple-looking gold pocket watch. 'The cord that attaches to the fob is made of braided hair that belonged to the owner's wife. She died during the birth of their first baby. The baby also died.' He clicks open the watch, and, set under glass on the inside of the case, there is the faintest wisp of soft blonde hair. 'The baby's hair.'

'There's something so moving about it,' I say. 'I understand it, that need to hold a memory in your hand. The fear that everything else might fade if you don't.'

The next room has no windows at all but a high, vaulted glass ceiling. I've lost track of where I am in the house, but I sense this is somewhere in the middle. Every inch of wall space is lined with photographs. As I focus on the images – children sleeping, family groups, young men standing next to a chair – I gasp and cover my mouth.

Hugh doesn't need to tell me that I am looking at photographs of the recently deceased, dressed in their Sunday best, posed with their living relatives.

'It horrifies us, and yet to them it was a miracle, a godsend,' Hugh says. 'At last there was an affordable way for every person to have a physical memory of someone they loved and lost. It was a marvel, a last chance to keep an image for eternity. These photographs gave an enormous amount of comfort to the masses, who would never be able to own a portrait or a carved marble statue.'

For some reason, I, who have washed and dressed so many of the dead, find the photographs almost impossible to look at. My eyes skim over them and I walk away, towards the door on the other side of the room, where I hesitate, wondering what is on the other side of it.

'Here.' Hugh opens the door for me. 'That's more or less all of the collection. Well, there are reams of documents, books and the like, but you won't want to see those. I think after the gallery you probably need a cup of tea.'

He leads me downstairs, the lights clicking on over our heads as we descend into a basement area, and to a maze of smaller rooms, leading off narrow corridors.

The kitchen is small, modern – more of an office environment than a traditional room. There's an industrial-sized tub of Nescafé, a box of tea bags and a bowl of tiny cartons of long-life milks.

'Are you going to go and see her, Grace?' I ask.

'I don't know,' he says, taking two white mugs from a cupboard. There's a sort of urn on the wall that he uses for hot water.

'I have already grieved for her. I missed her, I've loved her and hated her. I've grown up defined by her not being there. Every choice I've made is somehow influenced by her going. Her choosing to leave us. I've come to understand suicide, depression, to somehow understand what she did, or what I thought she did, and accept it. But now ...' He turns his face away from me. 'Now I just don't know. She died, in my heart. She died, and I remember her, the mum that always laughed and sang, the mum who'd spend Saturday mornings with me, making toast and drawing. I remember her. I don't know who this woman is that you have in your care. What if she isn't my mother at all? And even if she is, what good does it do either of us to grieve all over again? And don't forget, you said you delivered the letter too early. She hasn't asked to see me again; she doesn't want that. She just wanted me to know that she lied to me for years. Somehow that seems like the cruellest blow of all.'

'Who knows what she wants or doesn't want? And anyway, this mess, it's my fault. I started this. I ran away from what was hurting me, and I hurt you instead, without thinking about it, even though I knew what was in the letter. So don't blame Grace, blame me, and think about what you want. What will help you?'

Hugh sips his tea, and for a moment I have a sense of the two of us, in this small, brightly lit room in the basement of this secret, dark house. Alone, all the lights above snuffed out by stillness, surrounded by all the mass of density that is London, pressing in on all sides.

'Darwin ruined a lot for the Victorians,' Hugh says. 'They had this belief, this unshakable certainty, that they would go to a better place, after death, if they lived a Christian life. And then his big idea that made God seem irrelevant shocked society to its core. It's no coincidence that after the theory of evolution came to light, the practice of spiritualism, séances, a yearning for proof of the afterlife also followed.'

With a small, sad smile, Hugh reaches into his coat pocket and takes out a folded square of tatty yellowed paper, covered in childish writing. He unfolds it and lays it on the worktop.

I realise at once that this is what was supposed to be Grace's final letter, her suicide note. No wonder he knew it by heart; it's next to his heart that he keeps it.

'I so wanted it to be true that she wasn't gone,' he says. 'I kept this, read it and re-read it, looking for clues – anything to prove that she hadn't meant what she said, that this wasn't really a final goodbye. I hoped for years. I lived with my father's grief, and I watched it kill him, and all I had left to remember her by was a garage full of empty vodka bottles. They're still there, you know. And when I was offered this job through my work as a historian, it seemed fitting, somehow. Almost as if I thought I might find her face amongst the masks in the hallway, or a lock of her hair inside a watch fob. But even if I didn't, I still had this. Except now it turns out that I've been cherishing a false relic. And, honestly, now I have no idea what to do.'

'Yes, you do,' I tell him. 'You do; you fight that last battle, the very last one. You fight till your last breath for the people that you love, and your dreams, the future that you want. And you can fight for your past, too, because it's not too late to know how much it mattered to her, as well as to you. That's what you do. You fight. We fight. We fight for the people we love.'

Dear Angelina,

You have been named after me, not that actress woman.

I am your great grandmother. You are nine days old; I am ninety-three. I held you today. Funny, angry, red little thing, you are, with great big black eyes. I thought I could see a little touch of me around your eyes, perhaps in that stubborn little chin.

This letter is for you to read when you are eighteen years old, and is to accompany a silver locket, given to me by my grandmother, and hers. It's a tradition. Goodness only knows how the world will have changed in eighteen years' time, Angelina, but when you have lived as long as I, you learn one thing, which is humans do not change. So here is my best advice to you.

Do not trust a man with unkempt facial hair.

Vote. Even if they are all hopelessly inadequate, pick the least terrible one and vote. My mother fought hard to get you that vote.

Keep your own finances, and let your husband keep his.

Study hard. A good education is worth a thousand kisses.

Wear sturdy shoes, except at weddings or parties, and your back will thank you.

Good manners cost nothing. Bad manners can cost you everything.

Your mother will remember me; she may very well say I was a terrible old dragon, but she will be joking, because she and I have loved each other as much as any batty old granny and her granddaughter ever have.

Goodnight, sweet girl,

Angelina Elizabeth Stoke

CHAPTER TWENTY-NINE

HUGH

It seems illogical to come home from the museum, instead of going to her, but I do, because it's here in this house that it should make sense. I'd wondered why she never haunted me, why I didn't get a sense of her from time to time, and now I know.

I stand outside the house, my house, and look at it for a long time, as the rain drifts down in non-committal sheets, hazing around the street lamps. The render is old and cracked; the front yard is neglected and forlorn. I've come back to this house every single day since my mother left it. I thought that one day I would probably die in it. But now I'm not so sure. Is it a home? Or is it just some lesser version of the Liston James Museum – a mausoleum to all that I have lost?

A light clicks on in Sarah's house. Mikey's bedroom.

A moment later the window opens, and out slinks Jake, hopping deftly down from the sill and onto the porch, from where he drops silently onto the pavement, pausing briefly to sniff the air before slinking into the night, away from the two cosy identities he has made for himself, that

I know of, and off into the night. He doesn't even give me a second glance.

I see some movement behind the nets in Mikey's room, and the light goes off. And then I see her face for a moment, small and white at the window, and she sees me. I must look like the sort of weirdo who hangs around outside people's houses, hoping to catch a glimpse. And perhaps that is what I am doing. Talking to Stella, that helped; she's one of those people who I seem to understand right away, and who seem to get me. But I have never felt more like I need comfort for the longest time, and it strikes me that, in a life that's been carefully constructed with acquaintances and colleagues only, there is no one I know who I can ask to give me a hug.

I am opening my gate a few seconds later when her front door opens and she appears in a white T-shirt, with bare legs, make-up free, and with her long black hair tumbling loose over her shoulders, and I am quite uncertain as to where I should direct my gaze.

'You all right, Hugh?' She says my name as if it is an unfamiliar, foreign word, but I love the sound of it on her lips.

'Um … not really,' I confess. 'You know my mum, who I thought was dead? It seems rumours of her demise were greatly exaggerated.'

'She's not dead?' Sarah takes one barefooted step out onto the cold damp path. 'Are you sure?' She thinks for a moment. 'Is this you drunk?'

'I am reasonably sure,' I say. 'And I am not drunk; though actually, now I think about it, I don't know why not.'

'Fuck.' Sarah takes another couple of steps forward and peers at me. 'Hugh, you're crying.'

'Am I?' I let her take my hand – my numb fingers freezing against the warmth of her palm – and lead me inside her home.

'Sit there.' She points at her overstuffed sofa, and I oblige, shuddering as the warmth of the house works its way into my blood, feeling the cold in its aftermath, making my fingers itch. 'I've got some rum, somewhere. My ex used to drink it all the time. I hate it, but you never know when you might need emergency booze.'

After a quick hunt in the kitchen, she returns and thrusts a mug full of dark, potent-smelling liquor into my hand and sits in the armchair opposite, pulling her T-shirt down over her knees and leaning forward, her fingers entwined in one another. Without make-up, she looks younger; her naked eyes are wide and beautiful.

'You know what?' I say, feeling suddenly as if I am intruding. 'The last thing you need is me here, at this time of the night, or day, or whatever it is. You've got work, Mikey's got school ...'

'It's Sunday tomorrow, today, whatever.' Her expression settles into one of concern. 'And you look like you can use a mate. Go on, Hugh. Tell me about it.'

'I told you that my mum died, and I thought that was true. For twenty-five years, I have believed that was true,' I tell her. 'I didn't tell you that I thought she'd killed herself. But she hadn't, you see; she didn't go through with it. She just ran away. And now, well, a nurse at the local hospice where she is about to die at any minute came and delivered a letter in which she says, and I'm paraphrasing here, "I was a shit mother, so I thought I'd top myself, but then I didn't. But I love you anyway, and it was all for the best. And, oh, by the way, I know it's taken you most of your life to get over your abandonment issues, so I thought now would be the perfect time to fuck you up for another quarter of a century. Love, Mum."'

Sarah doesn't move; she only sits, chewing at the ball of her thumb.

'That's not really what it says, though, is it?' She reaches out her hand, palm facing upwards, and after a moment I deliver the letter to her and watch as she reads it.

I watch her as she reads, the shadows at the base of her throat, her neat bare feet, turned towards each other as if in quiet conversation.

'Brave woman,' she says finally, handing it back to me. I do not take it.

'Brave?' I say. 'Brave? The woman who ran away from everything until someone rescued her? Who had twenty-five years to come back and face up to what she did, but only decides to do that now, when she's dying?' I hear my voice rising, and I catch myself, covering my mouth. 'I'm sorry, I'm sorry. This gets to me, that's all.'

'Don't be,' Sarah says. She meets my eye and smiles gently. 'You have got every right to be fuming, but that doesn't take away the fact that this woman is brave.'

'Brave?' I ask her again.

'She could have died, and you would never have known. But she wrote you this letter to give you the one gift she could as a mother. She gave you the truth, because she reckons that the truth can heal, even if knowing it hurts you first. The truth will heal you in the end, but a lie will always fester. I think that's kind of brave.'

Closing my eyes, I feel the tears begin to flow then, free and easy, and I let myself go, let myself drown in them. I sense Sarah take the mug from my hands and replace it with her fingers. I bend my head and give in to the grief, like I never have. I let it tear at me, pull itself through me with every sob, and eventually I feel arms around my neck, her hair against my cheeks as I cry, and I cry and cry until there is nothing left in the small dark living room except silence and the ticking of a clock.

'Oh, Christ.' I pull away. 'You must think you've moved next door to a … I don't know. Nightmare.'

'I don't.' She pulls herself up from kneeling to sit beside me and hands me the mug of booze again. This time I knock it back, feeling it blister down my throat and hit my empty stomach with a queasy lurch. 'I've been through crap too, you know. I've cried my guts up, more than once. It's not easy, being in this world. Picking yourself up, getting yourself together, time after time, only for some bastard to whack you back down. But what else can you do? Right? If you keep on getting up, sooner or later something or someone is going to show the reason why it's worth keeping on trying. Sometimes they might be the last person in the world you'd think.' Her expression is perplexed as she looks at me, as if I puzzle her.

'Look, Hugh, your mum isn't dead. She's going to be dead really soon, though. Do you really think you want to live the next forty or fifty years knowing that you were too scared or pissed off to go and look her in the eye?'

'No,' I say. 'No, I don't want live like that. I don't plan to. Fight to the end, that's my motto. I just made it up tonight.'

'Good,' she says. 'Just lie down for a minute, rest your head. Close your eyes; get a little sleep. Everything will seem better when you wake up, I promise you.'

She gets up, and I let her lean me back against the cushions. And with a little effort, she takes off my shoes and drags my feet up onto the sofa. I'm so tired, suddenly. So very, very tired.

'I can't sleep – I have to go and see her,' I say. 'I don't know how long she has left.'

'You can't go like this. You can barely stand.'

'I could go home,' I say drowsily. 'It's only next door.'

'I think you've travelled far enough for one day. You can rest easy here.' At least, I think that's what she says, or perhaps I'm dreaming already.

Dear Irene,

Under the floorboard, in the dining room, back left-hand corner, by the window, there's a biscuit tin with £14,589 in it.

Don't tell anyone about. It started as cash I saved up over the years – a little bit I won on the horses. I didn't tell you because I knew you didn't like me gambling, and I felt bad about going behind your back. So my rule was only gamble money you've won gambling. That way I felt better about it.

To be honest, over the last twenty years I've lost a lot more than I won, but a few months ago, after the diagnosis, before I got my head together, I thought, sod it. I wanted to feel alive, to feel my heart racing again. So I took everything that was in the biscuit tin, which was nearly two grand, and I put it on an accumulator. I've never felt so alive in all my life. They all came in – every single one of the buggers came in.

It feels good to leave you something, so please, don't be too cross about the gambling.

Your Ron

THE SEVENTH
NIGHT

CHAPTER THIRTY

* *

HOPE

'Why does it always take so long to get out of these places?'
Mum says, a little too loudly, so that her voice carries down
the corridor. She has already packed my bag: everything
clean, neatly folded and rolled; everything dirty, still neatly
folded and rolled inside a carrier bag. I love her. I love her,
but I want to do my own laundry.

'I think we should all just feel lucky that she's getting to
come home,' my dad says, gently closing the door.

Mum shoots Dad a look – that look she gives him when
she's being all overdramatic and he's being sensible, and she
resents him for it.

'They're doing this as fast as they can,' I remind her. 'They
need this room for the next person; they're like gold dust. Do
you know, they only get eighteen per cent of their funding
from the NHS? The rest is from fundraising ... I was thinking,
I'd like to do something for them when I get out of here.'

'A sponsored run,' Dad says, with a smile.

'Well, let's not go crazy – a sponsored read could work,'
I say, thinking of Issy. 'Or maybe I could write a song, put
it on iTunes, or something ...'

Mum and Dad exchange a glance that they hope I don't see.

'What?' I say. 'Am I that bad?'

'Nothing. I think that's good, really good,' Mum says. 'We're not used to seeing you ... putting yourself out there. We're pleased, we are.'

'We are,' Dad says, because he never likes Mum to speak for him, although she always does.

I look out of the window. It's the last time I will see this view that I have gotten used to of late. The sun seemed to set so early, today; it was night again even before I noticed it, and I haven't heard from Ben all day. There are many reasons why I wouldn't have heard from him. The whole awkwardness of the sex-attempt thing, that would be reason enough, or because he does have a life – a sort of job, other friends. Reasons that I could happily obsess and dwell on, if it wasn't for the other thing: everything that he said last night.

I look out of the window, beyond the reflected room and into the night, hoping he might appear like he has every evening about this time; hoping that the natural world order might just have been miraculously restored.

We had both behaved as if it had been when he'd walked me home last night – with him telling me a long and hilarious story about an old man who came into his shop to ask about how to post an email. He'd left me at the green door, without so much as a second look. And when I got in, after I did my physio, I must have been exhausted, because I slept right through until two and the next lot of medication and physio. And then Mum and Dad arrived, and the last several hours has all been about waiting. Waiting to be allowed home, waiting for Ben to come, waiting to begin – not again, because I don't think I have ever really begun in the first place, not since I came home from university. Waiting to start my life – properly, this time.

I called Ben, and after he didn't answer his phone, I sent him a text: 'Am getting out today!' But there was no reply; he's busy, maybe. Selling phones, playing stupid customer bingo with his friends, hating me.

I pace, and my mum thinks it's because of my impatience to be out of here and back at home, tucked up on a winter's night in our sweet little semi, with the TV on and dinner on a tray. And in a way it is. In a way, I long for that safe and sheltered little life – the place behind a closed door where I don't have to worry any more – but that time is gone now. How many more second chances I'll get, I don't know. But what I do know is that the first thing I'm going to do on Monday is look for a house share. It might take me a while, and I'll need to start treating the book-cover-designing stuff like a business instead of a hobby, but the countdown to my moving out has started. Just no one tell Mum yet.

I check my phone again; still nothing. Honestly, anyone would think it was me who had done the romantic declaration about being in love – me who was on tenterhooks about hearing from him. Me and Ben as a thing, as an item; as a kissing, sexing item. I know what this is: this is like when we were about fourteen and he decided that he wanted to be Jewish. He just started telling everyone he was actually Jewish, even though he wasn't. When we finally got to the bottom of it all, he'd turned to me and said, 'I just hate being so boring, Hope. I hate being so normal.'

I'd told him right then and there that there was no chance of him ever being normal. It's laughable, really. If he thinks about it, if he really thinks about it, he'll laugh. I look at my watch.

'Still the same time as it was five minutes ago,' Dad says.

'Well, it's not,' I say. 'It's five minutes later.'

'A watched pot …'

'Who watches a pot?' I snap, and Dad shrugs apologetically. And it occurs to me that I am probably too old to be playing the cute but rebellious teen.

'I'm going out,' I say, feeling suddenly incredibly hot. 'For a breath of fresh air.'

'Going out?' My mum looks at my father, expecting him to stop me. My father plays his role to perfection.

'For a breath of fresh air,' he says. 'But …'

I know exactly how the conversation will play out as I let myself out on to the small patio, pausing to watch for a moment as they discuss whether or not I should be outside, not noticing that I have already left. I take my phone out of my pocket as I follow the path around the outside of the building, and call Ben's number. I'm going to talk to him, goddammit; he can't just say he loves me and then go underground. That's not how it works, is it? That's not what is supposed to happen. That's like … That's like swimming the Channel and then getting in a boat a hundred metres off Calais; that's like … like going on *X Factor* and deciding to read from a book. It's half-arsed, it's chickenshit, it's typical Ben – grand gesture one minute, ignoring you the next.

His phone is ringing, and an unfamiliar voice answers.

'What?'

'Um … is Ben there?'

'Wrong number.'

'No, this is Ben's number. Is he there?'

'This is Ben's stepdad, and this phone now belongs to me. I'm sick of him sponging off us …'

'Hey, give me that, you wanker …' It's Ben. For a moment, I am flooded with relief. Except that I can't hear him – maybe he sat on his phone or something? There's a noise, perhaps a movie, shouting, crashes. I can hear shouting. I open my mouth to do that thing, that thing where you yell 'hello', even though you know no one will hear you. I am going to do that anyway, when I hear the cry again, and I freeze. It's his mum crying, 'Stop it. Stop hitting him!'

I'm through the safe, green door and into the mayhem of the street before I know what I am doing. I'm not even at the end of the road and my legs are shaking, my chest is aching. There's no medical reason for me not to exert myself a reasonable amount; I need to build up my stamina, the doctors say. But, even so, the pain, the pain, and the fear that I might die if I run too fast, dog me. However, I don't stop. I won't die if I run, even though I'm not fit, but I won't die if I run, so I jog, as fast as I can go, into the heart of Camden. I jog out past the tube station and then, finally, out of breath, I pause to cough what feels like it might be my lungs up, then turn left into the estate where Ben lives.

He's always lived here, and I've always lived four streets away. He's always lived in a split-level flat on the fourth floor, with a balcony that runs the length of a row of front doors looking out on to the courtyard, where we used to play as kids. Now we're older it always seems to be full of menacing-looking teens not much younger than me. But I don't think about the fact that it's dark, or that my lungs are screaming. I just know I have to find out where he is, and the only place I can think of to start is his home. The lift, for once, is not out of order, which is good news. The bad news is that it terrifies me; it always smells of stale pee and disinfectant. It's cleaned all the time but you can still see the ghostly outlines of graffiti that has been and gone. The words 'You gonna die, bitch' loom out of the dark, taking shape as I stare for a long time at the place where they almost are. I hold my breath as the metal box rumbles up. I think about the last time I took a lift, with Ben, and remind myself to never get in a lift again. I'm always scared I'll get stuck in a lift, always; and, worse, I'm scared I'll get stuck in a lift needing a wee, and then what?

But the lift makes it to fourth floor and, after that terrifying moment of stillness, the doors open. It's more or less quiet along the balcony that fronts Ben's flat. Streets in the air – that's what they were designed to be once. There is a group of girls, smoking intensely, standing between me and Ben's front door. They are just girls, just girls like me, probably thinking and worrying about a lot of the same things, and yet they frighten me. I have no reason to believe they are going to hurt me, or even notice me, and yet I do believe that. I try to make myself small and avert my eyes as I hurry past. They gossip and laugh as I pass, and I am certain that they are talking about me.

And yet I still stop before I get to Ben's doorway.

It's been fifteen minutes, slightly less, since I heard what I thought was some kind of fight and ran out on my parents. What if I overreacted? What if it was just one of the normal run-of-the-mill shouting matches between Ben and his stepfather, and I've raced here, arriving dripping in sweat, to what … save the day? Make a cup of tea? What am I even doing here? And then I hear it again. The shouting is coming from inside his flat, and this time I can hear a woman screaming.

Glancing behind me at the girls, who seem oblivious or immune to the cries, I run to the door, press the doorbell several times, and bang hard on the glass. Seconds stretch out. Behind the frosted door I can see muffled figures tussle for a moment, tumbling into another room. I look back at the girls, unable to believe that they can so casually ignore what's happening.

'Can't you hear that?' I shout at them.

'It's always like that round here,' one says.

'Call the police!' I tell them. 'I think they are killing each other!'

'You call the police; they'll get here next Tuesday,' the same girl says, turning her back on me.

I hammer on the door again, but there is no reply. No matter how hard I knock, I don't think anyone can hear it over the yelling and the screaming. Looking around, I see a desolate-looking window box, full of dead soil and cigarette butts, leaning up against the railing. I pick it up and hurl it at the glass door before I know what I'm doing. It barely dents the toughened glass, but all I can think about is Ben, and getting to Ben, and the screams of his mother behind the door. Ben is tall and strong, but he's never been in a fight in his life, and Mark, his stepdad, Mark gets in a fight every Friday night.

'Fuck! Are you crazy?' one of the smoking girls asks me, suddenly switched on to what I'm doing.

Ignoring her, I kick at the dent in the glass, and it hurts – a pain shooting up into my thigh. I kick again, and again, with first one leg then the other, each exertion more painful than the last. I double over, an explosion of coughing halting my rescue attempt, a wave of fiery pain surging up through my lungs. Maybe I could die. Maybe, in my weakened state,

I could die. But it doesn't matter. I have to keep on trying, even if I do die. I go again, but the smoking girl steps in front of me.

'Fuck it,' she says. 'Stand back.'

She picks up the window box again and slams it hard and fast into the glass, again and again – clearly she's much fitter and stronger than me. When the glass finally gives way, she reaches inside and undoes the latch, releasing the door.

'I'll call the feds,' she says. 'I ain't saying who I am. You need any help, scream.'

I nod and barge my way into the flat. And for a tiny second, I catch myself and wonder what the hell I am doing, but then I charge on.

They are in the living room.

I see it all in a series of stills, like Polaroids coming into focus, with each swing of the naked light bulb in the centre of the room.

Ben's mum, in a T-shirt and nothing else, stands in the corner, her hands covering her face. She wails, she keens, she screams.

Ben goes down, tumbling against a table as his stepdad catches him under his jaw. I see that Mark has an eye that is swelling shut, blood tricking from his nose. If he's in a bad way, God only knows how Ben is. I scramble to the floor where Ben is trying to drag himself up, and put myself between him and Mark.

'STOP IT!' I shout. 'Stop it – the police are coming!'

Mark lunges towards me, grabbing my arm to drag me out of the way of his target, his fury blinding him to what he is doing. His grip is strong; it hurts at once, but I resist.

Fuck it.

Clambering up, I run at Ben's stepdad and shoulder into him, catching him off guard. He topples and I topple with him, screaming at the top of my voice, growling, yowling. I am a wild animal; I am a banshee. I only know that Mark has to stop what he is doing, and that it is going to be me who stops him.

'Hope?' Ben seems to come to as he sees me land hard on top of his stepdad, winding him, and he tries to reach me, while his mum is screaming and screaming. I see blood, fresh bruises forming on Ben's skin before my eyes. Staggering, he clambers to his feet and pulls me off of his stepfather, and together we stand unsteadily in each other's arms. Adrenaline races furiously through my blood. In this moment, I think I could defeat the world if it tried to hurt the person I care most about. The man that I love.

In obvious pain, Ben inserts himself between Mark and me.

'So a little girl going to stand up for you, is she?' Mark says. He's drunk, blindly, furiously drunk. 'A little sick girl got more fight than you, has she?'

'What are you doing?' Ben asks.

I dodge Ben, pressing forward, thrusting my face into the old man's. 'You're pathetic. You're just a pathetic old bully. You are disgusting ... Aren't you disgusted with yourself?'

'You little ...' He raises the back of his hand, but I don't move. And I see it in his eyes: as drunk and angry as he is, he knows that hitting me will have consequences; he knows that I wouldn't just take it.

'You've got no right coming round here, telling me how to live, you little bitch,' he says, but his hand retreats. 'He lives under my roof, by my rules. I deal with him as I see fit.'

'It's not your roof,' Ben's mum says, her hands trembling as she lights a cigarette. 'It's mine. I've put up with a lot of your crap, Mark, but not that. You are not getting into a fight with my son in my home.'

'He started it,' Mark protested. 'Did you see him start it, going on at me, baiting me?'

'Didn't take much, did it?' Ben says, straightening his shoulders. 'You've been itching for an excuse to beat the crap out of me since you moved in.'

'Not any more. Get your stuff, you're out.' Ben's mum's voice grows in strength with each drag on her cigarette.

'You can't throw me out,' Mark laughs. 'You can't even light a fag without popping some pills. The three of you can't throw me out.'

'Want to chance it?' I say, staring at him hard, and in my head I am six foot tall and invincible, imperious, powerful. I am Wonder Woman. I am an Amazon queen.

Ben steps past me and goes toe to toe with Mark; he's a good few inches taller.

'Get out, Mark. Just get out.'

The man stares at him for a long moment, and I wait. And then the sound of sirens can be heard in the background. Maybe they are on the way here, maybe not, but it doesn't matter – he grabs his coat.

'Fuck the lot of you,' he says as he exits. The second he is gone, Ben sinks down onto the sofa; his mother approaches him warily, blinking in bewilderment.

'What did you do that for?' she says, and her tone is full of confusion. 'It was like you were spoiling for a fight from the second you got in; you wanted that to happen.'

'I couldn't stand us living under his hair trigger all the time,' Ben said. 'He was waiting for an excuse, so I gave him one. Didn't take much, did it?'

For a moment I watch the two of them, mother and son, exchanging gazes full of hurt and wonder. I see what I have always known: how much they love each other and how little they understand each other, too.

'You need an X-ray,' I say, to break the deadlock. As I gingerly lift up the edge of Ben's T-shirt, the bruises on his stomach are already beginning to flower. 'Internal bleeding, maybe.'

He shakes his head. 'No. Hospital means police, police means interfering. And I was spoiling for a fight, Mum. You let these men come into your home and walk all over you. You've got to stop it; you've got to get your act together. I can't live here for ever, you know.'

'What do you mean?' she asks.

'I mean, I think I want to get away for a few months. Travel, maybe. I dunno,' he says. 'But I can't do that if you are like this – like a zombie. You've got to sort yourself out; for me, if not for you.'

She drops her gaze, twisting her fingers together. She look old, frail and frightened – not like a woman who can only be in her forties.

'Maybe a cup of tea?' I suggest, wanting to give her something to do.

'I'll make some tea,' she says, as if she hasn't heard me.

I wait for her to go to the kitchen before sitting down next to Ben. He refuses to look at me.

'What's going on?' I ask him.

'Do you care?' he asks angrily.

'Ben, what do you mean? Of course I care, of course I do. But this, this isn't you. Picking a fight with a bloke who's got love and hate tattooed on his knuckles!'

'How do you know?' he asks me. He winces as he tries to widen the gap between us. 'Do you think you really know me at all, Hope?'

He's hurt and angry, and still pumped up from the fight, and words aren't going to work now, so I move closer to him, and put my arms around his neck, and rest my head on his shoulder. After a while, one bruised and cut hand comes to rest on my knee.

'Were you impressed by how I came here and battered a door down to rescue you?' I ask him softly.

'I didn't need rescuing,' he points out, but the anger has ebbed out of his voice. 'But, actually, yes. Actually, I think it's the nicest thing anyone has ever done for me.'

There's the smallest wobble in his voice, and neither of us say a word or move a muscle until he is calmer.

'That door will need boarding up tonight,' Mrs Dargue calls from the kitchen, as if nothing very much has happened. 'We're out of milk.'

I take Ben's broken, bruised hands in mine. He has such long, fine fingers, gentle and kind fingers.

'Are you really going?' I ask him. 'Will you really go travelling?'

'I've got to do something, Hope,' he says. 'I can't spend my whole working in a phone shop and … hanging around with you. We're grown ups; we should probably start acting like it.'

'But it doesn't have to be, like, today, does it?' I ask him. 'We could start tomorrow, maybe – because I just got out of hospital, and I was thinking gluten-free pizza and a *Buffy The Vampire Slayer* marathon?'

He pauses for a moment, and the sweetest little smile lights just one corner of his mouth. 'Fine, but from tomorrow onwards we are all about maturity.'

'Ben.' His mother reappears, and it is as if she has erased the scene that has just happened from her mind entirely. 'What are we going to do about the door?'

'Leave it to me,' I say.

I go into the hallway. And I do what girls who are going to start being women tomorrow do. I call my dad. He arrives in less than twenty minutes with his toolbox and some plywood and my mum in tow. My mum runs a bath for Mrs Dargue. We try to persuade her to come and spend the night with us, four streets away in our nice Victorian semi, but she won't come.

'My flat,' she says. 'I'm not going anywhere.'

'But *you're* coming,' I tell Ben. 'Buffy.'

'Come on, son,' Dad says. 'Do as the girl tells you. You can't refuse that face, can you?'

I colour as Ben looks at me. 'Never have been able to say no to her yet.'

Dear Hugh,

I'm sorry to do this to you in a note, I really am, but I simply can't wait for you any more. Maybe that was the trouble between us. I wanted love and laughter and home-building. And you wanted fun – and never to be serious.

I thought that you and me were going to be together. I thought that I could change you, but I should have known better. The trouble is, Hugh, that I am not the right person to love you. We don't want the same things. You think you are happy, but you aren't, you know.

I'm leaving Jake with you because Angus is allergic to cats.

Good luck,

Mel x

CHAPTER THIRTY-ONE

· ·

HUGH

When I wake up, I am immersed in a shocking, sudden, cold drench of panic.

I fumble for my phone at once and call my new, but somehow already familiar, friend Stella.

'Is she …?'

'She's here. She's stable,' Stella says. 'I'm not on duty, but I wanted to come in, in case you needed me. I'm here and everything is fine for now.'

'I slept,' I tell her, sitting up, taking a moment to become orientated to my unfamiliar surroundings. 'I didn't mean to. It's what – seven? I must have slept all day.'

'Well, you must have needed it,' she says. 'How are you feeling?'

It troubles me that both Sarah and Mikey must have had to creep quietly around me all day, while I was completely oblivious to them. Either that or I kept them out of their own living room on one of the few days they get together. However, I'm also aware that I've not slept such a deep and dreamless sleep for so long, completely unaware of where I was or of the passing of time, which was running out.

'I'm OK, I think,' I say.

'What have you decided?' Stella asks me.

'I don't have to decide,' I say. 'In the end it's obvious there's no choice. I'm coming, now.'

'Do you want me to warn her?' she offers. 'After all, this is my fault.'

'I don't know,' I say. 'I have no idea how to do this.'

'Just come. We can talk when you get here.'

When I put down the phone, I see Mikey in the doorway watching me, curiously. He looks somehow younger out of school uniform, in a pair of jeans that are a fraction too short.

'Are you having a nervous breakdown?' he asks, matter-of-factly. 'Our maths teacher had a nervous breakdown. It was sort of our fault.'

'I'm sorry I crashed out on your sofa all day,' I say. 'I must have pissed you off, keeping you away from Zombie Death Fighters.'

'It's all right.' Mikey shrugs. 'Mum said you needed your rest. She said you'd had a bit of a hard time and gone flipping mental!'

'That's exactly what she said, is it?' I ask him.

'Well, not exactly. You all right now?' He advances further into the room to peer at me, like I am one of the more curious exhibits in my museum. 'She said your mum came back from the dead and it freaked you out. But not like a zombie. I thought, if your mum was a zombie, that would be cool.'

'Yes,' I say. 'That sums it up pretty well. And, no, not like a zombie.'

'I don't blame you,' Mikey says. 'I don't really see my dad much, and it's odd because when I don't see him, I miss him. But when I do see him, I feel like shit. So, you know, what's better?'

I'm touched that he's shared that experience with me, that somehow he's sensed that the one way to make me feel better is to feel less alone.

'Do you like fishing?' I ask him.

'No.' He looks offended.

'Have you ever tried it?'

'I'm not gay,' he says.

'Whether or not you like fishing isn't a marker of your sexual orientation.'

'You like long words, don't you?' he says. 'And bow ties. But I don't think you are gay because you fancy my mum.'

'I ...' Two spots of heat ignite on my cheeks, and he grins, pleased to have caught me out. 'I like fishing. Look, I've still got loads of kit, but I haven't been – not since my dad died. Would you come with me one Saturday, just to see if you like it? Because, you know, I've had a shit time and so have you.'

Mikey screws up his nub of a nose, looking thoughtful.

'Can Mum come?' he says.

'Sure,' I agree at once, because the idea of a Saturday with Mikey and Sarah makes me curiously happy in the middle of an ocean of sad.

'And you can work up to asking her out,' he says by way of agreeing. 'I'm going to put the telly on now.'

I stand up, stretching my arms above my head, then running one hand over my stubble, and that little bubble of tranquillity is replaced in my gut by churning, sickening nerves.

This is it.

It's time.

'Right. I'm off,' I say, to myself more than to him.

'No, wait,' Mikey says, as I pick up my coat. 'Wait a minute.'

'What's wrong?' I ask.

'Well, give me a chance to shout "Mum", and get my trainers on,' he says. 'We can't let you go there on your own. We can walk you, at least.'

As good as Mikey's word, he and Sarah walk me to the high street, where they say their goodbyes – Sarah grabbing my hand just before she leaves and squeezing my fingers, leaving a trace of her warmth behind as she departs. Then Stella meets me at a green wooden side door set into a rough brick wall. I follow her down a stone path, surprised by the sense of space.

'I never knew this was here – all the open grounds,' I say. 'It's rather beautiful.'

'Bequeathed in perpetuity by Marie Francis Bonne,' Stella tells me, as if she is quoting something. 'For the well-being and respite of the weary and sick.'

'Funny,' I say. 'All I have to bequeath is a fishing rod and some DVDs.' I'm babbling because I am terrified, heartbroken, furious and needful. And somehow I know that Stella knows that. She listens to me talk, opening the door for me and leading me to what I guess must be the nurses' station.

An older woman, with short hair and huge earrings, greets me with a polite but surprised smile.

'Mandy, this is my friend Hugh,' Stella says, adding quickly, 'Hugh is Grace's son.'

Mandy's eyes widen.

'Oh?' she says, looking at me, and then back at Stella. 'I thought she didn't have family; she never mentioned any.'

'Didn't she? She told me all about him,' Stella says.

'Well.' Mandy looks at me, her smile full of sympathy. 'It's wonderful that you are here. The doctor's on her rounds, but I'll get her to pop in and see you in between patients.'

'Ready?' Stella touches my arm briefly.

'No,' I say, and I feel my knees threaten to give way and my throat tighten. I am afraid. Stella takes my hand in hers and squeezes it hard – hard enough to hurt.

'You will be OK,' she says, looking into my eyes.

I nod, and she opens the door to where my lost mother is sleeping. And the strangest thing happens: Jake, my cat, looks up as I enter the room and gets off the bed, and trots towards me. Bending down, I scoop him up into my arms, heartened and confused at the same moment. How can Jake be here?

'That's Shadow,' Stella whispers, stroking his head. 'He visits us all the time.'

I want to tell her that this is not Shadow, or Ninja, but Jake – strange, mysterious Jake – but it doesn't matter, not right now. All that matters is that he is here, because this small, odd little black cat gives me something I thought I might not have: he gives me courage. He leaps out of my arms as I begin to walk into the room, and takes up his place on her bed, his head by her dormant hand.

The room is gently lit, and the woman, the old frail woman on the bed, is lying very still, her eyes closed. There's a rhythmic beat of some sort of monitor and the steady, if laboured, rise and fall of her chest that tells me she is alive.

I come to a halt when I see her, and I hear a sob, deep and threaded tight with longing, tear from my chest, but I catch it and push it away, bracing myself.

Carefully, Stella edges around, and walks to her bedside, picking up my mother's hand. I take off my coat. It's so cold outside, it takes a moment for my face to thaw enough to move.

'What?' Grace murmurs, so softly, to Stella, and I remember fragments, maybe memories, maybe dreams, of her whispering me goodnight. 'What's up, little one?'

Stella nods at me, and I hesitate for one second longer, brim-full of such perfect pain and rejection that I almost want to run – run away from this moment, which will surely hurt us both before any good can be done, and out into a night where there is still the promise of the sun about to rise, flooding every corner with light.

But I steel myself, every sinew in my body tensing as I walk towards her.

'Mum?' I say. The word sounds foreign, and tastes unfamiliar. She turns her head at the sound of my voice, her brow furrowed, confused.

'Am I dead?' she asks, quite calmly. I pick up her hand; it's warm and full of blood, pulsing just under the skin.

'Mum, it's Hugh. I … I found out you were here. I came to say … hello. Hello, Mum. I hope that's OK.'

Her eyes focus on me, and I catch my breath as her face fills at once with something akin to joy, something like pain.

'Son? Is it you, really?'

'Yes, it's me. Mum, is it OK, me being here? I know you didn't want to see me …'

'Of course I wanted to see you,' she says, seeming to overcome her drowsiness by sheer force of will. I watch as she tries to drag herself up into a sitting position, and Stella steps forward, raising her bed with a remote-control thing and rearranging her pillows. Mum never takes her eyes off me – she doesn't even seem to blink. I think she is afraid I might be a figment of my imagination. I take the time to study her face. Her beautiful elegant blonde hair is all but gone now, but I can still see the traces of her that I remember, and more than that: I can see me, my own face, hiding in amongst the shadows of hers. We can't stop looking at each other, as if two people who have been thirsty all their lives are suddenly offered a glass of cold water.

'Is it really you?' Her hand frees itself from my fingers and floats impossibly upward, lighting on my face. I take the greatest of care to control the storm of feelings that wants to shake me to pieces; I must not let that happen. I must keep myself so tightly sewn together that not one molecule of longing escapes. I don't want her to see what I didn't know until just this second: that I am still a little boy who needs a hug from his mother.

Stella looks like she is about to leave, so I send her a look, begging her to stay.

'Do you want me to go?' I ask my mother. 'I can, if that is what you want.'

'I don't deserve to have you here,' she says. 'I left you, and I didn't even have the courage to die. I ran away.'

There are some silent seconds, with nothing but the beat of the machines, the hum of the heating. It feels like I've been let loose somehow, set free of gravity and time; I'm just existing in this strange moment – almost like this is the afterlife and I've crossed over with her.

'That doesn't matter now,' I say at last, and she will never know how much it costs me to say those words. 'All that matters is this.'

She closes her eyes, and a tear tracks down her cheek.

'I tried,' she said. 'Every day I tried to get up and live this life as best I could … Not at first. At first I just drank, and hurt people, hurt myself, but the years went on and I realised. If I didn't have the guts to die, then I had to have to guts to stay alive.' She opens her eyes and grips hold of me so tightly. 'Just before I came here, I phoned you, the house, the old number; I knew it off by heart. It was your dad on the answerphone … I felt like I was calling you then, when you were ten years old. I felt like I was reaching into the past to say goodbye. Only I couldn't find the words – there were not words.'

The breaths on the other end of the line, the rush of traffic captured on my answering machine – it was her. It was Mum.

'I don't want to die, son. I don't want to die now you are here. I'm afraid.'

The anger, it's still there – still stronger than the sadness and the peculiar joy that seeing her brings. There is a large, childlike part of me that wants to tell this thin, fragile woman my own story of loss and sorrow. But I don't; I simply leave my hand in hers and listen as she talks, telling me about her life, her work, the children she's brought back from the brink of disaster, the good she has done becoming a surrogate mother for so many. Words pour out of her, defying the medication that she is under, as if her need to explain, to justify, to apologise is greater, has more life force, than even her body. I listen. I am gentle and kind; I speak softly and carefully. Yet in every angle in my body, with each breath, I want to ask, but what about me? Why didn't you care for me the way that you cared for those other children? And finally she stops talking and reaches for me. Uncertainly, following her lead, I lay my head on her shoulder, and she puts her arms around me.

'It's OK to cry, you know,' she says. 'Sometimes life just isn't fair.'

Beloved,

Do not miss me, because I will always be with you. In every drop of rain that touches your tongue, in every breath of air you inhale. In the tips of the leaves that you brush with your fingertips as you pass by. I will be there, in every moment. I am not gone, I am only altered, from this state of matter to another. For a moment, for too brief a moment, I was the man that loved you, but now that I am changed, I am the air, the moon, the stars. For we are all made of stars, my beloved.

You and I, and all of life, we were all born out of the death of a star, millions of billions of years ago. A star that lived long and then, before its death, burned at its brightest, its fiercest – an enflaming supernova. But when it died, it did not cease to exist; instead everything it was made of became part of the universe once again, and everything that is part of the universe will once more become part of us.

So do not miss me, because I do not die; I transform – into the wind in the tops of the trees, the wave on the ocean, the pebbles under your foot, the dust on your bookshelves, the midnight sky.

Wherever you look, I will be there.

Carl x

CHAPTER THIRTY-TWO

* *

HOPE

'What are you doing here?' Stella is surprised and worried to see me and Ben, coming in through the side door. And it's weird to see her not in her uniform but in just a sweater over some leggings and a battered old pair of surprisingly pink trainers. 'You only just left. Are you OK?'

'I'm OK,' I tell her. 'It's him.' I nod at Ben, who is hunched inside his great big coat. 'He got in a fight, and he's a bit bruised. I'm worried about him. I saw something about internal bleeding on TV the other day, and how you can just be fine one minute and then drop dead the next. He's refusing to go to hospital.' I give Stella and Mandy my best winning smile. 'Please would one of you just have the tiniest little look at him? I'll buy you cake and doughnuts.'

'I'll do it,' Stella says. 'I'm not officially on duty, though, so if I'm worried, you'll have to see the doctor and they may well insist that you go to hospital. There isn't a free room, so you'll have to come through here.' She leads us into the older part of the building, where there is what looks like an old-fashioned school nurse's office, with a cot bed at the side.

'Lie down,' she says to Ben.

He eases off his coat with a great deal of difficulty. Stella frowns as he lowers himself onto the bed, and I, with some newfound sense of intimacy that I choose not to analyse, reach across and sweep up his shirt. Even I draw in a sharp breath as I look again at the bruises that I am already too familiar with.

'A fight, you say?' Stella looks at him. 'Or a beating?'

'You know, live fast, die ... painfully,' Ben says. 'Anyway, you should have seen the other guy ... barely a scratch on him.'

'I'm going to have to get the on-call doctor to look at you,' Stella says. 'I can't take the risk of missing something, and if we've got her on board, we can maybe do an ultrasound – check for any free fluid. Wait here.'

As soon as she is gone, Ben tries to sit up.

'Come on, let's scarper,' he says. 'They've got people in here a lot worse off than me.'

'Ben, don't be an idiot,' I tell him. 'Imagine how annoyed I'd be if you died before me – now, and of stupidity, too. I'd be so pissed off. We haven't even ...'

'What haven't we even?' he says.

'Just lie still,' I say. 'And that includes your mouth.'

'Fine.' He lays back down, picks up my hand and starts to idly play with my fingers. His touch makes my stomach flutter.

It's been a curious few hours since I rescued him, which is how I am choosing to describe it – because it is driving him mad. They have been curious and dream-like, spent in my bedroom with the curtains drawn and my mother pacing anxiously outside the door.

'Do you want tea?' she called through the door more than once. And when I refused: 'Squash?'

'We are not having sex, Mum,' I called out to her. 'And even if we were, it would be legal.' And then I remembered how much I loved her, and how lucky I was that I had her. 'I love you, though!'

Ben slept for a while when we got back, just falling easily into a deep sleep; one minute he was there, the next he was gone. I wasn't surprised that he was tired. He curled up in my bed, his arms wrapped around one of my many teddies, and he was fast asleep almost before his head hit the pillow.

I read for a while. I thought of Issy and, logging on to Facebook, I found her mum's profile and sent her a friend request and then a private message, saying hi. I said it was probably too soon, but as soon as I was able, I wanted to do something to raise money for the hospice, and I suggested that maybe we could join forces. I'd already given her my phone number so I told her to call me. I put three kisses on the end of the message. After that, I watched TV and had a look on Twitter. I read the blogs of people I wished I was more like and watched a lot of videos of cats in dog beds until eventually the adrenaline, or whatever it was, wore off, exhaustion overtook me, and I slept too.

When I woke up, not too much later, Ben's arms were wrapped around my waist – his great big body curled around mine like a comma. For a few sleepy moments, I was aware of the rise and fall of his chest, and I think I was smiling to myself when I went back to sleep. I felt like I was smiling, anyway. And then hours after that I was very sure what woke me, because it was impossibly awkward and embarrassing. It was Ben's erection pressing against the small of my back.

I tried to wriggle away from it, but he caught me and pulled me closer, still sound asleep.

'Ben.' I prodded him till he opened one sleepy eye. 'Inappropriate hard on.'

He groaned as he rolled away from me, grabbing one of my poor teddies and holding it over the offending area.

'Is it that inappropriate? I mean, we did nearly have sex; we could do that now, if you like.'

'No!' I was appalled. 'We can't have sex now just because of your mechanical erection. That's not ...'

'What?' He looked at me, interested.

'Polite.' I was defensive. 'And, anyway, that ship has sailed, don't you think?'

'I guess so,' he said, and I let the little smooth pebble of disappointment sink to the bottom of my chest. 'And, anyway, I thank God that my penis is working. I don't think any other part of my body is up to much.'

And all these strange and curious, and frankly quite... erotic thoughts rushed through my head, so I grabbed his hand and pulled him out of bed. 'That's it, I'm taking you to Marie Francis to get checked out.'

'It's not *that* serious,' he'd protested.

'Not yet,' I'd told him. 'But if we stay here, I might kill you.'

'You are so brave,' I say now, quite suddenly, to Ben, who looks perturbed.

'I don't think so. I picked a fight with a psycho. I'm fairly sure that makes me stupid.'

'Yes, that was stupid, but that's not what I'm talking about,' I say. 'Before, in the hotel, when you said … you know.'

'No idea,' Ben says, and my eyes widen before I see that he is teasing me. 'When I said that at some point in the last couple of years, probably when I was drunk or on drugs, I fell in love with you. Yes, I remember.'

'You kept all this stuff inside for such a long time. You didn't tell me. Why? Am I a shit friend?'

'Yes.' Ben looks serious for just a moment, and then he smiles. 'No, of course you aren't a shit friend. I didn't tell you because … well, no one likes rejection.'

'But … you didn't give me a chance to respond,' I say.

'You didn't have to; you should have seen the look on your face! It was pure horror!'

'It wasn't! It wasn't horror,' I say. 'It was shock. And it was amazement. Because it just didn't seem real to me that you – the coolest, smartest, funniest person I know – could really like *me*.'

'I don't really like you,' Ben says. 'I fucking love you. I am in love with you, Hope. Big shit-scary, proper all-the-way-to-my-toes love. With you.'

'Well,' I say. 'Thing is, yeah, I think I fucking love you too.'

Ben suddenly drops my hand and covers his face.

'What? I say. 'What? Have you changed your mind?'

'I'm freaking crying,' he says.

'Dork,' I tell him, taking his hand away from his face and kissing it.

'So, we're doing emergency admissions now?' The tall and very beautiful Dr Kahn appears in the doorway, eyeing Ben, with Stella close behind. 'Well, come along, young man. Let's make sure you are not completely broken.'

'Oh, I'm not completely broken,' Ben says, a smile breaking out on his battered face. 'There's one bit of me that's working just fine.'

Dear Julie,

Well, now, the time has come ... and all that jazz. You know what a Sinatra nut I am, so please would you indulge me this one last wish and have 'My Way' played at the funeral? I know you never had much time for Ol' Blue Eyes but, for me, there was never anyone better.

We've always been different, you and I. Not a match made in heaven, but you have been a good wife, and I am sorry to leave you. I think sometimes you'll be quite glad to have me out from under your feet, but I think you'll miss me too — I like to think you will.

We didn't marry for love, did we? We married because of one silly Saturday night, and our Roy, who was the result of it. I thought my mum would die of shame, and I thought your dad would kill me. There was nothing else for it but to get married back then. And so we did. We stared at each other on the wedding day like we were terrified of each other. I was sorry that you didn't love me and I didn't love you. But I wasn't sorry we were married, or sorry about Roy when he arrived; he was the apple of both of our eyes.

But do you remember the day that it happened? Roy was about four and we'd taken him to Brighton for the bank holiday. Hot as Hades it was; him in his hat, moaning about the pebbles under his toes. We were walking along the shore behind him, not saying much. And then suddenly, out of nowhere, you just grabbed my hand and held it. We'd never held hands, but then we did, walking along like a couple in the first bloom.

Roy was wading in up to his knees, screaming and splashing. You shaded your eyes to look at me, and you said, 'I like being married to you, Brian Fletcher.'

And I said, because it hit me just then, 'I love being married you, Julie Fletcher. I love you, you know.'

CHAPTER THIRTY-THREE

* *

STELLA

Home. After leaving Hugh with his mother, and sending Hope back out into the night with her boy, I discovered I wanted more than anything to be at home – because that empty, unloved house suddenly felt exactly like that to me; it felt like home.

I walk around the house I have hardly lived in for the past two years and see it with fresh eyes. The wallpaper in the hallway left over from the last occupants: huge blousy red roses we swore would be gone as soon as we'd closed the door. The corner that Vincent ripped off with his thumb, revealing magnolia paint underneath. The box of non-specific kitchen items, still labelled and sealed in the space where a dishwasher should be. Clearly it's filled with objects that I never use, or need – objects that I can't remember – and so quite why I bothered to wrap them in newspaper and seal them in a box is anyone's guess. They must have seemed important once. A lot of things seemed important once that hardly matter at all now.

On the stairs there's some neatly folded laundry that I left there to take up a few weeks ago, now dusty and creased, and a mug of cold tea. In the bathroom is a desiccated sprig of lavender in a frosted glass vase, its shattered flower heads littering the windowsill like dead flies. In the bedroom, the cold green paint, the temporary wardrobe. And at the bottom of this is Vincent's bag from the hospital – all of his belongings still zipped up in an overnight bag that has never been unzipped since the day he got home. I don't know why neither of us touched it. Maybe we thought that unzipping it might somehow release all of the terror and pain of the first few days of surviving the accident out into this world, our world. Perhaps we didn't realise that had already happened.

It's heavier than it looks; I heft it onto the bed and unzip it to reveal musty, folded clothes on top. Taking a breath, I tip the bag upside down and shake the contents onto the bed. It's clothes, mostly – T-shirts, jogging bottoms with one leg cut off, underwear. But also there's a cheap plastic bag with a necklace in it – a small gold St Christopher, which Vincent had always worn for as long as I knew, but not since the injury, although I don't think I even noticed until now. A long time ago, soon after we met, I remember fingering the fine gold chain and catching the small octagonal medallion in the palm of my hand.

'Lucky charm?' I had asked him.

'Mum gave it to me when I joined up. She told me, that day, how proud she was of me. I think it's the only time I heard her say it. It isn't so much lucky; I guess it's just a reminder of that – it's a bit sad, really. You should give me something, too. You should give me something to keep in my pocket, to remind me of you.'

And he'd grabbed a pair of knickers from my drawer and waved them over his head, saying they were going with him back on tour, and I shrieked and chased him around the room until we fell into bed and made love again. I never did see those knickers again, though, but they aren't in this bag.

There is something else in amongst the jumble of clothes: a long white envelope. Perhaps discharge notes from the hospital? I pick it up and sit down on the bed with a bump. It's addressed to me. And it's written in Vincent's handwriting.

Vincent, who hates even having to write a shopping list, or a Christmas card, has written to me. But of course I know why. I know what this letter is; I just haven't ever known that it actually existed.

It's his last letter.

I hold it lightly, seeing how it trembles in my fingers. And even though it somehow feels like a betrayal – no, more like tempting fate – I force my thumb under the seal and rip it open. I take the letter out and unfold it. There it is, his handwriting, neat and boyish, a little laboured, but carefully written, thoughtful. Somehow I know that this wasn't the first draft; that'd he tried and tried again to get this missive exactly right. I see my name, but the other letters swim on the page – out of focus as tears blur my vision for a moment and I blink them away. I was only ever meant to read this if he died. And yet, once I am able to start reading, I cannot look away.

Dear Stella,

If you are reading this then I am gone. And it will be hard for you. When I think about it, you being alone, having to deal with what's happened, it feels like it will be hard for me too. It hurts to think about. But it won't be – I will be gone. It's not me I have to worry about – it's you.

We never talked about this, the possibility that I might be killed in action. Maybe we didn't want to tempt fate. Maybe we didn't want to acknowledge it. We always did like to believe, you and I, that together we are indestructible.

So, there are some things you must do to remember me. Don't change, Stella. Don't stop being brave, fierce, funny, sexy as hell and too clever for your own good. Don't stop reading all those books, or saving all those lives, or making people smile just by smiling at them. Don't lose the joy you have in living, which has made me want to stay alive more than anything I know.

Don't be lonely, not for me. Make sure your friends take you out at least once a week, even in the beginning. Make sure you go out and party. You love to party. Don't stop flirting. It hurts me to write that, but I want you to be happy. And one day, maybe in about a decade or so, you can try and meet someone new – though just make sure they always feel like they are living in my shadow.

Remember that, for you, I have been the best man, and the best soldier, that I can be. Since you became my wife, I grew up, I cared, I tried. I lived the best way I could, in every moment. And I will die the best way I can too.

Think of me, remember me. But never change who you are because of me. Always be you, perfect and happy. And somehow, some way, I will always be with you. If you are reading this letter, all that it means is that you and I were never meant to have our happy ending. But you can still have yours.

I love you,

    Vincent

And all at once I see for the first time what both of us have failed to realise all along. We have been separately mourning the life we used to have, missing what can never be returned to us, but it doesn't mean that we can't still be the people we were before. He told me, here in this letter, that if the greatest tragedy happened, I shouldn't change. And yet, it didn't happen – I got him back – but somehow we both changed. We both let it change us. And yet, it doesn't have to. We can be the same people; we can still love each other the same way, simply living life differently. And, above all else, simply living. We have both been ghosts, ghosts haunting an empty house. Ghosts made not by death but by our own lack of will to live, to fight for the life that made us happy.

I look around this bleak, empty building full of shadows and cold corners, and I know that without Vincent in it, without the man that I love it in, it is an empty shell. It's exactly as Hugh said: what is love if you don't have to fight to keep it? What is life if you don't fight every second to live it? We can still have our happy ending, together. Only it won't be an ending, it will be a beginning.

I know where Vincent is, right now.

I lace up my shoes, let myself out of the front door, glance up at what's left of the night, and I run.

CHAPTER THIRTY-FOUR

. . . .

HOPE

'Are you OK?'

Ben is leaning on me; he sounds a little out of breath. The doctor at Marie Francis checked him out and said everything seemed fine, other than severe soft-tissue damage and some cuts, but to keep an eye on him and get him to A&E if anything changed.

'Am I OK?' Ben laughs. 'I don't know. Am I? You tell me.'

I know he wants me to do or say something – the next thing that will move us on from where we are now to being more, to being lovers. And I'm terrified; to make someone that is so vital to me, so important, suddenly so … significant is scary. This isn't some boy I met at a summer festival; this matters. Right now, this matters more than anything else.

'I think you are OK,' I say, pulling him a little tighter to me. 'You've got me now. You've always had me, you just didn't seem to know that.'

The market is busy, bustling with cool kids and tourists, harassed-looking mums, people of all backgrounds and faiths jostling with each other for elbow room. I glance sideways at Ben; his head is down, his hair, minus all the product he usually shoves in it, is falling in his eyes. It makes him look younger, somehow – softer, sweeter. Without all the bravado and front that I love about him so much, and yet, somehow, without it, I love him even more.

'The thing is,' I say, 'I want it, what you want. But, Ben, I have to say it, because it wouldn't be fair not to. What about the whole CF thing? Because, apart from the fact that I am needy and desperate and moody, I might go and die on you. Possibly even before you get bored of me. And I'm not sure … should I let you put yourself through that?'

He stops suddenly. 'That's not your choice to make. And, anyway, if it happens, it won't make a difference if we are together or not, because if it happens, then … well, it's not going to happen.' He grabs the lapels of my coat and draws me closer to him. 'Hope, I love you. You don't get to decide how much I love you or not; that's a done deal. All you get to decide is whether you want to benefit from my masterly skills as a red-hot lover. That's really all you have to think about.'

I gasp and laugh at the same time. And I am about to kiss him when he releases me so suddenly I stumble back at little.

'Look where we are!' he says. 'It's a sign!'

We are standing outside the Market Tavern, and I remember that tonight is the night we were supposed to be on stage, in there, singing our song. There is this rush of horror, excitement and adrenaline all at once. I get the horrible feeling that I am about to be impulsive.

'Let's do it now!' he says, tugging at my sleeve and nodding at the sign. 'Come on, let's go in and do our song!'

'Now?' I am uncertain.

'No, next Tuesday. Yes, now!' Ben tugs at my hand. 'Yes, come on, this is what we need, isn't it? We both need to get our blood pumping and our hearts beating. To scare the shit out of ourselves and remember that we are young and alive and in reasonably good health, considering. Don't we? Well, what better way than doing this? This is what we said we would do.'

'I can't even breathe properly, at the moment, never mind sing,' I say.

'You can never sing,' he says. 'You just think you can and people don't seem to mind.'

'Cheeky git. I'll show you!' He laughs, but then his face stills as he sees something in my expression. 'You actually want to do this now?'

'Yes, I do. I'm tired of waiting; my life is in limbo. I'm tired of being stuck inside my own head all the time, so much that I missed the fact that the boy I love is in love with me. I might have been dealt a crappy hand of cards, but I don't have to let it determine what kind of person I am. I want to get out there, and live, and be … well, like you.'

'We don't have guitars,' Ben says, a little cautiously.

'It's a room full of wannabe musicians; I think there will be a couple lying around.' This time I grab his lapel and drag him towards the door.

'Wait.' He stops me. 'I wanted to say something.'

'Um, is it something about grabbing life, going for it, not standing about in the street talking instead of doing something exciting?' I say, recapping.

'No,' he says. 'I want to say that I can't wait to kiss you again. Oh, and try not to sing out of key.'

✸

The pub is full to the rafters, noisy and beery, and there are three dudes with beards on stage, singing something surprisingly folksy. It's five-deep at the bar, and a man with a suspicious-looking hat is sitting next to the stage with a clipboard.

'Hi, can we put our names down?' I ask him. 'I know we are a bit late, sorry.'

He looks me up and down, and definitely judges the toggles on my duffle coat, then glances at Ben.

'We're full, love,' he says. 'You have to get here when we open if you want a slot.'

'Can't you just squeeze us in? We only want to do one song.'

'They all only want to do one song – and, trust me, one song is usually too many.'

'Look.' Ben leans across me. 'You've probably heard of my band, The Black Angels? If you can do us a favour, I'll make sure you get a gig from the band. We always draw a full house.'

'Oh well, that changes everything,' the guy says.

'Really?' I say.

'No, not really. Never heard of you. Now look, I'm already up to my ears in overentitled, middle-class, talentless school kids pouring their bile into my ears as it is. Come back next week and put your name on the list in advance.'

'It's just that I'm dying, you see,' I say, and the words come out of my mouth in a rush. 'Cystic fibrosis. And this is like one of the items on my bucket list. If I don't do it tonight, who knows when I will get the chance. Might be dead next week.'

'Boo hoo. I'm weeping for you,' the bloke says.

'Well, man, I hope you don't believe in karma,' Ben says. 'Come on, Hope. You tried. We'll tell that journalist that you just didn't have the luck to meet someone who cares ...'

'Wait ...' Ugly Hat pauses. 'Really? You're really sick?'

'Yes,' I say. That part at least isn't a lie, and I did *nearly* die quite recently. Maybe I should feel a little bad about using my CF this way, but bugger it – it owes me at least one favour.

'Fine. All right, then; you can go on after the next guy. I just hope you don't get bottled off.'

'Wow, thank you. You are really kind,' I tell him, not entirely sarcastically. Now all we need is two guitars.

✳

Of course Ben has been on stage a hundred times before, a million times – every paving square or passing park bench is a stage for him – but I never have, and this small triangle of a platform stage, in the corner of a Camden pub, is pretty much the most terrifying thing I have ever encountered. The crowd talked over us while we set up. Ben said 'one, two' into his mic, and then I did too, because that's what you do, although I have never really worked out why. We tuned two guitars, borrowed from some guys Ben knows, and then our benefactor coughed loudly from the side of the stage and gave me a look that said, 'You're not the only one on a deadline.'

My voice is too thin, too quiet and too high for the first few bars, but Ben covers me with his too-loud, not-quite-in-tune-but-oddly-melodic tone. I remind myself I have less than three minutes to do this, and only one shot, so I close my eyes and pretend that the crowd isn't looking or listening to me, which mostly it isn't because people are talking amongst themselves. I just tune into the music and to Ben, and we sing. A few bars more and it's just us and the song, and I feel myself smiling as we become entwined in each other's voices. Our music soars; every hair on my arms is standing on end. I can feel my lungs working properly, my heart thundering. It's a perfect, wonderful two minutes and fifty seconds, and then it is done. I open my eyes. There is a ripple of disinterested applause and a half-hearted cheer from the back, but I don't actually care. I feel like Wembley Stadium just gave me a standing ovation.

'We thank you!' Ben says. 'Talent scouts, see me after!'

He bows, and I bow with him, a microsecond too late.

A few minutes later and we are running outside, laughing like loons.

'That was brilliant!' I say. 'We were awesome!'

'Uh-oh, you've got the gigging bug,' he says, grinning fondly at me. 'You were great, though, too good. Everyone in there was intimidated and resentful of your beauty and talent.'

'What shall we do now?' I ask him. 'I feel like I need to do something!'

'Pub? Dinner? Back home to your mum's house for some more tea and biscuits?' he asks me.

'Let go for a walk to Primrose Hill,' I say. 'It's a nice mild night, and it's only a few minutes; we might even see some stars!'

Ben shrugs and lets me tuck my arm through his, and we make our way through the park, walking in silence, both of us lost in deep thought. Somehow, finding him, saving him from his stepdad's beating, changed everything. It changed my life even more than being born with CF, or surviving near-death, or knowing that my life will probably be really short. I have been too long in this cocoon that I spun myself, but it was a cocoon that didn't just protect me from the world, it kept me from it, too. It kept me from experiencing … well, everything. I was so busy feeling sad, scared, anxious, angry that I never had time to feel happy, scared, joyous, lucky. But now, tonight, I do feel lucky. I do. I feel like the luckiest girl in the world.

By the time we reach the top of the hill, Ben is flagging a little, and we stop by mutual consent to sit on a bench. For a few moments, we sit and look at the city below us, a skyline of landmarks stretching out, reaching upwards towards the heavens.

'That thing you said,' Ben says. I hold my breath. 'That thing about "the boy I love".'

'Yes?' I hold my breath.

'Does that mean I can just kiss you when I want to now?'

'Yes,' I say. 'Yes, that would be perfectly fine.'

'I'm really scared, right now,' he says, and I can feel him trembling. 'It's scary to feel this much stuff, and admit to it. I'm terrified.'

'I know,' I say. 'But we already decided. From now on, we are going to be brave.' I place my hands on either side of his face, drawing him to me. His arms wrap around me, his huge coat enveloping me, and this kiss is the one that I will always remember to the day I die. This wonderful kiss that floats on clouds of joy and longing, and that is, at last, about to be quenched.

CHAPTER THIRTY-FIVE

* *

HUGH

When I come out of Mum's room for a moment, I'm surprised to find Sarah sitting in the corridor outside her room.

'You came here? You didn't have to do that,' I tell her, though I am glad, deep in my heart, that she has.

I really had talked myself into believing that I didn't really need anyone, and that I was OK – happy going through life, passing through a series of not-that-close encounters. I was footloose and fancy-free. I made myself believe that, even though my dad taught me that it wasn't true. And then Mum came back, from the dead, turning my life full circle in one fluid moment, and I let myself feel again. All the love that I had felt for her before and pushed down and away for so long, all the fury and the bitterness, all the anger and the need, came flooding back and reignited me. Somehow, right at the last, she has saved me. Only now the doctors have told me this is likely to be her last night. I must go and be with the mother I lost, so many years ago, and watch as I lose her again. Yet there is hope in my heart as I stand outside her room. Because this time I get to look in my mum's eyes; I get to tell her goodbye.

'Well, Mikey's mate invited him for a sleepover, and so I thought … well, I thought you might like someone here,' Sarah tells me with a small smile. 'I think that you need people around you during times like this. Someone to hold your hand and make you tea.'

I take a breath and look back at the door. 'It means a lot that you are here.'

'Are you OK?' she asks, catching hold of my hand.

'Not OK, no,' I say. 'Not tonight; tonight I'm not OK. But one day. I feel like one day, at last, I will be OK. Does that sound weird?'

'Everything you say sounds weird to me.' Sarah smiles very slightly, and then, leaning forward, kisses me softly, briefly, on the cheek. 'I'll be here, when it's over. I'll take you home and we'll make you tea and toast. We'll look after you, all right? Me and Mikey, and even Ninja. I mean Jake.'

'Talking of the cat of many names …' I tell her the story of how I found my, our, cat here, curled up on my mum's bed. 'Here he is called Shadow.'

'I thought he was just some scraggy little back cat,' Sarah whispers. 'Turns out he's the Mayor of London.'

'Well, as long as I don't find out that he's also my boss,' I say. I look into her brown eyes and feel steadied.

'Time to go back?' she asks.

I nod once and go back into my mother's room.

Hours go by, and Mum sleeps with me by her side, keeping vigil. I don't know how long I watch the rise and fall of her chest, or listen for her every breath; it doesn't matter. It's timeless, this moment. It's never and for ever all at once. I am here with my mother, she is with me, and we will always be like this, somehow.

Sometime late, late into the night, she opens her eyes and speaks.

'Do you remember, son?' she says to me. 'Do you remember when you were so little, and we'd go camping in the night-time?'

'I think so,' I say, taking her hand. 'I think I remember being fast asleep and warm one minute, then, the next, you'd have pulled some sheets over some chairs to make a tent. And we'd be sitting on the grass staring at the sky, and you'd be telling me what the constellations were and what they meant.'

'I made it all up, you know.' Her laugh is like lace – finely spun and delicate; like a spider's web that might fall apart in your hands. It is barely a breath on my cheek.

'I did find that out a few years later, when I tried to tell my teacher that Ursa Major was a bear on roller skates going for a milkshake,' I say, smiling. I'm lying next to her, my face very close to hers. Our eyes meet and never stray for a moment. She is holding my hand in hers; my fingers are wrapped in hers.

'I was a terrible mother, the worst,' she says.

'You weren't textbook,' I admit, gently. 'But I never felt sad, or frightened, or neglected. And I laughed all the time, and I never guessed for one second that you were so sad, so unhappy. You protected me from it all – right up until the moment you left. I wasn't sad until you left.'

She closes her eyes for one long moment, and I catch my breath, but she opens them again, slowly. I watch her pale gold lashes, few in number, the colour fading out of her eyes, sheened in silver.

'But I still left. I left you.'

'Yes,' I say. 'And it hurt me, and it broke Dad's heart. But Mum, you came back. You came back and put it right with me, before it was too late. This day, this time with you; it's made me whole again. You've done that.'

'I wish I hadn't been so scared,' she says. 'I thought if I could save everyone, everyone else that I met, get them set right in the world, then the pain and the longing would cease. But it didn't; it never did. Not until I saw your face again. I'm so sorry.'

The effort of speaking exhausts her, and gently I lean my forehead against hers. There are no tears. I thought there might be, but I don't want to cry yet. There is peace – just peace, quiet and contentment.

'Shall we go outside and see the stars?' she says suddenly, with a spark of something, a smile. Joy.

'I'm not …' The words don't even reach my lips. Now is not the time to say no to her. 'Of course, why not?' I say. 'Wait a moment.'

Climbing off the bed, I take as many blankets as I can out of the cupboard and open the double doors that lead out on to her private patio. It will take more than just me to move the bed outside, so I open the door just a crack and catch Mandy's eyes.

Mandy detaches Mum from all of the beeps and buzzers, and just brings the drip out with us, as together we push the bed out into the night. It's cool, but not freezing, crisp and clear. The air is fresh, as if recently laundered, and the moon is bright and full, sailing above the treetops that seem to surround us. And in between their bare, balletic branches, I can see the first glimpse of dawn lighten the hems of the horizon.

'Aren't they beautiful?' Mum says. 'Can you see the stars? Can you see the fire? Ball of fires burning so brightly in the sky. I can feel their heat on my cheeks – can you? It's just like when you were little, and we lay out on the grass and watched the moon rise.'

I look at the same patch of sky that she is gazing at, where I see the barest few stars that are strong enough to filter though the light pollution.

'It's amazing,' I agree. Mandy brings me a chair and I sit beside Mum, gazing upwards.

'I loved your dad so much,' she says, and I am not sure if she is telling me or telling the heavens. 'He was a man who was too good for me, from the start, right from the start. He always had a smile on his face, always full of light.

I thought if a man like that loved me back, he'd turn every dark corner I have into sunshine; he'd love the blackness out of me, and I'd be happy again. And he did love me – he loved me so much. But all I did was pour the darkness into him, turn his happy life into a tragic one.'

'That isn't true,' I whisper. 'Not true at all. I know that for a fact. He talked about you all the time; he made me talk about you all the time. The adventures we had, our Saturday mornings, our nights under the heavens. That holiday we'd had in Margate, when you entered the talent competition and came second and pushed the winner off the stage. And we all had to run away, down to the beach, laughing and screaming. We ate fish and chips on the sand and stayed up so late. You sang for us; you took your shoes off and danced in the surf and sang for us. And afterwards I gave you a rock I'd found on the beach as a prize. Those were the things Dad talked about. He never talked about your hard times, the depression, the drinking – not until I was a lot older. And, even then, never with any regret.'

'I've never believed in God,' she says. 'But if there is something, anything else, I hope your dad is there. I hope he is there and that he will forgive me.'

'He forgave you a long, long time ago.'

'You take after him,' she says. 'You have his sunshine in your heart.'

Thinking of my job – the rows of white faces, the endless strands of hair caught in glass – I wonder if that is true. I want it to be. I want to be like my father. But I want to be like this woman, too – this woman who failed in her eyes so unforgivably, but who somehow came back to life. More than that: she lived for other people. She came back from the dead to be amongst the living. And I – I choose to spend almost all my time amongst the dead, trying to work out, if anything, what their passing meant. Suddenly I realise, with a rush of clarity, that it means nothing, not to me. To the historian, the writer, the morbidly curious, it's interesting: a fascinating insight into a time gone by. But every one of those white faces in the hallway at the museum only had meaning while there was still someone who had once known them – still alive to look at them and miss them. Once, their deaths meant everything, and now they mean nothing; just a footnote in a textbook that no one will read. This is what matters: this moment, this present, *this* life, *this* death.

'There's this kid moved in next door, and his mum. They are going to make me tea, and I'm going to take them fishing like Dad did. The boy, Mikey, he's funny, sweet and thinks he's tough. And Sarah, she's kind and … sort of gentle. I like her a lot.'

At first I don't think she's heard me, but then she smiles and says softly, 'I'm glad you have someone.'

She raises a hand just a few inches off the bed.

'That one,' she says, pointing at the morning star, shining brightly, over the crest of the tree. 'Do you know what that star means?'

'I don't, Mum.' I smile, resting my cheek against hers.

'It means I love you,' she says. 'I love you, Hugh.'

Carefully, I wrap my arms around her and hold her, and we watch the star shining so brightly it can outshine a city. And we watch as the sky becomes the deepest purple, erupting into streaks and gold and orange, reaching out bright tendrils into the night. And just before the dawn, just before the warmth of the sun can find us, I feel her breathing slow and stop, followed by one long sigh that seems so full of relief. I bury my face in her hair, and I weep.

CHAPTER THIRTY-SIX

HOPE

'We've stayed up all night,' I say, leaning back against Ben's chest, both of us wrapped in the warmth of his huge coat, looking out across the city. 'Not bad since you were getting the crap beaten out of you when this night began.'

'I know, me up all night with a hot girl, *talking*,' he says. 'I've lost my touch.'

'Talking and kissing,' I say, turning my head to smile up at him. 'And going for a midnight all-day breakfast in that café. And quite a lot of heavy petting, too.'

'Mm.' Ben's hands, which had been resting beneath my shirt, begin to roam again. 'The anticipation is certainly building. You totally sure you don't want to do it on a bench?'

'I am,' I say. 'And, besides, I want to enjoy this part for a little while longer.'

'I'm really fucking happy,' he says. 'I'm so happy that I'm scared. I don't think I've ever had anything I was afraid of losing before, except for you. And now … now I'm twice as terrified that I'll fuck it up.'

'You won't,' I tell him. 'I won't. We've both changed.'

'Well, we might have, but the world hasn't.' He sounds apprehensive. 'I still work in a phone shop; my mum is always going to be a space cadet. Your mum is still going to worry about you …'

'Worry about me – she's going to kill me,' I say.

'Why? You told her you were with me, and that everything was fine.'

'Yeah, but I've been out all night, in a park, in November. Without my vest on.'

'Or your bra,' Ben says. 'And I have to say, after several years of wondering, I was right: your breasts are magnificent.'

'Ben!' The happiness, the laughter, it just bubbles up in me, like a lava lamp or a hot spring. Like someone has finally pulled the plug that was keeping me from feeling these things, knowing these things that I have always skirted around before: desire, delight, happiness.

'Well it's true,' Ben says. 'And, anyway, your mum can't be cross about you staying out all night; you are twenty-one years old, Hope. You are a woman. All woman, as it turns out.' Turning, I kiss him again, and quickly we are both caught up in the moment of desire.

'We need to find a bed,' I say, breaking the kiss abruptly.

'Are you OK? Are you tired?' he asks me, his face full of concern. 'Do you need to lie down?'

'No, you idiot. I really want to have sex with you. Right now.'

Ben takes a ragged breath.

'I don't know what we are sitting here for, then,' he says, pulling me to my feet. He slips his coat off and wraps it around me.

'Won't you be cold?' I ask him.

'I think something like the equivalent of a cold shower is exactly what I need right now,' he says.

As we start to go down the hill, we stop for a moment and watch gold pouring into the dawn, streaking the sky with bronzes and ruby pinks, turning the dirty city into a gilded landscape, touching everything with beauty.'

'Oh, Ben,' I say, breathless with joy. 'This is it. This is the day that everything begins.' And somehow I know, whatever comes next will be wonderful.

CHAPTER THIRTY-SEVEN

* *

STELLA

The moon, battling off the arrival of dawn, travels with me as I race along the streets of London, keeping a steady, strong pace. Days, months of exhaustion, drop away under its benign gaze – full and round, silver and flat. And soon, the breathlessness drops away and I begin to feel strong again. Strong and certain. It's wonderful.

London seems to bow to me as I weave through her maze of streets. Knowing roughly where I need to go, I take right turns and left turns as the mood takes me – never slowing, never faltering. I run past lit windows and dark ones, hunched figures in doorways, new couples pressed urgently against lamp posts, groups of girls in sequins squealing, party-goers, dancers, men on a mission and cabbies leaning against their cars, grabbing a quick smoke.

Each step I take brings me nearer to him.

Nearer to what I need to say.

Through Victoria, past the palace, I run, only pausing for the great rush of traffic that never ceases in the centre of this city. Past the station and down Vauxhall Bridge Road; past quaint exhausted little Georgian houses, leaning against red-brick modern apartment blocks. Past pubs that are still lit from within – the muffle of voices sounding through reinforced glass. The pavements shine with yesterday's rain; the puddles of dirty water are turned into sudden bright worlds that shatter and reform as I run through them.

Vauxhall Bridge greets me with wide open eyes as I dodge a red light to leap onto her. And for a moment, just a pulse, I pause and look at my city, stretching out either way, tumbling along the river's shore. I find myself smiling as I sprint on, forward into the night. Under the railway bridge, silent and still, and onwards, past the tall, dark towers and the one thousand sleeping lives, until I stop suddenly – my hands acting as a break against the wall of the tower block where Vincent is.

Somehow I need to get in, without pressing the doorbell where he is staying. I don't want to be turned away down here, fifteen floors from making amends. And yet, looking at my watch, I see that it is almost 5 a.m. Someone in the great, vast, self-contained town must be pacing the floors now. I close my eyes and press button after button after button, silently apologising for the sleep that I'm disturbing; careful to avoid the one button that I am afraid of. Finally the intercom crackles into life.

'Sweets, that you?' I hear.

'Yeah,' I say, wondering who sweets is and what she or he sounds like.

The buzzer sounds and I push the door open, making my way to the lift.

It's not until its door slides open to reveal the floor where Vincent is staying that I start to doubt myself.

The corridor is dark and long, lined with doors on either side. As I walk along towards 1543, my invincible legs begin to tremble, my strong heart starts to falter, my step slows a little more with each one taken. And yet I am here, and I cannot turn back, so on I go until I stand outside his door.

I lean my head against it and listen. It's almost quiet inside but I think I can hear the sound of a TV or a radio. That will be Vincent in his nightly vigil to keep away the demons, memories and dreams that have haunted him ever since the moment he woke up alive – I'm almost certain of it.

I knock gently at first – so quietly it clearly can't be heard. There is no sound of shifting from within, no approaching footsteps. So I knock again, a little louder, and then louder after that. And, finally, there's the sound of someone approaching, accompanied by muttered swearing. I stand back so I can be viewed through the spyhole.

'Shit! Is that you, Stella?'

It's not Vincent who opens the door to me, but his mate, Frenchie, Sergeant William French, whose place this is.

'Mate, it's fucking five a.m.,' he says. 'What you doing here?'

'Vincent's here, isn't he?' I say, trying to see past him, to catch a glimpse of my husband.

'Yeah, yeah, he's here.' Frenchie runs his fingers through his ruffled hair. 'But, babe, he's sleeping. I know you guys are having trouble, but waking him up now for a barney – I'm not sure that's the way to go. Know what I mean?'

'He's asleep?'

'Yeah, like a baby. He's slept pretty much since he got here. Snores like a fucking pig as well. I want you two to get it sorted, I tell you. I'm fucking knackered.'

'Please, Frenchie, just let me see him, please. I'm not here to argue. I've come a long way. Don't turn me away, please.'

'Fuck if I know what women are thinking.' Frenchie shrugs and steps aside to let me in. I walk into the hallway, catching sight of myself in the mirror – flushed, damp with sweat, soaking clothes, dirty shoes. Self-consciously I take my muddy trainers off and leave them by the door.

'He's in there.' Frenchie nods at a closed door with the name Danielle emblazoned across it in pink letters. 'It's my weekend to have her, next weekend, so if you can make it up before then, I'd be grateful. I'm watching telly. I'll come if it sounds like it's getting violent; otherwise I'll leave you to it.'

Slowly, hesitantly, I push the door open and close it softly behind me. It takes a moment for my eyes to adjust to the dark. A pink night light glows softly on a shelf, and I see him then, sprawled on his stomach on the bed. My heart lurches. His leg is propped up against the wall, and he's sleeping in a pair of white boxers. He is sleeping, deeply. His face is relaxed and calm. He looks so beautiful.

He takes up most of the single bed, but I strip off my damp leggings and wet top and climb in next to him, winding my arms around his chest, moulding myself to the curve of his back. He adjusts slightly, moving over to make room for me in his sleep. His arms shift to cover mine, securing them, and then he settles back into deep sleep.

For the longest time, I am tense and nervous. I am cold and cramped, waiting for him to wake up and push me away, but he doesn't. After a few minutes, I realise my neck is at a painful angle, my shoulder is pressed against something hard and uncomfortable, but I do not move; I dare not move. Instead, I just let the warmth and strength of Vincent's body seep into mine. And slowly my heartbeat steadies, my eyes grow heavy and dreams start to weave their way into my thoughts.

*

I am not sure if I sleep for moments, minutes or hours, but when he moves my eyes fly open. He turns in bed, his hand running sleepily, absently, down my flanks, and then his eyes blink open.

'Stella?' His voice is dry, sparse. 'Are you real?'

'Yes,' I whisper. 'I came to see you.'

He shifts a little, and as he starts to wake up, suddenly conscious of his hand on my hip, he withdraws it.

'I want to say I'm sorry,' I tell him. 'And I wanted to say that I was wrong. That I've failed you. Because all I've seen for last the year and a half are the problems, and all

I've tried to do is fix things: fix you, make you better, be a nurse. But you don't need fixing. Not by me. You are perfect – more than perfect. You are remarkable and brave and fierce and honourable. And I am so proud of you and everything you have achieved. And I'm not sorry that you stayed alive for me; I'll never be sorry about that. I'm glad and grateful and relieved that you stayed alive for me. I'm sorry that I've seen only problems, and issues and injuries, since you came back. I'm sorry that I haven't seen you. Beautiful, beautiful you.'

Vincent doesn't speak for a moment. His solemn, silent eyes are watchful, searching. I let him think. I wait.

'I went to see Kip's widow, Maeve,' he says. 'Before I came here, I went to see her and I told her. I told her what happened. I read her this letter I've been trying to write.'

'What did she say?' I take his hand in mine, looping my fingers through his, and he does not pull away.

'She said if it had been him – if Kip hadn't done the same thing – she would have killed him anyway. She said I did the right thing. She said it would be OK.' He pauses, dropping his chin. 'They've got this little girl, tiny little kid. She's so sweet, Stella, so full of joy – joy for life, even when her Dad is gone. I want to help her, help Maeve and Casey. Be part of their lives, if they'll let me. Maybe take the little girl out, sometimes. Make sure her mum gets back on her feet. I want do that.'

'I think that's a very good idea,' I say.

'After I spoke to her, I slept. I've been sleeping without dreaming. At least, without the bad dreams. And it's like … it's like all I had to do was to tell her what had happened for my brain to let me rest.'

I nod and wrap my arms around him, pulling our bodies close together and holding him.

'We aren't those people, are we?' I say. 'The girl that likes sitting and the squaddie that couldn't keep still. We aren't those people that met and fell in love any more. I get that now; I get what you've been trying to make me see.'

'No, we're not,' Vincent agrees. His arms tighten around my waist; his finger trails down my spine.

'I've been so sad, so heartbroken and lost. So alone and looking for answers that don't exist. Trying to fix things that I can't fix. I lost myself, Vincent, but I think … I think I am on my way back now. Except I know that whoever I am next, I will never be that girl you met one summer's morning any more.'

'I know that, too,' Vincent says. 'And, well, I won't ever be the same, either. I can't grow a leg back, can I? And I won't ever feel invincible again, or have this idea that I'm somehow superhuman; that I'm one sort of man when I'm not. The leg – well, yeah, I miss it, sometimes. But I can live without it. My sense of who I am, what I'm like – losing that, it nearly drove me mad, Stella. It nearly drove me into the ground. And now … now I need to find out who I am again. But I do know that I will never be the man you first met again. I might not have died out there, in the heat and dust, but he did.'

I nod, and in the half-light of a winter morning, we look at each other anew, like strangers who have never met, but who know each other as well as they know themselves.

'I loved him, that Vincent. I loved how brash and crazy, and silly and funny and fun he was,' I say. 'I loved him. And, the thing is, you might have changed, but that love, it hasn't. It has never wavered, not even for one second. Not even when you couldn't look at me; I still loved you. Not even when you made me so mad I wanted to punch you; I still loved you. And that's what it's about, isn't it? Love? Love's about making it last, making it stick, making it count – even when it hurts, when times are hard, when people change, when life changes them. If you love someone, then you have to want to love them, whoever they are ... And if you don't, then that isn't love.'

Sitting up, I draw myself into a kneeling position on the bed.

'I read your last letter,' I confess. 'The one I was only supposed to see if you died.'

Vincent shifts uncomfortably, pulling himself up into a sitting position.

'Do you remember what you wrote?'

He nods again, his gaze falling away from me and to the place where his leg used to be.

'Whatever happens, however we have changed, the man that survived, the man that I ran across London to see, he's the man that I love. And we can. We can still have our happy ending – if we are ready to fight for it. It might be a different ending, but I know that I am ready to fight for you. But … if I've changed more than you can stand, then I will understand. And I will love you, and leave you, and wish you well.'

A thin strand of grey light filters in through the white curtain, casting shadows on Vincent's face – the bump in his nose, the dimple in his chin, thrown into relief, his lashes lowered still. I thought that in this moment I would feel stricken with grief, anguished, nervous, terrified that he will say no, that he cannot love me any more, but I don't. I feel peaceful and strong. And I know that whatever he says, I will survive it, because somehow during the months and weeks that I lost myself, I found something else: a will to be alive, to inhabit every moment with my life, in every way that I can. Whatever Vincent says next, I know I will be OK. Heartbroken, maybe, but OK.

'I don't think I have a choice,' he says at last.

I nod. 'I understand.'

Carefully, I start to rise, but he catches my wrist.

'I don't think I have a choice but to love you, Stella. To love you with all of our changes and with all of my heart. And, anyway, whatever else happens, you still have the same eyes, like two sunrises greeting me every morning. I'll fight alongside you, if you'll have me.'

Reaching out, I touch his scarred cheek, run my fingertips over the shiny, textured skin and down his chest, along his thigh to where it ends abruptly.

'Well, I already did my romantic speech,' I say, with a small smile. 'I haven't got anything left to say, but yes.'

Vincent leans forward, his strong arms encircling me, pulling me astride his lap. We kiss each other fiercely, hungrily. He drags off my vest top, and I tug at his boxers, lifting myself a little to allow me to pull them down over his hips. Closing my eyes, I lower myself back onto him, and we are still, just for a heartbeat – his eyes looking into mine. And then slowly, slowly, I begin to move on top of him, losing myself in his kisses, in the complete connection between us. Our momentum builds until I cry out and fall against him, feeling him shudder against my chest. After a while, I move beside him; he lets himself sink down in the bed, and I rest my head on his chest, his arm around me. With my eyes closed, and the rarest sensation of contentment spreading through me, it takes me a little while to realise that the gentle warmth that caresses my back is sunshine. Twisting around a little, I look out of the window and see a bright blue sky.

EPILOGUE

Dear Vincent,

You're probably wondering why you've received a letter in the post addressed to you in your wife's handwriting, aren't you? Because right now I am sitting across the breakfast table from you. But don't ask me; don't say anything. Just keep reading.

While I was working at Marie Francis, I wrote a lot of letters for other people – letters that marked the most important moments of their lives. I learned that what people say has a thousand times more meaning when it's written down. On the page, the words become immortal, beautiful, personal, heartfelt and special. They are words that will always be there, to be read again and again, and again. A letter is a memory that will never be lost, will never fade, or be forgotten. And long after we are gone, perhaps one day, a long time from now, our children, or our children's children, will read these words, and they will be there too, in this moment with us, for ever.

We've come such a long way in the last few weeks, fighting side by side. And there is still a long road ahead. One, I hope, that will take us the rest of our lives to travel.

But it won't just be you and me any more, Vincent. Because just before I sat down to write this letter, I found out that we are expecting a baby.

You are going to be a father.

Now before you cry, or throw this letter down and reach across the table and kiss me and tell me how much you love me, just read the final sentence, please.

We are winning, Vincent. We are winning.

All my love, always,
    Stella

ACKNOWLEDGEMENTS

This book was one of those books that would not share its secrets with me until it was almost finished, which made me a little bit crazy. So I have a lot of people to thank for their patience and support during the writing process.

Firstly, thank you to Gillian Green, my wonderful, supportive and brilliant editor who helped me figure it out, and to all the amazing team at Ebury, especially Emily Yau, Amelia Harvell and Louise Jones, and that fantastic sales team. What a wonderful home for my book to have.

Huge thanks always to my agent, Lizzy Kremer, who keeps me going with many pep talks and refusals of letting me give up being a writer to get a 'real job'. I couldn't do it without you, Lizzy. And thanks to the brilliant Harriet Moore, Laura West, Alice Howe and all the team at David Higham Associates.

To my amazing, dear, writer friends: Julie Cohen, Cally Taylor, Kate Harrison, Katy Regan, Miranda Dickinson, Tamsyn Murray, Amanda Jennings, Lucy Robinson, Lucy Dillon, Cesca Major – thank you for writing your books, for being part of the group that is always cheering each other on, for being funny, kind and inspirational.

Thank you so much to my oldest friends in the world. I might not see you very often, but somehow I always know you are there: Jenny Matthews, Cathy Carter, Sarah Darby, Rosie Mahony, Margie Harris, Kirstie Robertson, Catherine Ashley.

A special thank you to nurse Rachel Dixon for helping me out with some insight into a difficult and crucial job. Thank you to the Hospice of St Francis for inviting me to see just a little of the incredible, life-affirming work you do. The hospice in this book is entirely fictional, as are all the patients and staff, but the love and infinite care is inspired by this real place.

Finally, but most importantly, thank you to my family. Thank you to my Mum, and to my lovely husband Adam, and my brilliant, wonderful, funny, exhausting, incredible, delightful children. And to Blossom my dog, who arrived in my life soon after I started writing this book, and has been asking to be let in and out of my office ever since.

With love, Rowan
April 2015